Julie Wassmer is a professional television drama writer who has worked on various series including ITV's *London's Burning*, C5's *Family Affairs* and BBC's *EastEnders* – which she wrote for almost 20 years.

Her autobiography, *More Than Just Coincidence*, was Mumsnet Book of the Year 2011.

Find details of author events and other information about the Whitstable Pearl Mysteries at:
www.juliewassmer.com

STRICTLY MURDER

A Whitstable Pearl Mystery

JULIE WASSMER

CONSTABLE

CONSTABLE

First published in Great Britain in 2021 by Constable

A CIP catalogue record for this book is
available from the British Library.

ISBN: 978-1-47213-444-8

Typeset in Caslon Pro by SX Composing DTP, Rayleigh, Essex
Printed and bound in Great Britain by Clays Ltd, Elcograf S.p.A.

Papers used by Constable are from well-managed forests
and other responsible sources.

Constable
An imprint of
Little, Brown Book Group
Carmelite House
50 Victoria Embankment
London EC4Y 0DZ

An Hachette UK Company
www.hachette.co.uk

www.littlebrown.co.uk

In loving memory of
Maureen Moesgaard-Kjeldsen

'Dancing with the feet is one thing,
but dancing with the heart is another.'

Anonymous

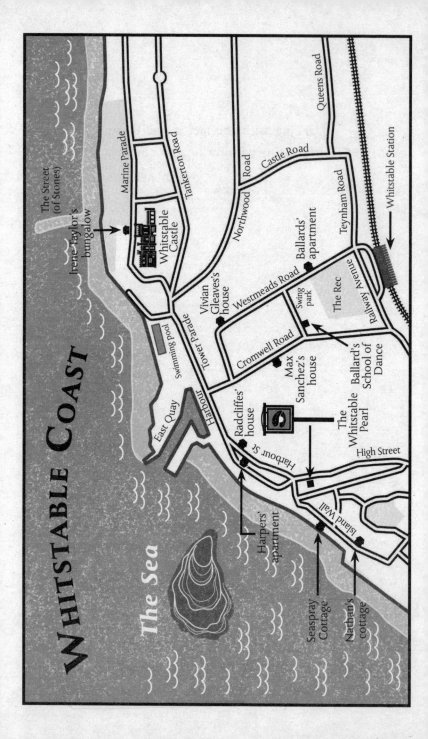

Chapter One

Depending on the weather, Whitstable's estuary waters could so often take on a dull pewter-like hue, or even a sepia-brown tone, after the shell-encrusted mudflats of the coastal bed were disturbed by heavy winds, but on this fine August morning Pearl Nolan found herself staring out at a calm sea of cobalt blue. She allowed her gaze to linger on the scene, framed by the square of window in the beach hut in her garden that she used as her office for Nolan's Detective Agency. How she wished she was outside on the pebbled beach itself, hearing the waves washing up on the shore, instead of having to listen to the pompous drone of Councillor Peter Radcliffe's voice blathering on behind her.

'Excuse me,' she said quickly, having heard quite enough. 'I think we could do with a bit of fresh air, don't you?'

She moved to open the window and allowed the soft tinkle of a small set of wind chimes to enter the room on the sea air. Then she took a deep breath, closed her eyes and imagined for a moment that she was sailing her dinghy out on the rising tide with the warm breeze flowing through her long dark hair – free of all cares . . .

At this time of year, an early-morning swim or sail before the crowds gathered to the magnetic pull of Whitstable's shore was always a welcome pleasure, but Pearl knew that both would have to wait. Radcliffe, or 'Ratty' as he was known to most of his constituents – a nickname acquired from the toupee the councillor wore, which looked like something wild animals had fought over – had managed to extend his appointment beyond the usual time allotted and Pearl now recognised that if she failed to take control of this meeting, she would be late for opening her High Street restaurant, The Whitstable Pearl. She turned to see Radcliffe using a handkerchief to dab beads of sweat emerging from his toupee, and she couldn't help wondering what his wife, Hilary, seated beside him, could possibly find attractive in her husband – other than Radcliffe's status and perhaps his recent purchase of the historic home they now shared. The Old Captain's House was a fine piece of Georgian architecture, situated in the heart of the town near the harbour. White-walled and sporting mullion windows, it had gained its name from a series of maritime owners, including one with connections to the deep-sea diving industry that Whitstable had pioneered in the nineteenth century after a local man had invented the diving helmet. That fact went largely un-commemorated save for a few artefacts in the local museum and the naming of a street of dwellings as 'Dollar Row', after it had been built with the proceeds of a salvage operation of a ship full of silver dollars. But the Old Captain's House stood as a reminder of that era while providing a suitable residence for Councillor Radcliffe, from which he enjoyed lording it over this little north Kent fishing town that was most famous for its native oysters.

'So,' said Pearl, 'you're absolutely sure that these items of clothing *have* been stolen?'

'Sure? Of course I'm sure,' the councillor bellowed. 'And this isn't mere "clothing", you know,' he added with a disparaging sneer. 'I've told you, the "items" are of the highest quality. Explain, Hilary.'

Hilary Radcliffe cleared her throat, producing, as she did so, a single high note like a ship's whistle piping aboard a passenger, before confirming: 'Peter's right. It's an exclusive selection, sold only in Paris, London and Rome. Five items from the Scarlet Woman range, six from the Black Widow and four from . . . Virgin Queen.' She looked slightly abashed.

'Fifteen items in total!' Radcliffe exploded – entirely unabashed. 'The cost runs into thousands!'

'But you haven't notified the police,' said Pearl. 'If you did that, you could claim on—'

'Insurance – I know, I know,' Radcliffe broke in testily, 'but I'd only end up paying a higher premium. Besides,' he added, 'considering the delicate nature of the items, I can't say I trust the local police not to leak the details to the press. I have a public image to maintain, you know.' He preened and dabbed his sweaty forehead once more.

'And you think your wife's stolen underwear might affect that?' said Pearl starkly.

'I've told you,' said Radcliffe, holding Pearl's gaze, 'it isn't any old underwear, it's—'

'Exclusive lingerie,' said Hilary, breaking in. 'Torn from our washing line,' she added with a wounded look.

Radcliffe nodded. 'And by what I can only assume to be a local pervert.'

'Or,' said Hilary, 'a covetous woman with exquisite taste.' She offered a tight smile and for a moment, Pearl questioned whether she really wanted to go searching for the thief of Hilary Radcliffe's underwear. If the stolen goods weren't recovered quickly, the case would surely require prolonged contact with the Radcliffes – an idea Pearl didn't exactly relish, especially at this time of year. Did she really need to burden herself with a mundane case from potentially difficult clients when The Whitstable Pearl, and the town itself, were busy with holidaymakers taking advantage of a final staycation before the school holidays ended? Pearl knew she could rely on her assistant chef, Dean Samson, in the restaurant that bore her name, as well as her small but hardworking band of devoted staff whom she considered more like family than employees, but there had been a dearth of cases recently for Nolan's Detective Agency, nothing to tax the skills Pearl knew she possessed, but which she had failed to make use of following the police training she had undertaken as a young woman. The training had been abandoned by Pearl when she had discovered she was pregnant with her son, Charlie. Now, over twenty years later, Charlie was away, enjoying a working holiday on an organic farm in Burgundy with a family who made their own wine and olive oil, having a wonderful summer while his mother was at something of a loose end . . .

'So,' said Pearl, trying to wrap up the appointment with the Radcliffes, 'what you want to know is if I can discover who's responsible for this theft and recover all the items?'

'Precisely,' said Radcliffe, adding, '*and* how much that's likely to cost me.'

Pearl plucked a leaflet from her desk and handed it to Radcliffe. 'My rates and conditions.'

Radcliffe quickly ran his beady eyes across the text, raising caterpillar-like eyebrows and patting his sweaty brow once more.

'Fine,' he announced. 'I'll give you a retainer right now.' He plucked a chequebook from his pocket, followed swiftly by a gold biro. 'Who do I make this payable to – you?' He was still staring down at his chequebook when Pearl replied.

'The Whitstable Carnival.'

At this, Ratty looked up and saw Pearl's slow smile. 'The carnival committee is in need of funds,' she explained. 'I said I'd help by donating the fee from my next case to them.'

Hilary squealed. 'What a lovely idea! We could help with a donation too, couldn't we, Peter?'

She looked to her husband for a response, but Radcliffe seemed ready to scotch the idea until Pearl intervened with: 'The committee will be listing every single donor in the carnival programme – which goes out to practically the whole town – just before the next council elections.'

'Is that a fact?' said Ratty, ruminating on this for only a moment before he made a hasty decision and, with a flourish of his gold pen, quickly signed two cheques and handed them both to Pearl. 'You'll be keeping me fully updated?'

'About the carnival funding?' asked Pearl, casting her eye over the sums on his cheques.

'About my wife's missing lingerie,' Radcliffe said tersely.

'Of course,' said Pearl, relieved to see that the Radcliffes were finally getting to their feet. 'I'll come to the house tomorrow and check out exactly where the items were stolen from. Will you be home around ten?'

'I'll make sure I am,' said Hilary before she remembered the folded newspaper lying on top of her stylish designer bag. 'And I suppose we'll be seeing you tomorrow evening, too?'

'Tomorrow . . .?'

'For the new dance class.'

Hilary noted Pearl's confused expression and exclaimed: 'Oh my goodness! I thought you would have enrolled by now. Tango – with Tony and Tanya Ballard?' At Pearl's lost look, Hilary explained: 'They're the leading exponents. Look . . .' She handed the newspaper to Pearl, who unfolded it to reveal a front-page photo featuring an attractive couple in flamboyant Latin costume. Tanya Ballard wore impossibly high stiletto heels and a low-cut, figure-hugging scarlet dress, the black frills of which stood out horizontally suggesting she had just completed a very rapid spin. Her partner, Tony, sported a tight-fitting black shirt and trousers, together with red braces and a white trilby hat pulled low over one eye.

'They've taken over Taylor's Dance School. It's now Ballard's,' Hilary went on. 'The new tango classes begin at eight tomorrow evening.' She offered a knowing smile. 'Perhaps you could invite your friend, the police detective. I haven't seen him around for a while?'

Pearl noted the smile playing on Hilary's lips. 'No,' she said flatly, 'DCI McGuire is away on a training course.'

Peter Radcliffe gave a derisive snort. 'Fancy that,' he said. 'You'd have thought once they reach the rank of DCI they might already be fully trained.' He took Hilary's arm. 'Come on, my dear.'

With a self-satisfied smile, Radcliffe steered his wife to the door. As it closed behind the departing couple, Pearl heaved a sigh of relief then looked down again at the photo in the newspaper. How had news of Whitstable's intriguing new dance duo passed her by?

Chapter Two

'What on earth possessed you to take on a case from Radcliffe?' asked Pearl's mother, Dolly Nolan, as she chopped parsley in a quiet corner of the restaurant kitchen.

'It was really for Hilary,' said Pearl, before taking a sip of the mignonette sauce she had just prepared for a selection of Pacific rock and native oysters. She paused to savour the sharp blend of minced shallot, white wine and rice vinegar then added some white peppercorns while Dolly pointed out: 'Paid for by Ratty.'

'But the proceeds will go to the carnival fund,' Pearl explained. 'Radcliffe's also given a donation, so, all in all, it will make a nice tidy sum for the committee. You know how desperate they were this summer. But if we start fundraising now, as early as possible, next year should be so much easier for them.' Pearl handed the mignonette sauce to her kitchen hand, Ahmed, who ferried it across to chef Dean, a young man who had proved himself more

9

than capable of replicating all Pearl's most popular dishes – and a few more besides.

Dolly lowered her voice before commenting: 'So desperate you had to take on trying to find Hilary Radcliffe's knickers?'

Pearl said nothing, waiting until Ahmed had crossed the kitchen to the sink before she looked back at her mother and explained, 'I've only told you about this in case you happen to hear anything, but I expect you to keep it strictly confidential, understood?'

Dolly gave a reluctant nod. 'All right,' she agreed, 'but why couldn't she have just put it all in the tumble dryer like anyone else, instead of flaunting it for all her neighbours to see?'

'Because,' said Pearl, 'they're not the kind of pieces you'd trust to the tumble dryer.'

'Oh?' Dolly's curiosity was suddenly piqued.

'They're from an exclusive range, a gift from—'

'Don't tell me,' said Dolly, grimacing. 'Naughty nicks, courtesy of Ratty? What a horrible thought.'

'It's actually a beautiful range from an exclusive company,' said Pearl, producing the catalogue from her bag. 'You can't say she doesn't have taste.'

'Not in men,' said Dolly. 'If you ask me, Hilary Radcliffe is a traitor to the sisterhood – an attractive woman like that succumbing to Ratty? She's nothing more than his trophy wife.'

'Yes, I'm sure there's a price to pay.'

'And it'd be far too high for me.' Dolly shoved the

catalogue back at Pearl, who watched her mother huffing over her chopped parsley. Although Dolly was in her sixties she was nevertheless sporting a newly dyed turquoise fringe while each of her fingernails was painted a different colour. Beneath her Whitstable Pearl apron she wore one of her own handmade artist smocks – another riot of colour that screamed, *Ignore me at your peril*.

'Well,' said Pearl, 'I don't think you have much to worry about: I don't think you're Ratty's type.'

Dolly looked up sharply. 'I'll take that as a compliment,' she said proudly.

'Meanwhile,' Pearl went on, trying now to change the subject, 'Hilary happened to mention this . . .' She produced a copy of the local paper and Dolly smiled as she saw the front page.

'Ah, so news has hit the *Chronicle*.'

'You knew about this?'

'Of course,' said Dolly, wiping her hands on her apron. 'Tanya Ballard is Irene's niece.'

'Irene . . .?'

'Taylor. Irene was Susanne's sister – that's Tanya's mother. She was a dancer too. Modern – not ballroom.' Dolly looked wistful for a moment, as she recalled something. 'Beautiful young thing she was, a pocket Venus. There was something quite . . . ethereal about her – especially when she danced. Like a little sylph.' Dolly mused on this for a moment before continuing: 'She joined a dance group – four girls – only teenagers at the time but they became quite a success . . . a phenomenon. Long before you were born, of course – I'm talking about the sixties. *Skip to my Lou*. Dreadful name, but the group's leader was called Louise, if I remember rightly. They were all very talented, and pretty, of course, or they would never have got on to TV, where they spent most of their time prancing around to hits of the day on a chart show. They must have made quite a bit of money, though – enough for Susanne to start up the dance school. It's a fair-sized building, you know, used to be an old chapel and would have cost quite a lot even back then. Irene ended up running it because Susanne disappeared off to India to study Transcendental Meditation with the "giggling guru" – the Maharishi – and all the other "beautiful people" he attracted at the time: the Beatles, Mia Farrow—'

'What happened?' Pearl broke in, curious. 'To Susanne, I mean?'

Dolly shrugged. 'She met a rock star and moved to California. Became a fully fledged Flower Child and never returned. A decade later, she had Tanya and . . .' Dolly paused for a moment, her brow furrowing. 'Well, she became rather a casualty of it all.'

'Of . . .?'

'Sex and drugs and rock 'n' roll, of course. I think there were clinic referrals . . . psychological problems . . . substance abuse? The poor woman died some years ago.'

'And the dance school?'

'It's managed to carry on, despite being a bit off the beaten track. Susanne may have started it up, but Irene's always done most of the work. She never married, so in many ways it's been her baby – her pride and joy – as is Tanya, too. Irene's a remarkable woman – strong, persevering, responsible. The complete opposite of her sister, who always seemed so vulnerable.' She paused and looked at Pearl. 'If only I could have got you to Taylor's when you were young, but you never showed the slightest interest in ballet or tap – you were much happier out with your dad on his boat.'

Pearl smiled as she watched her mother now ladling herrings in Madeira sauce on to slices of homemade sourdough bread. It was true that Pearl had adored the company of her late father Tommy, accompanying him out to sea as often as she could to fish Whitstable's waters for oysters. From a young age Pearl had learned the routine: the heavy dredge, lowered off the stern, dragging along the seabed to fetch up a catch from which unwanted intruders would be plucked. Crabs were capable of cracking open the shells of young oysters but starfish remained the oysterman's nemesis, seemingly innocent baby fingers clamping on to the oyster's shell to suck the life from it. As a child, Pearl had helped her father to wrench them from their prey, sorting through his catch, on the culling table at the boat's stern, before returning on the lowering tide with full baskets of oysters to mark a good day at sea. With her gipsy black hair and grey eyes the colour of moonstone, Pearl even resembled her late father – a rebel at heart, who had been able to trace his roots back to Galway. In contrast, Dolly was from

Whitstable stock; short and stout, she appeared to have passed nothing down to her daughter – beyond her own indomitable spirit.

'You're the dancer,' Pearl reminded her mother.

Dolly sighed. 'If only,' she said. 'Imagine being paid to dance for a living? I can't think of anything nicer.' For a second Dolly considered all her former terpsichorean exploits – from belly dancing to flamenco, not to mention a stint in an eccentric local troupe known as the Fish Slappers, whose aquatic costumes – featuring scallop-shaped bras and cod headdresses – had caused quite a stir at local Oyster Festival parades in years gone by. She heaved a sigh. 'These days,' she continued, 'I lack even the basic requirement.'

'Rhythm?'

'A centre of gravity,' Dolly admitted, staring down glumly at her plump figure in contrast to Pearl's willowy frame. 'And the flamenco really did play havoc with my knees, you know?' she added. 'All that stamping?' She rallied now with a smile. 'But I'm sure I'll do better with tango.'

Pearl turned to her. 'You mean, you're actually going to enrol?'

'Already have,' said Dolly, wiping her hands on her apron. 'You have to get in quick, you know. Tanya and Tony are a class act. Coming along?'

Pearl shook her head. 'I don't think so.'

'Why ever not?'

'Because,' said Pearl, 'as the newspaper headline states: "It Takes Two to Tango", and somehow I don't think you and I would make the best partners.' She stood close to Dolly and by doing so, underscored their difference in height.

'You're right,' Dolly agreed, 'which is why Ruby's agreed to partner me.'

'Ruby?' Pearl glanced across the kitchen towards her young waitress, who was just heading out, with a platter of oysters, on to the restaurant floor.

'Yes,' said Dolly. 'Her friend Florrie works at the school and she's managed to get us both in for classes. I'll ask her to put you down too – plus one – in case Nathan needs a partner.'

'Nathan's up for this too?' asked Pearl, surprised to hear this about her journalist friend and neighbour – especially since he had only just returned from researching a travel piece in Italy.

'Along with half of Whitstable, I'd imagine,' said Dolly, 'once they've seen this headline.' She slapped the newspaper and handed it back to her daughter as she remarked knowingly: 'Strange that the "X-ray specs" of our town should be so slow off the mark about this?' Dolly moved off with her herrings, leaving Pearl to wonder how someone who prided herself on knowing most of what took place in her town could possibly have remained ignorant about this development. Before she could respond, Ruby Hill came back into the kitchen, this time with a cordless phone in her hand.

'Customer,' she explained hurriedly. 'Says she'd like to book a table for tomorrow but asked to speak to you personally?' Ruby handed over the phone and allowed her boss to take the call.

'Pearl Nolan. Can I help?'

The woman on the end of the line carefully explained: 'I realise this is short notice,' she began, 'but I'd like to make a group booking for tomorrow lunchtime, if at all possible?'

'For how many?' asked Pearl, moving to her computer screen.

'Eight,' said the caller. 'I know you're always busy and I really should have called sooner, but a relative told me that if I mentioned the name Dolly Nolan you might be able to work some magic for us?'

'A relative?' asked Pearl, curious.

'Yes, my aunt, Irene Taylor. She's an old friend of your mother's.'

'And you are . . .?'

'Tanya Ballard – from the dance school.'

'Tanya and . . .'

The woman spoke quickly. 'Tanya and Tony, that's right,' she said. 'To be honest, I'd like to treat my staff by taking them somewhere special before classes begin tomorrow. Everyone agreed there was only one place to go – The Whitstable Pearl.'

Pearl took this in and checked her seating plan, realising that with a bit of juggling she could make room for a single table near the window.

'How does one o'clock sound?'

'Wonderful!' said Tanya Ballard, clearly relieved. 'Thank you so much.'

'It's a pleasure,' Pearl replied. 'I look forward to meeting you then.'

Replacing the receiver, Pearl stared down at the newspaper, her curiosity piqued as she realised how much she actually meant this.

Later that evening, Pearl dropped in on her neighbour, Nathan Roscoe. Nathan's cottage lay on the opposite side to Pearl's, on a street known as Island Wall, which ran parallel to the seafront. While Pearl's home, Seaspray Cottage, was located on the north side and came with a sea-facing garden, Nathan's home was on the land side, low-lying and bordered by a large fence that screened it from other back gardens nearer the town. The fence sported a mural – nothing figurative, but an abstract style that perfectly matched the clean minimalist lines of Nathan's home and outdoor space. A redwood deck, lined with a few large planters containing evergreen topiary cones, led down to a paved area containing several stylish rattan armchairs, and a settee on which Pearl now sat, relaxing after a hard day at the restaurant as she listened to the sound of birdsong and the gentle flow from a water sculpture cascading over a block of Carrara marble. An attractive man in his early forties, Nathan was wearing a long white shirt that hung loose over linen trousers, not creased, but rather perfectly crumpled. His designer stubble was peppered with grey but his thick, cropped hair remained a rich warm brown. Nathan could easily have passed for ten years younger as his taut physique was honed by regular visits to the gym. He remained perfectly groomed – as ever – pouring Limoncello over ice cubes before handing a glass to Pearl. She smiled and eyed the syrupy yellow liquid before thanking him.

'A pleasure,' said Nathan in the soft Californian drawl he had failed to lose in spite of having lived twenty years in Whitstable after a brief stint in Chelsea. He touched Pearl's glass with his own and they each took a sip, savouring their drinks before Nathan sighed and noted: 'It's been far too long since we've done this.'

'Yes,' Pearl agreed. 'But if you will keep running away from me . . .'

'Never, sweetie,' said Nathan, raising an admonishing finger. 'I was hijacked by work – forced to spend weeks on the Neapolitan Riviera.'

'Amalfi,' said Pearl, musing, 'Naples, Sorrento . . .'

'Yes, *povero me*,' said Nathan. 'Held captive on the shores of the deep blue Tyrrhenian Sea . . .'

'The Sea of the Etruscans.'

'That's right.' Nathan nodded, impressed. 'Dotted with islands like Capri, Elba and Ischia . . .'

'Citrus and olive trees . . .'

'The best seafood pasta – apart from yours, of course,' he added.

'Not to mention Limoncello,' said Pearl, considering the drink in her hand.

'And a forty-thousand-word travel guide to write in a very short space of time,' Nathan continued, adding: 'Luckily, as ever, I managed to fit my huge itinerary into my very tight schedule.' He raised an eyebrow. 'So now I'm able to enjoy some well-earned R and R, sweetie.'

He leaned back in his chair and closed his eyes, tilting his suntanned features to the lowering sun. Pearl smiled as she observed him with affection. Were it not for the fact that Nathan was gay, Pearl liked to think they might have made the perfect couple.

'And . . .' she began, 'learning how to tango will be part of that?'

Nathan opened one eye. 'I should have known nothing would get past you.'

'Strangely,' said Pearl, 'Tanya and Tony Ballard *did* get past me. I'd never heard of them before today.'

'Where on earth have you been?' Nathan exclaimed. 'They're the Fred and Ginger of tango!'

'I know that,' said Pearl, 'now! But somehow their celebrity status seems to have passed me by.'

Nathan took another sip of his drink and pointed a finger at Pearl. 'You really must get out more.'

'You're right,' said Pearl, acknowledging even more discomfort at feeling out of the loop. 'They're booked into the restaurant tomorrow for lunch, though,' she told him, adding: 'A staff outing of sorts.'

'Ah,' said Nathan. 'Then you're bound to meet my old friend Max.'

'Max?'

'Max Sanchez. Have I never mentioned him? He's from across the pond, like me, but Max is Afro-Cuban – his parents were originally from Havana – and he's a *very* talented dancer and choreographer. Tap's his speciality. He's toured the world in stage musicals – *Chicago*, *Ain't Misbehaving*, *Follies* – but now he lives on Cromwell Road. Must be almost sixty, and suffering the scourge of all dancers – arthritis.' Nathan paused to sip his drink. 'He's been teaching at the school for some time. A "temporary measure", he once told me – but that was two years ago,' he added with a knowing look before explaining: 'I don't think he's been doing much else and I get the impression he'd like to move on, though he won't actually admit it.' Nathan sipped his drink once more. 'He did suspect his classes might be cut – with the new takeover? But I think his concern might be misplaced. Tanya and Tony appear to be breathing new life into the place.' He gave a smile. 'In fact, it was Max who asked me to support this new class by going along tomorrow night – so I said I would. How about you, sweetie? Up for it?'

'Not my kind of thing.'

'No?'

'Mum's going.'

'I wouldn't have expected anything else.'

'Meanwhile, I have a new case,' said Pearl, trying to change the subject.

'Murder?' Nathan gave an ominous look but Pearl shook her head.

'Hardly.' She sighed then explained diplomatically: 'Let's just say I'm trying to retrieve some stolen property.'

'A matter for the police, surely?'

'Ordinarily,' said Pearl, 'but my clients want a low-key investigation. It's all quite simple – and totally unchallenging,' she added with another sigh. 'In fact,' she went on, 'things have been quiet for far too long.'

'As far as serious crime goes, you mean?'

Pearl gave Nathan a look that he read immediately. 'I see,' he said. 'You're thinking this may be . . . the calm before the storm?'

Pearl frowned. 'Just a feeling I have.' She studied the last of the Limoncello in her glass then drained it. 'But I hope I'm wrong.' Putting her glass down, she stretched her long suntanned arms and sighed. 'You know, I could quite easily stay here all evening, but I really must go.'

'A date with a tall handsome policeman?'

Pearl shrugged. 'McGuire's away,' she said. 'Stuck in the depths of the Hampshire countryside on an S.I.O. course.'

Nathan looked blank.

'Senior Investigating Officer,' Pearl explained. 'Seems like his superintendent comes up with these things just to get him away from Canterbury.'

Nathan raised an eyebrow. Pearl explained: 'McGuire's a DFL, remember? A Down From Londoner, like you?'

'Of course,' said Nathan. 'And the poor unsuspecting inspector was only meant to be here temporarily, wasn't he?' He looked at Pearl. 'I wonder what could possibly have tempted him to stay so long – or should I say "who"?' He gave a slow smile – which Pearl returned.

'I wonder,' she said enigmatically. As she got to her feet, Nathan followed.

'Sweetie,' he said, 'I know I can't possibly fill the space left by your . . . sexy S.I.O., but until he returns, I *am* here for you.' He leaned forward and gave her a peck on the cheek.

Pearl smiled. 'It's good to have you back,' she said sincerely before she turned and headed for the garden gate.

Nathan quickly called to her: 'Hold on!'

Disappearing into his kitchen he returned bearing a chilled bottle of Limoncello. 'This one's special,' he said, 'made from Amalfi lemons, so don't go giving it away to your customers. It's just for you. As are these.' He handed her a sealed plastic bag, inside which Pearl quickly identified some plump Sicilian olives.

'*Grazie mille.*' Pearl smiled.

'*Prego!*' Nathan winked.

Ten minutes later, Pearl slipped her key into the front door of Seaspray Cottage and entered her home, leaning back against the door as she stared around her empty living room. Her two tabby cats, Pilchard and Sprat, were nowhere to be seen, and with her spirits enlivened by Nathan's company, and his Limoncello, she suddenly felt in limbo – and somewhat abandoned. Tossing her bag on to an armchair, she strolled across to the window and gazed out to see the tide had yet to return but a few hunched figures were dotted on the mudflats digging for bait. Strains of music carried across on the air from the direction of the Old Neptune – the white weatherboarded pub that had stood on the beach, in one form or another, for almost two centuries – in the eye of estuary storms and gales. Hearing the sound of voices and laughter echoing across the shore, for a moment Pearl considered taking a stroll to the pub in order to join in the evening ritual of watching the sun slowly falling behind the Isle of Sheppey. She was sure she would find a familiar face or two there, sitting at the tables outside or on the timber groynes that broke up the waves at high tide – but something stopped her. It wasn't exactly loneliness Pearl felt in that moment but the nagging sense of something missing. With Charlie away, and work at both the agency and the restaurant undemanding, she was forced to admit to herself that over the last few weeks she had really missed McGuire. The detective had found a place in her life – and her heart – so much so that she now felt his absence as strongly as a presence. Although busy with his course, and in an area of poor mobile reception, McGuire had done his best to keep in touch, but Pearl had missed several of his calls due to problems with her own mobile. Having bought a brand-new smartphone, she now took it from her bag and plugged it into a charger, then headed off to the kitchen to fix some supper, when she suddenly noticed a light signalling a voicemail on her answerphone. She pressed the 'play' button and a familiar voice suddenly filled the room.

'Pearl, are you there?' A moment's silence before McGuire spoke again. 'Looks like I've missed you again, but never mind. That's it,' he continued. 'Course finished. I'm out of here tomorrow, Pearl. I'm finally coming home.'

Chapter Three

The front door of the Old Captain's House led into a narrow hallway, off which two open doors allowed Pearl to glimpse a comfy front room on one side and an intimate dining room on the other. Hilary Radcliffe led the way for Pearl towards the back of the house as she explained: 'Peter's at a council licensing committee meeting at the moment, opposing a new cocktail bar in Harbour Street – just another haunt for the DFLs.' She gave a dismissive sniff and walked on, entering a spacious living room beyond which a smart kitchen led out through a set of French windows to the garden. For a moment, Pearl stood motionless, stunned by the sight before her. Old photos of the historic house had always shown a beautiful garden, full of mature trees and shrubs, with an expansive area laid to lawn, housing a Gustavian table for dining alfresco and a concealed folly used by the previous owners as a secluded hideaway. In contrast, Pearl now found herself facing only a bare and uninspiring plot resembling something from a low-budget TV garden makeover. The property's historic walled garden consisted now of a large area of Astroturf, from which sprouted only a few croquet hooks. A striped sunlounger was positioned near to a kitsch pagoda beside a low rattan table on which sat a bottle of expensive suntan lotion, a long drink in an iced tumbler and a novel, the cover of which showed a pretty young nurse in a passionate clinch with what appeared to be a handsome white-coated doctor with a stethoscope hanging around his neck.

'I hope I'm not disturbing you,' said Pearl, feeling some sympathy for Hilary Radcliffe's apparent need to resort to fictional romance. Her client was dressed only in a stylish red-and-white polka-dot swimsuit with a crimson sarong tied around her neat waist.

'No problem,' Hilary said. 'I was just trying to enjoy a little sun. At this time of year, the beach is far too busy, don't you find?'

'In places,' said Pearl. 'But I do have the dinghy and it's always peaceful at sea.'

'Not for me,' said Hilary, wrinkling her nose. 'I don't have a head for waves – or should that be stomach? I am a martyr to my *mal de mer*. We took a first-class cruise last summer to Venice and Peter *swore* I wouldn't even notice when we left port but my equilibrium is *so* delicate I suffered for the entire trip and could barely stagger across Piazza San Marco to Florian's.' She gave a small shudder at the thought.

'The line,' said Pearl, trying to drag her client back to the purpose of the visit.

'I'm sorry?' Hilary asked, still lost for a moment.

'Your washing line? The one on which you hung your—'

'Oh, yes!' said Hilary, quickly breaking in. 'Follow me and I'll show you.' She led the way for Pearl, adding: 'I do hope you'll be able to solve this mystery. I have great faith in you.' Heading down to the end of the garden, she indicated a rotary washing line set into the Astroturf lawn and smiled. 'It's a lightweight top spinner,' she declared proudly, 'turns effortlessly on the slightest breeze.' She gave it a push with her manicured hand and set the contraption turning like a merry-go-round.

Pearl waited for it to slow down then moved forward to investigate. 'It's set into a tube in the ground,' she noted.

'Yes,' said Hilary. 'But the spinner lifts out, you see.' She raised the central pole from which the drying arms sprang and nodded towards a large shed near the wall. 'We store it in there when it's not in use. Like I say, it's lightweight. Top of the range.'

'And everything was hanging on this?' asked Pearl.

'Until it all disappeared,' said Hilary, glumly surveying her empty top spinner as Pearl eyed two ivy-clad walls on either side of the garden while noting that the rear wall led to a narrow alley accessed by an old wooden gate that was securely locked.

'Your garden walls are all quite high,' Pearl noted. 'Were there signs of anyone having scaled them?'

'Signs?' echoed Hilary, confused. 'Such as?'

'Footprints in the soil near those shrubs? Or on the . . . lawn?' she asked, for want of a better term to describe the Astroturf.

Hilary shook her head. 'Nothing at all,' she replied. 'It was as though everything had simply vanished into thin air. All that was left were a few pegs – though most were on the ground.'

Pearl considered this.

'What're you thinking?' asked Hilary, curious.

'Pegs on the ground suggest the items had been snatched . . .'

'Yes!' said Hilary quickly. 'And violently. I found a thin shred of red silk clinging to the line – no doubt from my favourite Scarlet Woman camisole.' She pressed a hand-kerchief to her lips.

'I'm sorry,' said Pearl. 'I know it's upsetting.'

Hilary nodded mutely and Pearl turned to check out the walls – as well as the height of the rotary washing line – before she finally made a decision. 'I'll come back tomorrow with some suitable cameras,' she said, 'and once they're in place, I'll set up a sting.'

'A trap, you mean?'

Pearl nodded. 'It will mean having to peg out some more articles.' Hilary looked alarmed, so Pearl quickly explained: 'Nothing quite so exclusive this time.'

'I see,' said Hilary. 'You mean . . .'

'Decoy items.'

Looking up, Pearl registered that several surrounding

houses seemed to have a clear view straight down into the Radcliffes' garden.

'Now that the mature trees have gone, you're quite overlooked here.'

'That's true,' agreed Hilary. 'But the garden was so dark and dismal when we moved in and I am a sun worshipper, after all,' she announced proudly. 'You have to make a house a home, don't you?'

'Of course,' said Pearl. 'But the Old Captain's House has always been very special.'

Hilary looked at Pearl. 'Do you really think so?' she remarked with some surprise, as she led the way back inside through the French windows. 'To be perfectly honest,' she confided, 'I'd be far happier living somewhere else.'

Pearl turned. 'Really?'

'Oh yes.' Hilary nodded. 'Peter likes the idea of being the new . . . skipper at the helm.' She indicated a white captain's hat hanging on a coat stand by the front door. 'But I'd rather be living somewhere modern.' She glanced around with disdain. 'This place is so . . . dated and fusty. Noisy, too! The old windows let in far too much racket from the traffic.' She took a deep breath and exhaled with a long sigh. 'If only we could get Harbour Street pedestrianised.'

Pearl gaped at her client in horror. 'But . . . that would mean directing traffic in a virtual ring road around town . . . creating rat runs and problems elsewhere . . .'

'Maybe.' Hilary shrugged, unconcerned. 'But imagine how peaceful it would be here in Harbour Street – a lovely little enclave filled with cobbled streets and café society?'

She opened the door, still waiting for a response, but all Pearl offered was a simple sentence. 'I'll be back tomorrow.'

A few hours later, Pearl had managed to distract herself from the Radcliffe case by busying herself in The Whitstable Pearl, dressing a large round table near the window and setting a vase of pink sweet peas on her crisp white linen tablecloth while Ruby straightened the last of the napkins. Pearl watched the girl at work, smiling at the way Ruby took pride in her work and a great deal of pleasure in her job. Although she was only nineteen years old, Ruby had been working at the restaurant for a couple of years, during which time she had found a place for herself in The Whitstable Pearl 'family', as if she had been born into it. Pearl felt not only a great deal of affection for Ruby but also a sense of protection as the girl had no natural family of her own following her grandmother's death a few years ago.

'Will your friend be coming along today?' asked Pearl. 'Florrie, is it? The girl who works at the dance school?'

Ruby nodded. 'She's an assistant there and it's actually her twentieth birthday tomorrow so this'll be a bit of an added treat.' She leaned in to Pearl and confided: 'She hasn't told anyone, though – only me. We're going to Canterbury for a concert at the Marlowe Theatre.'

'Catching a meal there first?' asked Pearl. 'I hear there's a new tapas bar opened near the station?'

'Yeah, and it's meant to be good too, but I don't think we'll have time to try it. We'll probably just get a drink first. Florrie's working and you know how unreliable the buses can be.'

'Well,' said Pearl, 'maybe I could give you a lift in, if that helps?'

'Really?'

'Why not? I'll come and pick you up when I leave here.'

'Thanks,' said Ruby with a smile. 'I'll find out exactly what time Florrie will be finished. Around six, I think.' She secured a strand of her fair hair back into her ponytail, her smile quickly vanishing as she noted something through the window. 'Look – they're here already.'

Pearl turned and recognised Tony Ballard from the local newspaper story, ushering in a slender woman wearing an eye-catching white sundress. A wide-brimmed scarlet hat covered the upper part of the woman's face so that all Pearl could really see of it were her full crimson lips until she took off the hat, shook out her shiny long dark hair and offered her hand – and a smile.

'You must be Pearl?' She introduced herself: 'Tanya Ballard. I booked the table.'

'And it's all ready for you,' said Pearl. 'A window table, so I hope you won't feel on display?'

At this, Tony Ballard gave a smile. 'I don't think Tanya will mind too much about that, will you, darling? Tanya's more than used to being "on display".' He offered a wink and his hand to Pearl. 'I'm Tony, Tanya's husband.' His handshake was firm but the smile he offered was friendly.

'Oh, isn't this lovely!' trilled a young girl, clearly delighted by the attractive table and the paintings lining the restaurant's walls, which served as an informal gallery for Charlie and Dolly's work. While Pearl's son's efforts were bold, striking and graphic in style, Dolly's paintings consisted mainly of a collection of seascapes and collages featuring various *objets trouvés* such as driftwood and dried seaweed.

Ruby leaned in to Pearl and whispered: 'That's Florrie.' At this, the girl offered a broad innocent grin. Pearl noted she was slim but buxom, with tow-coloured hair and bright baby-blue eyes.

'So pleased to meet you,' the young woman gushed. 'Ruby's told me all about you.' She continued to beam at Pearl while five other guests entered, waiting patiently by the door to be seated.

'Please make yourselves comfortable,' said Pearl quickly before asking Ruby to bring some prosecco. As Ruby headed off, Pearl turned back to the guests, explaining: 'On the house. A special welcome for you all.'

'How kind,' said Tanya Ballard, seating herself first before gesturing to the others to take their places. 'Tony can sit here beside me. Jack? You should be here on my right – and then Laura beside you, of course.'

She gave a smile and Pearl watched as a tall young man with long fair hair did exactly as he was told, seating himself beside Tanya, while a blonde woman in her mid-thirties took her place beside him.

'Then Florrie,' Tanya continued. 'Max . . . Vivian . . . and Auntie Irene.' She gave a sweet smile as the other three guests obediently took their places at the table.

Just as Nathan had described, Max Sanchez looked to Pearl to be in his late fifties. A short, handsome man with lively features and skin the colour of carob, he was dressed flamboyantly in a white silk shirt with red braces, and found himself sandwiched between young Florrie and the woman called Vivian, who sat beside Tanya's aunt, Irene Taylor. Pearl also noted that Tanya had placed herself fully on display, facing straight out towards the High Street, so that anyone passing would see her. Before Pearl could say another word, Dolly appeared with Ruby from the kitchen, ferrying prosecco and olives. 'Irene, my love! How are you?' she called.

At that moment, Irene Taylor, a tall but unremarkable-looking woman whose short grey hair did little to enhance her drained complexion, looked a little embarrassed. Pearl couldn't be sure if this was due to Dolly's effusive greeting or perhaps because Tanya might feel upstaged by it in some way. Certainly, Irene lowered her gaze modestly as she replied, 'I'm fine, Dolly,' before quickly indicating Tanya across the table.

'My goodness,' Dolly remarked, 'I don't expect you'll remember me, Tanya, because the last time we met you were barely a young teenager, but it's wonderful to have you back in Whitstable, and I'm really looking forward to your class this evening.'

Tanya smiled. 'I'm glad you're coming, Dolly. We'll all be there,' she added, glancing around the table.

'All?' asked Dolly.

'Yes. All of us,' Tanya replied, with a sweeping gesture

that took in every person seated at the table. 'Everyone involved in our school,' she explained. 'After all, it's a new start, and we need to show our joint commitment to its success.'

Tanya was still smiling, although Pearl noted that the only enthusiastic expression was on Florrie's young face. Nonetheless Tanya continued, 'Let me introduce you,' she began. 'My husband and dance partner of twenty years, Tony Ballard.'

Tony gave a charming smile and a nod of his head before Tanya went on. 'Jack Harper,' she continued, with a quick look at the fair-haired young man beside her, 'our pianist and music coordinator.' Jack Harper offered a nervous smile before glancing at the blonde woman beside him and taking her hand as Tanya explained, 'And that's Jack's lovely wife, Laura.'

'I . . . don't actually work at the school,' Laura explained nervously, 'so it's very nice of you to include me.'

'Nonsense!' said Tony. 'We're all one big happy family.' He winked at Laura and she looked away, back at her young husband, who squeezed her hand. Tanya continued, once more: 'Florrie Johnson is our able assistant – and currently taking care of our extensive wardrobe.' Florrie looked pleased as punch with this description. 'And,' Tanya went on, 'Max Sanchez, you'll recognise from his many stage performances.'

'But of course,' said Dolly. 'The King of Tap!'

Max tipped his head in appreciation of Dolly's comment. 'That's me,' he said in a lazy American drawl. 'Or it was – last time I checked.' He gave Pearl a wry look.

'And Vivian Gleaves,' said Tanya, moving swiftly on, 'our ballet mistress.'

The woman Tanya introduced was in her late fifties with auburn hair scraped back into a neat French pleat. She sat poker straight at the table but turned her head slowly to Pearl and added almost in a whisper, 'Formerly of the Royal Ballet.' She offered a proud smile, then looked down at the table, giving a slight cough, as if suddenly ashamed of having said too much.

'And finally,' added Tanya, 'my amazing aunt, Irene Taylor, who's given so much of her time to the school over the years.' Tanya gave her a warm smile.

'You're all most welcome,' said Pearl. 'And I hope you'll enjoy your lunch. You'll find today's menu chalked on the blackboard and, of course, being Whitstable, oysters are always a speciality.'

'Except when there isn't an "r" in the month,' said Tony.

'Not true,' said Pearl. 'You can enjoy our Pacific rock oysters any time of the year – it's only the native oysters that are seasonal.'

Dolly, never a fan of oysters at the best of times, suddenly suggested: 'How about I go and put on some music?'

Before Pearl could stop her, Dolly beetled off towards the kitchen, leaving Pearl to offer an apologetic smile and an explanation: 'Mum's very excited about the classes this evening. She's a great fan of dance.'

'And you?' asked Tanya.

Before Pearl could reply, strains of music began wafting from overhead speakers.

'Oh, what a surprise,' sighed Max, unimpressed. 'More tango.'

Picking up on his bored tone, Tanya looked sharply at him but Max explained: 'You *can* have enough of a good thing, you know.' He glanced at Pearl as he explained: 'I've heard nothing else for days.'

'I'll take it off,' said Pearl, about to move to the kitchen.

'No,' said Tony Ballard. 'Leave it, please. This is a great recording,' he added as he began nodding along to an orchestral introduction featuring lush strings and piano.

'Yes,' Jack Harper agreed, appearing to recognise the track. 'Héctor Varela's orchestra, isn't it?'

'"*Fueron Tres Anos*",' said Max, with perfect Spanish pronunciation. Everyone at the table now began to pay attention.

'And probably his most famous number,' Tony added in a slightly wistful tone, just before another instrument was heard.

'Oh, I *love* the sound of an accordion,' said Florrie.

'That's not actually an accordion,' said Jack patiently, 'it's a—'

'Bandoneon!' said Dolly, as she arrived back at the table. 'Very Argentinian – and very tango!'

Florrie looked confused. 'What's the difference?'

'Well,' said Jack, about to explain, but Max took advantage of the young man's pause and went on himself.

'The bandoneon is part of the concertina family,' he said with authority. Smiling at Florrie, he took the girl's hands gently in his own and demonstrated patiently to her. 'It's held like this,' he said, his hands guiding hers, 'and played by squeezing the air through the bellows rather than pressing any buttons.'

He smiled again but Florrie quickly seemed to lose interest and turned again to Jack to ask: 'Will you be playing tonight at the class?'

Jack nodded. 'Sure. And I'm looking forward to it.' He gave a smile for the girl but before she could respond, Tanya qualified: 'We'll need you on piano only for the steps, Jack. But for the performance, we've decided on the full orchestra recording, which you can cue, okay?'

Jack Harper simply nodded, while his wife Laura stared at him with what looked to Pearl to be some concern.

'You'll be performing as well?' asked Dolly, impressed, as she helped Pearl serve flutes of prosecco to the guests.

'If my knee holds out,' said Tony.

'Oh?' said Dolly. 'Problems?'

Tony nodded but Tanya explained: 'It's no secret Tony had a knee replacement earlier this year. His recovery's been . . . slower than expected. That's preventing us from touring at the moment, but I'm sure we'll be able to manage a tango demonstration for our pupils this evening – after all, it's important we give everyone something to aspire to.'

She smiled, a little too sweetly, thought Pearl – though this seemed to go unnoticed by Florrie, who gushed: 'I can't wait to see you dance.'

'Well,' said Vivian, the ballet mistress, 'let's not forget, our students will be there to learn.'

'Meaning?' asked Tanya.

'Meaning,' said Max, 'it's not a floor show. It's a lesson. But then you *are* new to teaching, darling.' He picked up his flute of prosecco and watched the bubbles fizzing at the surface.

In spite of the endearment he used, Tanya looked stung, but Irene quickly commented: 'I'm sure Tanya's right. Everyone in the new class will welcome some inspiration.' She raised her own glass and offered a toast. 'To the school.'

The other guests picked up their flutes, but Tanya interrupted the proposed toast.

'Shouldn't that be "To tango"?' she said quickly, raising an eyebrow. 'After all, that's what this is all about – and why everyone will be coming this evening – to witness . . . magic.' She looked at Tony and went on: 'A man and a woman stepping out on to a dance floor, their arms entwined around each other, body to body, in the special tango embrace – the *abrazo* – that must always remain unbroken . . . conveying the shared emotion, the passion we hear in this music.'

As Dolly's choice of tango music played on in the background, a man's voice suddenly joined in with the melody, plaintive and heartfelt, setting just the right tone for the orchestral backing. Jack Harper's hand tightened around Laura's as he explained: 'That's Argentino Ledesma singing. A legend. An amazing talent.'

Beside him, Laura smiled and nodded, but Florrie turned to Jack and shook her head, puzzled. 'But . . . I don't understand the lyrics. They're all . . . foreign?'

'Spanish,' said Max. 'And you don't need to understand them, Florrie; it's all there in the tone of his voice. He's describing to his lover his heartbreak at their separation. *Fueron tres anos . . .* It's been three years since they kissed, but he still feels her lips on his own.' Max's voice had lowered to a whisper and everyone fell silent, listening as the song finally came to a dramatic end.

Pearl noted the reactions of the guests at the table: Jack Harper still held his wife's hand tightly as he tapped out a silent rhythm on the table; Tanya's eyes were on her husband, Tony, as he stared down into his glass; Max Sanchez offered a smile to Florrie but she, in turn, was looking across at either Tanya or Tony, Pearl couldn't be sure. Vivian glanced at Irene Taylor, whose eyes remained fixed on Tanya, who finally broke the spell by suddenly raising her glass to say: '*That* is the magic of tango.' Everyone followed by raising their glasses and finally joined in with Tanya's toast: 'To tango!'

For a few seconds more, Pearl found herself lost in the moment until Ruby caught her attention by nodding towards the window and giving a little cough. Taking her waitress's gaze, Pearl noticed someone was standing directly outside on the pavement: a man dressed casually in a white T-shirt and jeans with a linen jacket slung across one shoulder.

For a moment, Pearl thought she was imagining it until McGuire lifted the sunglasses he wore, pushing them up on to his head before offering a smile.

'Excuse me,' she said to her guests, before turning to

whisper to Ruby, 'Take the orders and I'll be right back.' She headed quickly outside.

Out on the hot street, Pearl pushed a hand through her long dark curls as her eyes met McGuire's. Instantly, he swept her up into his arms, lifting her off her feet for a moment before setting her down again and holding her tight. Then he tipped his head towards the restaurant and asked: 'Busy?'

Pearl glanced back through the window and nodded. 'A full house.' Staring into McGuire's blue eyes, she suddenly felt like an awkward teenager and compensated by putting some idle conversation between them. 'How was your course?'

'Too long,' said McGuire, holding her gaze. 'I missed you.'

Pearl smiled. 'Good.'

'Any chance you could get away?'

She sighed, torn. 'Your timing's rotten.'

'But my intentions are good. How about later? I could come back after you've finished. Take you somewhere nice?'

Pearl's eyes locked with his. 'What do you have in mind?'

McGuire leaned his face so close to hers Pearl could feel his breath on her cheek. 'Anything you like.'

'Anything?'

McGuire slowly nodded.

From inside the restaurant, Pearl heard more tango music playing – something livelier this time. Through the window she saw her customers from the dance school were now animated – perhaps from the new rhythm or from the effects of the prosecco – but Tanya Ballard's gaze was fixed on Pearl, or, thought Pearl, perhaps she was actually looking at McGuire and trying to work out what was going on. In that moment, Pearl remembered Tanya's words about tango – and the magic she had managed to convey: *A man and a woman stepping out on to a dance floor, their arms entwined around each other, body to body, in the special tango embrace – the* abrazo *– that must always remain unbroken . . . conveying the shared emotion, the passion you hear in this music . . .*

'How about you meet me outside St Alfred's Church tonight just before eight?'

McGuire looked taken aback. 'Church?'

'Don't worry,' said Pearl. 'I'm not planning on introducing you to the vicar.'

'So what *are* you planning?' he asked, intrigued.

'A surprise,' said Pearl innocently.

Staring into Pearl's moonstone-grey eyes, any suspicions on McGuire's part now suddenly evaporated. Leaning further forward his lips met Pearl's as he whispered: 'I can't wait.'

His face remained close to Pearl's as he breathed in her floral perfume – the delicate fragrance of lilies he could never quite conjure up for himself until he was with her once more. He knew she had other things on her mind right now – customers to attend to, meals to supervise – but tonight he would return . . . and Pearl would be all his.

Chapter Four

Later that same day, having left the restaurant's evening shift in chef Dean's capable hands, Pearl checked her appearance in a full-length mirror in her bedroom. She'd tried on several outfits, deciding in the end to abandon her favourite summer dresses – the vintage fifties frocks with their nipped-in waists and full skirts that so suited her tall slim figure – and opting instead for a slinky red dress with a deep V-shaped backline that dipped almost to the waist. The dress was cut on the bias so that it flowed out at the hem, allowing Pearl the freedom of movement she imagined she would need in a dance class. Turning from side to side, she watched the base of her dress rippling out like waves on a beach.

While she didn't feel herself to be a good dancer, Pearl was nevertheless a fan of most kinds of music, and she now picked up her brand-new smartphone and began to search for the song that Dolly had played at the restaurant earlier. It didn't take too long to find it. The music of Héctor Varela's orchestra suddenly filled Pearl's living room; strings and piano sounding the long instrumental introduction to *'Fueron Tres Anos'*, punctuated by chords from the bandoneon before Argentino Ledesma began to sing a melody that seemed even more plaintive now that Pearl understood the story behind it. She listened, transported, catching the odd Spanish word – *'tormento . . .* *'adios . . .'* – but it was the singer's voice and the music itself that conveyed the heartache of a man in torment, separated from his love . . .

As the song played on, Pearl recalled once more Tanya's description of a couple stepping out on to a dance floor to take up the tango's special *abrazo*. She closed her eyes, imagining herself locked in such an embrace with McGuire. Perhaps it was true that 'absence made the heart grow fonder'. Certainly, Pearl knew she had missed her lover – but in spite of what he had told her, could she really trust that he felt the same way? McGuire was an attractive man but he was also something of a conundrum. He had formed a good relationship with Pearl's son, Charlie, and had even managed to charm Dolly, who, as a natural rebel against all authority, had never been a fan of the police. Being steady and responsible, Pearl felt sure McGuire would have made a good father, but at forty years old he remained single, a loner, and seemingly content to allow his work to dominate his life while seeing Pearl in his spare time. Pearl recognised she had a rival – McGuire was married to his job – which was surely the reason he had not been snapped up by another woman, someone who would demand far more of his time than Pearl had ever done to date. Perhaps, she thought, this was the reason their relationship worked – because she had wanted nothing more . . . until now. Dolly had always complained that when it came to men, her daughter was far too picky, while Pearl had argued that it was no bad thing to have high standards. There had been plenty of dates with local men, like her local fruit and vegetable supplier Marty Smith – who still held a candle for Pearl – and also some relationships with DFLs – handsome, moneyed characters who had held some fascination for Pearl until she had realised she was, for them, just part of the landscape, while they were little more for her than a summer romance, as Charlie's father Carl had been. In truth, over two decades, there had been many times when Pearl would have loved a man to rely on, but she had managed well without one – and that had only served to fuel her own sense of fierce independence. But listening now to the music sounding in Seaspray Cottage, she imagined how it might feel to have a lover singing to her so passionately that his voice reached her soul. She swayed to the music, allowing herself to believe it was McGuire she was dancing with, feeling his strong arms around her in the empty room, seeing his face before her, his deep blue eyes locked with hers – as though this might be a prelude to him offering some form of commitment beyond the relationship they already enjoyed . . . She sighed. It was all wishful thinking, a reverie, because Pearl knew full well that McGuire wasn't the kind of man to allow passion to overtake him. He was a hardened detective who played his cards close to his chest and relied on procedure – formal procedure – to solve his cases. Unlike Pearl, who preferred to act on instinct, McGuire was cautious, considered, and perhaps because of that, he was in many ways reliable – if predictable. And yet, Pearl smiled to herself, there was still a chance that McGuire might yet surprise her . . .

It wasn't until she heard the bells of St Alfred's Church sounding on the evening air that Pearl remembered to check the time before quickly switching off her new smartphone – and the music. Picking up her bag, she hesitated and studied her reflection once more as she realised she had forgotten something. Moving quickly to her dressing table, she opened the shell-decorated lid of her jewellery box and rooted inside for a simple necklace of scarlet glass beads. Once she had put them on, she applied a slash of red lipstick to match, then shook out her long black curls and prepared to meet McGuire.

As she left Seaspray Cottage by the garden gate leading out on to the prom, the beachfront air was thick with the smell of charcoal and barbecued fish. Above Pearl, against the clear blue sky, an ultralight glided past, so high it appeared like a butterfly on the sea breeze. Children were still playing on the beach, collecting shells in plastic buckets, while parents sat close to the timber groynes as they prepared shoreline suppers. A young couple passed Pearl on the prom, their arms entwined so closely around each other they appeared like Siamese twins – oblivious to their surroundings. Pearl watched them as they moved on, saw them share a kiss, silhouetted against the lowering sun. She smiled to herself, thinking that perhaps this was just how she and her first love, Charlie's father Carl, had once appeared to others as they had walked along the same prom more than twenty years ago. Twenty years . . . So much had happened since Charlie's birth, including the birth of The Whitstable Pearl restaurant, which had supported the whole family throughout the years that had passed so quickly. Charlie was now grown, the restaurant was in good shape and even the secondary business Pearl had begun, Nolan's Detective Agency, had brought Pearl some success. But it had also brought her into contact with McGuire. Pearl recalled her recent conversation with Nathan – everything she had told him was true – at this point in time, life seemed unchallenging, though Pearl knew her greatest challenge was McGuire: the man who had become her partner in crime but who she still could not envisage as a life partner. McGuire was too elusive for that, too caught up with his cases, his trials and training – and yet, at times like this, when he came back into her life, everything seemed just right . . .

Pearl moved on, heading inland into an area known as Keam's Yard. Centuries ago, it had been a boat yard responsible for the construction of yawls that had fished Whitstable's shores for native oysters. Now it was a concrete car park servicing the visitors who powered the town's new industry – tourism. Crossing the car park, Pearl acknowledged a pair of community police officers: two fresh-faced young constables who prompted her to reflect on the time when she, herself, had joined the force – equally fresh-faced and with a keen ambition to become a DCI – just like McGuire. An unplanned pregnancy had caused Pearl to abandon her dream and take up another role, becoming Charlie's mum. But once Pearl's son had become his own man, she had seized the chance to prove, if only to herself, that she could still use her 'people person' skills to solve crimes in her home town. If only there was a suitable case to exercise those skills . . .

The bells of St Alfred's rang out once more and Pearl hurried on, taking a short cut through Kemp Alley, one of the many ancient alleyways that, for hundreds of years, had been used to access the town's main business place – the sea. In years gone by, passageways like Kemp and Squeeze Gut Alley had formed handy escape routes for smugglers, but now local people simply relied on them to cut short their journeys around town. Pearl emerged on to the High Street at the side of the local playhouse. Straight ahead lay St Alfred's Church, a Union Flag flapping in the breeze on the church tower. St Alfred's remained at the heart of the local community, both geographically and in relation to those it served, not solely for religious purposes and to commemorate births, deaths and marriages, but also because it offered itself for public meetings on a variety of issues concerning the town – ably chaired by its vicar, the Reverend Prudence Lawson, a spirited woman with a compressed sense of power about her, like a charged battery.

Pearl was not particularly religious and had never been a regular churchgoer, though as a child she had attended

Sunday school and learned her Scriptures, but she had always felt the presence of the Church in the fabric of her life. St Alfred's held a special place in what had been principally, for so many years, a fishing town. Members of its parish had inevitably been lost at sea and ministers had offered solace and a suitable memorial service. As Pearl crossed the road she looked up at the church's stained-glass windows, which depicted biblical scenes familiar from her childhood: images of Christ preaching from a boat on the Sea of Galilee – a resonance for the congregation of a fishing town. Pearl had attended weddings of friends and relatives in this church as well as funerals – including that of her father and an oyster fisherman by the name of Vinnie Rowe, whose death a few years ago had first brought her into contact with McGuire. Charlie had been christened here, too, and although it was true that people now seemed to prefer using their Sundays to worship at the altar of consumerism – with visits to supermarkets whose size matched those of some cathedrals – a parish church like St Alfred's still held significance in the lives of its community.

Pearl's eyes scanned the church lawn for signs of McGuire, but he was nowhere to be seen – so she moved to a bench and sat down to wait. After a few moments she bit her lower lip, considering whether perhaps she should have hinted to McGuire what her 'surprise' might consist of. Could he possibly have got wind of what she was planning? She thought again – maybe he was simply held up in the busy evening traffic heading out of Canterbury.

She checked her phone and found no messages. Bringing up a stored number she was just about to call when an incoming text sounded. From McGuire, it read:

> Sorry, Pearl. Still tied up in a meeting.
> Can I meet you somewhere?

Reflecting on the hurried text, she replied – 'Yes' – then quickly tapped out an address before adding:

> Meet me there as soon as you can.

She hesitated for a moment before pressing 'send'. After dropping her phone back into her bag, she set off alone.

Chapter Five

Whitstable's only dance school was located in what had once been an old Methodist chapel, situated off the beaten track in a residential road between the High Street and the local railway station. It was set back from the pavement and backed on to some open land that formed part of a recreational area which included a children's swing park. Pearl arrived to find the school's forecourt packed with cars. The school had always seemed an unprepossessing establishment with dated signage bearing Irene Taylor's surname, but Pearl noted a more sophisticated design was now in place, featuring the new name – Ballard's School of Dance – with an artist's impression of Tony and Tanya Ballard in a dramatic tango pose: heads cast downwards as though scrutinising whoever might enter. Pushing open the door, Pearl found her waitress, Ruby, standing behind a desk in the foyer beside her friend, Florrie Johnson, who was acting as receptionist. The walls were plastered with inspiring dance images that included photographs of classes throughout the years – ballet, tap, ballroom, clog and Irish step dancing – but a large banner was strung across the entrance to the main studio emblazoned with two words: 'TANGO TIME!'

Both Ruby and Florrie had dressed up for the occasion in colourful figure-hugging frocks. Florrie's tow-coloured hair was pulled back into a ponytail, an artificial red rose pinned close to her ear. The girl had experimented with make-up and appeared to be wearing some pale foundation set with face powder. Her thin lips wore a slick of crimson lipstick.

'Good evening,' she said with a warm smile. 'I don't have to ask for your name, but if you could sign in this register that would be lovely.'

'Of course,' said Pearl, noticing as Florrie offered the register, a small tattoo was visible on the underside of the girl's wrist; what looked to Pearl much like a lightning strike. Signing her name beneath a long list of others, Pearl then handed the pen back to Florrie.

'You certainly both look the part.'

'Getting in the mood,' said Ruby.

'Yes,' said Florrie, 'I'm dying to see Tanya and Tony dance.'

Pearl commented on the loud rumble of voices sounding from the dance studio.

'Quite a few here already?'

It was Ruby who replied: 'You bet.' She nodded. 'Dolly's here and raring to go. It's going to be a lot of fun.'

'Thanks for partnering her,' said Pearl.

'Actually, she's going to have Irene as her partner now,' said Ruby.

'Oh?'

'Tanya's put me with Max,' Florrie explained. 'Jack will be dancing with his wife, Laura. So, if you need a partner—'

'No, it's fine,' said Pearl quickly. 'A friend's going to be joining me. He's just a bit delayed.' She glanced anxiously back towards the door, but there was still no sign of McGuire.

'No problem.' Florrie smiled. 'Just go straight through and have a great time!'

Pearl entered through swing doors to find the dance studio was packed. Before she could properly take stock of who was there, Nathan stepped forward.

'You made it!' He kissed Pearl on the cheek then indicated the man beside him. 'I hear you've already met Max?'

Max Sanchez offered a smile for Pearl. 'And the pleasure was all mine,' he said. 'That was a fabulous lunch you put on for us. And may I say,' he paused for a moment surveying Pearl's red dress, 'you look a million dollars.' He reached for Pearl's hand and brushed it lightly with his lips.

'I can't say my dancing will be worth as much,' said Pearl. 'But this is a community venture – so I'm here to support it.'

'As are we all.' Max gave a lazy sigh and looked back into the busy room as Pearl caught sight of Dolly, who, to her relief, was wearing her old flamenco dress and not her Fish Slapper's outfit. Dolly waved ostentatiously before continuing to chat to Irene Taylor. The two women were standing close to a grand piano on which Jack Harper was stacking some sheet music as his wife waited patiently for him. Laura Harper's blonde hair hung loose about her shoulders and with her bobbed fringe, she reminded Pearl of an illustration of Alice in Wonderland from one of Pearl's own childhood books.

Noticing Pearl's line of sight, Max commented: 'Laura's been drafted in too. Though I can't say any of us had much choice in the matter. Tanya's arranged everything – including who we partner. Even poor Tony's under strict orders to perform tonight.' He nodded towards Tony Ballard, seated in a chair near the grand piano, and explained: 'That knee operation of his was quite some time ago, but he still doesn't seem to be over it. Still, you know what we troupers always say,' he continued: 'The show must go on? And it *will* be more of a show than a lesson,' he stressed.

'What do you mean?' asked Nathan.

'I mean, my friend, we shall soon all find ourselves part of Tanya Ballard's audience.' He looked at Pearl and added: 'She needs one.'

Stunned by his honesty, Pearl hesitated, trying to think how to respond, but before she could do so, a voice suddenly sounded behind her.

'Well, well, I didn't count on *you* being here.'

Pearl didn't have to be a detective to realise that her old

suitor, Marty Smith, had just arrived: his booming voice and the overpowering smell of his musky aftershave clearly announced his presence. Bracing herself, she turned to find Marty beaming at her with newly bleached teeth and his dark hair slicked back with so much shine product it was glinting like black plastic beneath the lights. His shirt was open, unbuttoned almost to the waist, exposing his suntanned chest. Pearl was sure she saw him flex a pectoral before he asked the inevitable question: 'So . . . looking for a partner?' He winked – then waited expectantly for Pearl's reply.

'Well . . .' Pearl hesitated, recognising she was sure only of one thing: she could do without partnering Marty for a tango.

'She has one,' Nathan said quickly, springing to Pearl's rescue. 'I've stolen Pearl for this evening,' he lied, offering a broad smile.

Marty's own wide grin faded as he stared between them. 'I see,' he said, crestfallen. 'Well, be sure you give her back,' he went on, 'cos there's always a next time, eh, Pearl?' He winked once more, still offering the expectant look Pearl knew so well.

Having long since dashed his hopes for a relationship, Pearl didn't feel able to dash his hopes for a dance completely. 'Maybe,' she said politely.

Satisfied, Marty moved off, and Pearl spotted Peter and Hilary Radcliffe across the room, chatting to Whitstable's vicar, Rev Pru. Hilary, wearing a flimsy sequinned dress, offered a little rippling wave to Pearl while Radcliffe adjusted his toupee, which appeared to have had a restyle for the occasion, presumably, thought Pearl, to prevent it from making a bid for freedom during the class. A moment later, it looked to Pearl as though Ratty might be about to cross the studio towards her but she was saved from his presence when voices suddenly dropped, and an expectant murmur spread around the studio.

Tanya Ballard appeared through a door at the rear of the hall, wearing a striking black and red dress, impossibly high stiletto-heeled shoes and what looked like a hastily acquired gleaming suntan.

'Good evening, everyone!' she called out. Once she knew she had everyone's attention, she nodded to Tony, who appeared to brace himself before getting up from his chair. Having done so, he hesitated for a moment then gave a professional smile before slapping a white trilby hat on his head and moving across to his wife to take the slender hand she offered, her long fingernails painted crimson for the occasion. A look passed between them before Tanya continued: 'Welcome to Ballard's School of Dance . . . and our new class: Tango Time!'

Seated at the piano, Jack Harper played a series of dramatic tango chords, and another murmur went around the room as Tony suddenly released Tanya from his grasp, allowing his wife to perform three quick turns before he grabbed her once more and leaned her backwards, so low in his arms that Tanya's long dark hair almost touched the floor. A gasp went up from everyone, including Pearl, before Tanya sprang up again with a flourish of her arm.

Spontaneous applause rang out – an indication that the pair had a good home crowd for this evening's lesson.

'Tony and I,' said Tanya, 'are so pleased to be here in Whitstable tonight, sharing with you the principles of the dance we fell in love with more than two decades ago.' She paused and smiled at Tony, but the smile appeared to falter as her husband seemed unable to return it. Instead, Pearl perceived a look of pain etched on Tony Ballard's face. Nevertheless, Tanya continued: 'Why were we so captivated by tango above all other dances?' She looked again at her husband. 'Tony?'

'Because,' said Tony, shifting his weight from one leg to another, 'tango is more than just a dance.'

Tanya gave a small nod to what appeared to be a well-rehearsed answer. 'That's right,' she said. 'Someone once said that "tango is a sad thought danced",' she went on, her eyes searching out every figure crowded into the studio. 'Certainly, tango is a feeling – a passionate connection that has to continue throughout the whole dance. Everything that happens during tango takes place while we maintain the embrace.' She looked at Tony. 'It is never broken. And though tango could be described, very simply as . . .'

'A walking dance,' Tony supplied.

Tanya smiled and nodded. 'Tango is relaxed but with its own special energy that adapts to the beat of the music. It changes according to the space available in which to perform it, the style of music and, of course . . .'

She looked at Tony once more, who commented: 'The connection between the dancers at that moment.'

'That's right, Tony,' said Tanya. 'Tango relies on emotion. Without it, partners are simply . . . performing steps. But what must be conveyed is the emotion that is shared between two people in the special tango embrace – what's known as the *abrazo*. It's an emotion that's summoned up by music – and the embrace, the dance itself, is the means of conveying this. *That* . . . is tango – and its first rule is that it must start from here.' She turned to Tony and pressed the palm of her hand against his heart, holding his gaze as she went on.

'A passion . . . shared between two people. If the passion isn't there – it just isn't tango.' She smiled and turned to the class as she continued, 'What we know as the walking dance of the streets of Buenos Aires, the Argentine Tango, was to become the ballroom version that Tony and I are most known for.' She smiled at Tony. 'But tonight, before we begin any instruction at all on the steps, Tony and I will demonstrate for you the dance in its simplest form – to reveal the passion that is tango!'

Looking across to Jack Harper, Tanya gestured for him to begin the music. Jack duly got up from the piano and stepped across to the music deck. After a moment, a slow tango rhythm began to sound and Tanya turned back to face her husband – her cue for him to pull her towards him in an opening embrace. Tony did so, staring into Tanya's eyes, but he held the pose for only a second more before he suddenly gave a gasp of pain and shook his head, his hand moving quickly to his right knee.

'I'm sorry,' he said, grimacing as he looked up at Tanya.

'I can't do this.' Pain still written on his face, Tony Ballard reached out his other hand and Florrie quickly left Ruby's side to support Tony as he limped across the studio to his chair. A collective groan went around the room.

Tanya Ballard looked stunned but Max leaned in to Nathan and Pearl, and whispered: 'I'm not surprised one bit. I warned her but she wouldn't listen. He isn't up to it.' Max gave a confirmed look and Pearl stared across to see Irene and Florrie now tending to Tony. Tanya, still reeling from the shock, finally came to her senses and placated her class.

'I'm . . . sorry, everyone,' she began. 'But it's nothing to worry about. Tony will be okay.' She looked to Irene and Florrie for reassurance and both women nodded to her before they helped Tony out of the rear door.

Gathering her senses, Tanya continued: 'As I was saying, tango can be as simple or sophisticated as required, so . . . I wonder—' She broke off for a moment, staring around the class before adding: 'I . . . *could* continue with another partner . . .?'

Pearl saw Ratty Radcliffe taking a step forward while straightening his tie. As he did so, Marty Smith gave an audible cough and patted his bare chest to gain Tanya's attention. In desperation, Tanya stared instead towards Max, but he looked away, muttering under his breath: 'For God's sake, let her find another victim.'

At that moment, Tanya's face broke into a smile, like sunshine after rain, as she caught sight of someone entering the hall. Pearl turned . . . and saw it was McGuire. He was scanning the packed room, looking vaguely confused, but before he had a chance to spot Pearl, Tanya Ballard pounced.

'Fate!' she exclaimed. 'Please join me.' She was offering her hand to McGuire, who opened his mouth to speak – but Tanya was quicker. 'Your name?'

Uncomfortable, McGuire replied: 'Mike . . . But I'm here to—'

'Mike!' Tanya spoke over him. 'Come on, now. Don't be shy.'

Pearl looked on, mouth agape, as Tanya Ballard took hold of DCI Mike McGuire's arm and dragged him into the centre of the room, where she nodded quickly to Jack to cue the music once more. Laura Harper dimmed the lights so that only a central spotlight remained as Jack began the music track. Feeling guilty, Pearl sank into the shadows as she watched Tanya Ballard taking McGuire's right hand and positioning it around her waist, while holding his left hand firmly in her right.

'Just follow me,' Tanya said with a smile, fixing the detective's gaze with her own.

As the opening chords to a slow tango began, Pearl knew it was time to rescue McGuire. She moved forward – only for Nathan to lay a hand on her shoulder as he signalled with a look that she should stay put. Pearl now registered what Nathan could see from his vantage point – McGuire was actually compliant with Tanya, looking confident in the opening tango stance. Tanya slid out her left foot and drew a small circle on the floor with the toe of her high, black stiletto. Straight after, McGuire copied the move with his own foot then suddenly stepped out to one side, appearing to take the lead as he and Tanya moved off across the dance floor with three quick steps before pausing. Tanya seemed as surprised as Pearl, but a smile slowly spread across her face. She now moved her head close to McGuire's and allowed him to lead her in a slow promenade around the centre of the room.

Pearl glanced across at Dolly and saw her mother was equally entranced. The Radcliffes also stood motionless as McGuire turned Tanya in an efficient spin. Pearl craned her head, trying to gain McGuire's attention, but it was clear his concentration was focused on the dance.

Max leaned in to Nathan, whispering: 'This guy's good.'

Pearl frowned. '*This guy* is—' But before she could utter another word, McGuire had pulled Tanya Ballard even closer to him, slipping his knee between hers and holding the pose for two or more beats before executing a rocking step in time with the music then sweeping Tanya across the studio floor once more. The class gave a gasp but Pearl was dumbstruck, feeling in that moment a weight of complex emotions as she continued to observe McGuire holding another woman tightly in his grasp, his eyes fixed so closely on Tanya Ballard that he failed to notice Pearl in the shadows. The music came to a crescendo and McGuire finally leaned Tanya slowly back in his arms and the room erupted in a loud burst of applause.

Nathan moved closer to Pearl. 'Are you sure that wasn't

a dance course he's been on?' he asked, clapping furiously along with everyone else – everyone except for one person – Pearl – who remained looking on, dazed by what she had just seen.

Chapter Six

Pearl opened the front door to Seaspray Cottage and waited for McGuire to follow her in before she turned to him – still stunned by what she had witnessed at the dance school. 'I never thought in a million years you'd be able to—'

'What?' asked McGuire. 'Put one foot in front of the other?' He offered a smile.

'You did more than that,' said Pearl, heading straight for her drinks tray, where she poured a high ball of bourbon and handed it to him. 'How did you manage to keep that from me?'

She held his gaze while McGuire took a sip of his drink and pointed to her as he noted: 'You kept pretty quiet about the fact we were meeting at a dance school.'

'"School" being the operative word,' said Pearl, 'but you clearly needed no lessons.' Dropping some ice into a glass, she poured herself a vodka and tonic and turned back to McGuire. 'So,' she began, 'where did you learn to dance like that?'

McGuire stared at her for a moment, lost in her beautiful grey eyes. He was half tempted to explain, but thought better of it. 'You don't want to know.' He sat down on the sofa.

'Are you kidding?' said Pearl. 'I've never wanted to know anything more.' She sipped her drink and sat close beside him, waiting for his reply.

He turned and smiled. 'A "nice surprise", you said. You tricked me, Pearl. I was ambushed. When I walked into that studio, I didn't have a clue what was going on.'

'But you soon caught on,' Pearl countered with a knowing look.

'That woman jumped on me as soon as I set foot in the door—'

'That "woman" is Tanya Ballard.'

'I know that,' said McGuire, 'now.'

'And you also know how to tango,' said Pearl. 'So how did you learn?'

McGuire heaved a sigh, aware that Pearl was not about to give up. 'You really know how to break a man down, don't you?' He smiled before confessing: 'Streatham Academy of Dance.'

Pearl almost choked on her drink. McGuire gave a helpless shrug. 'My mother happened to have a thing about Patrick Swayze so . . .' He paused for a moment, then: 'She enrolled me for classes. At eight years old I didn't exactly have much say in the matter, but I got out of it as soon as I could and took up judo.'

Pearl looked at him, mystified. 'Why?'

'Why?' echoed McGuire. 'Because I figured I wouldn't be able to tango my way out of trouble in Streatham on a dark night, that's why.' He sipped his drink then gave another smile. 'I guess I was lucky she didn't have me down for ballet.'

Getting to his feet he walked to the window, where he stared out at the fast-disappearing sun. Pearl joined him there.

'And . . . you've kept this a secret since then?'

'I'm a cop.'

'A cop who knows how to tango.'

'Not something I'm keen to broadcast.'

'Then maybe you should have thought about that before you took to the floor this evening?'

McGuire looked back at her. 'If this gets back to the station . . . I'm finished.'

'Don't exaggerate.'

'I mean it,' said McGuire in all seriousness. 'I can't have anyone at the station finding out.'

'Like Welch?'

'*Especially* Welch.'

Pearl nodded. 'Okay. Point taken. But one good thing,' she added, 'is that Mum won't be able to call you a Flat Foot any more.' McGuire smiled. Pearl sipped her drink and went on: 'You have a hidden talent. You should be proud of it.'

'It's not a talent – just a skill, that's all. You go through the motions, over and over, until it becomes automatic – like driving a car.'

'Some people never get to pass their test?'

'Maybe they start lessons too late. Believe me, Pearl. Like riding a bike, you never forget how to do it.'

'Well, you certainly didn't look like you were losing your balance with Tanya.'

McGuire gently tilted Pearl's chin towards him as he realised something. 'Are you trying to tell me you were jealous?'

'Me?' Pearl shook her head. 'Of course not . . .' She trailed off before admitting: 'It was . . . a surprise. And now I'm wondering just how many other hidden "skills" you might have.'

McGuire held her look. 'We could try to find out?' He leaned in to kiss her but Pearl suddenly moved away and set down her drink. '*I'll* keep quiet,' she said, 'as long as you do something for me in return?'

McGuire frowned, suspicious, as he watched Pearl search in her bag for something, then she held out her hand to him. 'Come on.'

McGuire allowed Pearl to lead him through the kitchen and out into the garden, where the setting sun had left the sky several shades of indigo with a single stripe of flame on the western horizon. Pearl took a deep breath, sensing that with a rising full moon, this late summer night would be magical – one in which day would never properly end and night would never fall – a night that was not to be wasted in sleep but perhaps watching stars wheeling across the sky until dawn . . .

Having scrolled quickly through her smartphone she set it down on the patio table before turning again to McGuire with a determined look. 'Show me how to tango.'

McGuire looked sidelong at her. 'Are you serious?'

'Perfectly serious. I want you to teach me.'

Before he could say a word, McGuire was silenced by music that was suddenly sounding from Pearl's phone: strings and a bandoneon playing the introductory bars of *'Fueron Tres Anos'*. He hesitated then looked again at Pearl with new eyes as she stood before him in her slinky red dress that seemed to glow in the evening twilight. She raised her arms to shoulder height as the singer's voice began – and McGuire knew Pearl wasn't fooling – she really meant it. He slipped his arm softly around her waist, placing the palm of his hand flat against her spine, feeling her warm skin exposed by the deep V-shape of the back of her dress. Then he took her other hand and pulled her close.

For a moment, Pearl thought he was about to kiss her, but McGuire simply moved his face so close to hers they were barely separated and whispered to her: 'Just follow me, okay?'

He pressed his thigh tightly against her own and took a single step to the left before moving forward with his right foot and using his left to trace a small circle on the ground. Holding Pearl's look, he whispered again. 'A *lapiz*. Like your foot's a pencil drawing a circle on the ground.'

He swept Pearl around and brought her to a gentle stop by placing his foot against hers. '*Parada*,' he explained, 'a stop – like I'm breaking your step?' Pearl nodded and gave a smile, which McGuire returned before he leaned back a little and supported Pearl's spine as she did the same. '*Colgada*,' he went on, 'that means we're . . . suspended . . . hanging.' McGuire quickly spun Pearl around before drawing her even closer in his arms. Without saying another word, they now moved as one, McGuire still holding Pearl's gaze as he took several steps forward in perfect time to the music. The oppressive heat of the day was fading and a cool breeze blew in from the sea, enveloping them both in its embrace as the detective's arms closed more tightly about Pearl's body. Then he swept her around, his hand clasped around her waist, and she felt herself gliding with him until he stopped and stared down at the grass beneath their feet, then back at Pearl, as though signalling to her. She braced herself and traced a *lapiz* with her own foot upon the lawn. McGuire smiled and gave a small nod of his head, then guided her in a series of steps and swivels that Pearl followed until McGuire swung her backwards in a dramatic move. In a timeless moment, Pearl found herself suspended by McGuire's strong arms as she stared up at him, breathless, expectant.

A shooting star suddenly rose on the backdrop of the sky and McGuire leaned forward once more, his face drawn slowly to Pearl's, until, with the final beat of the music, his lips met Pearl's with the kind of hot kiss he never imagined he would owe to tango lessons from Streatham Academy of Dance.

Chapter Seven

The next morning, Pearl lay dozing with the warm sun streaming in through her bedroom window. A smile formed on her lips as she recalled her night with McGuire and she reached out lazily to touch him but her fingertips met only with an empty pillow.

Opening one eye, Pearl saw her two cats, Pilchard and Sprat, staring quizzically back at her, having usurped the space McGuire had occupied, then she spotted something on her bedside table – a single red rose, cut from her garden, sitting in a glass of water. A brief note, propped against it, read:

> *To the best partner I could ever have.*
> *Talk later.*
>
> *M x*

Pearl's sleepy smile returned as her fingers began tracing the delicate petals of the blood-red flower McGuire had left. Her new smartphone sounded.

'How are you feeling this morning?' McGuire asked.

'Fine,' said Pearl. 'I'm just wondering how you managed to escape.'

'You were fast asleep. I didn't want to wake you.'

'So you . . . haven't disappeared back to Hampshire?'

'I'm on shift at the station. Early start; briefings and a meeting with Welch later.'

'Lucky you.'

'Can you get off work tonight?'

'Why?'

'Because I'd like to take you for dinner, that's why, seeing as I didn't get to do that last night.'

'Because you were dancing with another woman?'

'I ended up dancing with you.'

'So you did.'

'Well?'

'I'm not working tonight—'

'Great.'

'But,' said Pearl, quickly remembering, 'I did promise to give Ruby a lift into Canterbury. She's celebrating a friend's birthday – the girl with the red rose in her hair last night?'

'Can't say I noticed,' said McGuire. 'I only had eyes for you. Why don't you drop the girls off and meet me here in Canterbury?'

'You're going to cook?'

'If I did that, it wouldn't exactly be much of a treat for you – or me,' he said. 'I'll see where I can book a table and call you later to confirm?'

'I can't wait.'

'Pearl?'

'Yes?'

'I just wanted to say . . .'

A paused followed. 'What?'

At that moment, Pearl suddenly realised her phone was out of battery. Getting up out of bed, she rued not having remembered to put it on charge the night before, but did so now, and then moved to her bedroom window and stared out. A fresh tide was rolling up on to the beach, bringing with it a gentle breeze. Pushing open the window she breathed in deeply, wondering to herself if she would ever have the measure of McGuire, and feeling a mixture of emotions in that moment as she remembered her shock at seeing him dancing with Tanya Ballard, bodies entwined, eyes fixed upon one another as everyone else in the class looked on, enthralled. A surge of possessiveness, and perhaps a twinge of jealousy, rose once more as she recalled how fascinated she had been by the performance, so much so that on returning home, she knew she had to be held in McGuire's arms in exactly the same way. She knew she would never match Tanya's tango skills, but still Pearl remembered the look in McGuire's eyes as he had danced with her in her garden under the setting sun, his hand pressed against her naked back, holding her tightly as he guided her through the steps – and then the kiss . . . perhaps a kiss she would remember more than any other. Pearl looked at the rose beside her. For all McGuire's reliance on the formality of procedure in his work, perhaps there was some passion within him to match her own, no matter how hard he might try to deny it . . .

An hour later, Pearl found herself at the Old Captain's House, with the express purpose of setting up a pair of small cameras in the Radcliffes' garden, relieved that neither of them were there to get in her way – or to comment on McGuire's tango prowess. Peter Radcliffe was attending yet another council meeting while Hilary, having managed to book an urgent hair appointment, had dropped off a spare key for Pearl at the restaurant on her way to Michel Angelo's – the most expensive hair salon in Whitstable.

Pearl worked quickly, deciding on the best location for her two surveillance cameras in order to capture Hilary's lingerie thief in flagrante delicto. If he or she had struck once, there was a good chance they would be tempted to do so again. Pearl confirmed to herself that the only possible entry point into the garden was via the gate in the rear wall – either by climbing it or by somehow managing to pick the lock. The gate led out into one of Whitstable's many alleys, but the two other walls, either side of the garden, were far too high to be scaled and were topped with a series of metal spikes set at regular intervals. After some deliberation, Pearl secured the cameras amid a thick crop of ivy on the wall near to Hilary's rotary washing line, confident that if the thief returned, her cameras would gain a clear record of the culprit for identification.

Staring up at the surrounding properties overlooking the Old Captain's House, Pearl considered that the Radcliffes' neighbours must surely have been much happier when they had gazed down at the old leafy garden rather than this soulless plot that now served as Hilary's sunbathing area. Nonetheless, Pearl couldn't rule out the possibility that someone very close by, and perhaps with a bird's-eye view into the garden, might have become fixated with Hilary Radcliffe – an attractive woman who clearly spent a small fortune keeping herself that way with regular visits to Whitstable's beauty salon, Whitstabelle, and a hairdressing bill to match Pearl's mortgage. Time, and Pearl's cameras, would surely tell. Zipping up her bag, Pearl headed back into the house, carefully locking the French windows behind her before moving into the living room, where she deposited Hilary's spare key on a coffee table. She then quickly scribbled a note that read:

> *Cameras all set. Hang the decoy items on the line after dark.*

After leaving the note conspicuously beside the key, Pearl turned to glance around the room. There were various photos on display in ostentatious frames, most showing Peter and Hilary on holiday around the globe – at the Pyramids in Giza; in a gondola on the Grand Canal; wearing cowboy hats in the Grand Canyon . . . Musing on this, Pearl realised that, by contrast, she and McGuire had only ever managed a single weekend away together to Bruges, though now she imagined herself in every one of the settings shown in the Radcliffes' photographs – and a few more besides. Pearl had always wanted to visit Rome but had never made it there, so she closed her eyes and conjured up a vision of being there with McGuire, tossing a coin into the Trevi Fountain . . .

She smiled and opened her eyes once more and noted a whole shelf lined with trophies – mostly for cricket but some for outdoor bowls. They sat perched alongside framed certificates and accolades for Ratty's municipal achievements – all displayed in the kind of conspicuous arrangement only someone of Peter Radcliffe's vanity might think appropriate. Pearl hoped that her security cameras bore fruit tonight so she could solve this case and offload her clients as soon as possible. At that moment her phone sounded an incoming text. Checking it, she saw it was from Dolly.

> *Pearl, I'm suffering. Can you get here?*
> *Use your key.*

Quick to respond to Dolly's SOS, Pearl arrived within minutes at her mother's home on Harbour Street, which was situated beneath the Bohemian little holiday flat – known as Dolly's Attic – which was rented out to visitors all year round. At the front of the building on the ground floor was Dolly's Pots, the shop from which Pearl's mother sold her 'shabby chic' ceramics and the artwork she created from 'treasures' found on her beach recces. Letting herself in with her own key, Pearl found Dolly reclining against batik cushions on a comfortable daybed in her conservatory

– the temperature of which was uncomfortably stuffy from the heat of the morning sun.

'At last . . .' groaned Dolly.

'What on earth's wrong?' asked Pearl, concerned.

'What do you think?' Dolly sighed.

'Your back?'

Dolly nodded. 'I'm such a slave to this disc.' She closed her eyes before adding, 'I should've known not to throw myself into those moves last night, but it was impossible to hold back.' Opening one eye, she now looked at Pearl and said: 'But who would have thought it . . .?'

'Thought what?'

'That a flat foot could have such a flair for tango?'

Pearl noted Dolly's mischievous look and turned away from it, busying herself by mixing two glasses of elderflower cordial as she commented: 'He'd rather you forgot about that.'

'How can I?' said Dolly, taking one of the glasses from Pearl. 'I've seen him in a totally new light now. Come to think of it, so has everyone. Did you notice the looks he got – especially from the women?'

'No,' said Pearl with a sigh. 'At the time, I was rather distracted.'

Dolly gave her a look, noting the firm set of her daughter's lips, before Pearl finally admitted: 'To be honest, I had no idea he could dance.'

'Oh, I see,' said Dolly. She took a sip of cordial. 'A new string to your beau's bow? I wonder how many other hidden talents he possesses.' Her smile immediately transformed into a grimace of pain to which Pearl quickly responded.

'Do you want me to call the doctor?'

'No, of course I don't,' said Dolly tetchily. 'I'll take some of my homeopathic remedies in a minute and rest up, which means,' she continued, 'I'm afraid I shan't be able to help out in the restaurant today.'

'Don't worry,' said Pearl, unperturbed, knowing she would be able to manage – not least because, unlike Pearl herself, cookery was not exactly Dolly's forte. In fact, Pearl had never forgotten how her mother had once shown such disdain for cuisine she had actually substituted peanuts on a dish of *truite aux amandes*. In truth, Dolly's extrovert nature was far better suited to duties 'front of house'.

'You'll be missed, but we'll manage,' said Pearl, though she remained concerned about Dolly's disc. 'Are you sure there's nothing I can do?'

'Nothing,' Dolly replied, before adding quickly: 'Apart from feeding Mojo. His kibbles are over there.' She nodded towards a jar of cat biscuits on a shelf that also housed a variety of items since the conservatory served as Dolly's own artist's *atelier*. Large white enamel jugs housed paintbrushes and palette knives, jostling for space amongst a vast collection of old blue apothecary bottles and items in which Dolly found inspiration: pebbles from the shore, clumps of heather and the skull of a sheep, bleached white as chalk. Within minutes of setting foot in her mother's home, Pearl always felt the need to tidy up and instil some kind of order, though Dolly always insisted that everything was, in fact, in its place. A psychologist might have linked Pearl's love of order, her need to find solutions and tie up all loose ends, as a counter-balance to a childhood that, for the most part, had been carefree and unrestrictive. It was certainly true that Pearl had thrived within the disciplined framework offered by her basic police training, but during her probationary period she had also demonstrated that she was someone who not only engaged well with the public, but displayed a sharp, instinctive understanding of people in general. It was this skill, above all, that had singled Pearl out as a potential candidate for criminal investigation, until a positive reading on a pregnancy test had prompted her resignation, leaving Dolly to quietly celebrate, since she was infinitely more comfortable with the idea of her daughter as a single mum than a 'lackey of the State'. Pearl opened the jar of cat biscuits and set a saucer for Mojo near the conservatory doors. She surveyed Dolly's overgrown garden, which had been taken over by so much rampant bamboo it could easily provide a location for a remake of *Apocalypse Now*, and called Mojo's name, waiting for a few moments before she shrugged and asked: 'So where is he?'

'I've no idea,' said Dolly glumly. 'You know what he's like when the weather's as warm as this – he can take off for days – but I don't want him to forget where his home is. If I don't feed him, someone else will and then he'll be gone for good.'

'I doubt it,' said Pearl. 'Mojo knows where his bread is buttered.'

77

'True,' said Dolly, appeased. 'And he does indeed enjoy a buttered slice every now and then – as well as a dippy egg.' She winked at Pearl, who leaned forward and kissed her mother.

'Let me know if there's anything else I can do.'

'There won't be,' Dolly insisted. 'Irene's picking me up a few things.'

'Irene? You mean—'

'Tanya's aunt, yes, she's popping round in a while so don't forget to leave your spare key for her beneath the bay tree pot outside?'

'I will,' Pearl agreed. She had begun heading for the door when she suddenly paused and asked: 'Was she pleased?'

'Pleased?'

'Irene Taylor – about how the class went last night?'

'Oh yes,' said Dolly. 'And Tanya, too – though it seems poor Tony is still as incapacitated as I am. I hear he's on some very strong painkillers. Irene offered to bring me some over but I told her—'

'You eschew Big Pharma and prefer holistic medicine?'

'But of course,' said Dolly.

Pearl thought for a moment. 'It . . . was a knee op, wasn't it?' she asked. 'Tony Ballard, I mean. Tanya mentioned it at the restaurant, remember?'

Dolly nodded. 'That's right. I understand from Irene that it was a straightforward replacement; he had it done several months ago, in the New Year, so it's taken a while to heal.' She frowned as she considered this. 'It's odd, because I have a whole host of friends with plastic knees these days and most are back to normal activities within six weeks of surgery – though the GP did warn Gloria from the bakers that it might take up to three months for her pain to subside, but then she's carrying a lot of weight these days. To be honest, she's as fat as butter from her addiction to gypsy tarts . . . but Tony Ballard looks incredibly fit.'

'Yes,' Pearl agreed, equally puzzled. 'Well, take care,' she said with a smile. 'Rest up and I'll talk to you later.'

Pearl moved again to the door but this time Dolly spoke. 'You're going to have to learn, you know.'

'Learn what?' asked Pearl, turning.

'How to tango, of course,' said Dolly, 'if you want to keep up with that man of yours.' She gave a sly smile, which made Pearl wonder if Dolly hadn't, in fact, meant: if you want to 'keep hold' of McGuire . . .

With another fine day and Dolly out of action, Pearl found herself occupied with a busy lunchtime session at the restaurant, but having organised some part-time waiting staff for the evening shift, she was relieved to have some spare time ahead of her once she'd fulfilled her promise to Ruby of a lift in to Canterbury to celebrate Florrie Johnson's birthday. McGuire had not yet confirmed where they might be meeting for dinner, though Pearl was sure he would do so once he was freed from the grasp of his nemesis, Superintendent Maurice Welch. No doubt the detective also had plenty of work to catch up with, including some new cases that would surely prove more compelling than Pearl's investigation into the theft of a washing line of underwear – no matter how exclusive the lingerie might be. She finished taking payment from a group of tipsy young women – DFLs, judging by their champagne tastes and salon tans – and watched as they teetered off in their high heels towards the door, where they crossed with someone entering. Tanya Ballard glanced quickly around before spotting Pearl at the sea-food bar and headed over.

'Pearl,' she said with a genial smile. 'I'm just on my way to meet Aunt Irene – but I couldn't possibly walk past without saying hello.' She indicated a bar stool at the counter and asked: 'May I?'

'Of course,' said Pearl. 'What can I get you?'

Tanya shook her head. 'Nothing. I really must fly but . . . I just wanted to say a huge thank-you for inviting along your friend last night. With Tony out of action, and just when I needed him most, the whole tango launch could have ended up the most horrendous flop. As it was, Michael saved the day. It . . . is Michael, isn't it?' she asked, fishing for information.

'DCI McGuire,' said Pearl, shocked to realise she was bristling in response to Tanya's question.

'When I saw you together yesterday,' Tanya went on, 'outside this restaurant, I had no idea he was actually a policeman.' She paused. 'But then my aunt tells me you were in the force once too?'

'A long time ago,' said Pearl. 'And only as a cadet.'

'I see,' said Tanya, 'and now you have a detective agency as well as this restaurant?' She smiled once more. 'I presume that's what you and . . . Michael . . . have in common, is it? Crime.'

'Mike,' said Pearl, now feeling the need to stress some informality.

Tanya gave a nod then asked tentatively: 'And will . . . Mike . . . be coming along next week?'

'I'm not sure,' said Pearl. 'His work keeps him very busy.'

'Of course.' Tanya seemed to reflect on this for a moment before she reached into her bag and took out a business card which she handed across the counter to Pearl. It showed a logo using the same image as the new sign at Ballard's School of Dance, together with Tanya's name and mobile number.

'I wonder if you would be kind enough to pass this on to Mike? If he did want to come along again, perhaps I could persuade him to partner me for another demonstration?'

Pearl's mouth gaped open before she looked from the card in her hand to Tanya, and asked: 'I take it Tony's condition is serious?'

Tanya looked helpless for a moment. 'It really shouldn't be,' she said, tense. 'A simple knee replacement, and he's had plenty of time to recover, but he did suffer some post-operative nerve trouble. It happens sometimes. He has a good specialist but . . . well, I can't help thinking that perhaps the whole experience has made him lose a little confidence. So I find myself, for the first time in my life, without a partner.'

'What a shame,' said Pearl, trying to summon up conviction.

Picking up on Pearl's tone, Tanya eyed her for a moment, then managed a brief smile before a voice sounded behind her.

'Tanya?' Irene Taylor looked surprised to see her niece as she approached. She pointed back to the door. 'I just happened to see you through the window,' she explained. 'I thought we were meeting at your flat?'

'We are,' said Tanya. 'I was just on my way back.' She leaned forward and kissed her aunt.

Irene then turned to Pearl. 'It would be lovely to stay and spend more time with you, but Tanya and I have some work to do – accounts to go through – but I've just left Dolly.'

'How is she now?' asked Pearl.

'Much brighter than when I arrived,' Irene explained. 'We had a chat and she even managed a brief turn around the garden – looking for her cat.'

'Mojo,' said Pearl. 'Did she find him?'

Irene shook her head. ''Fraid not, but she says he's apt to take off?'

'From time to time,' Pearl agreed. 'I think he does it on purpose, knowing Mum will spoil him rotten once he returns.'

'Yes,' said Irene, 'that sometimes happens with errant males.' She raised a knowing smile and said: 'I do hope her back improves soon.' Turning to Tanya she went on, 'I suggested some of Tony's medication – a painkiller and a powerful anti-inflammatory – but Dolly's GP would have to prescribe it and I don't think your mother approves of conventional medicine?'

'Mum hasn't seen her GP for fifteen years or more,' said Pearl. 'She prefers what she calls—'

'"Holistic medicine"?' said Tanya. She gave a sigh. 'My mother was the same. We lived in a commune for a while,' she went on. 'Big Sur, California. Mum relied a little too much on "herbal medicine" – home-grown pot mainly. I can't say it helped her much in the end.'

'Tanya . . .' Irene gently reproached her.

'What?' said Tanya, unabashed. 'It's no secret, is it?' She turned back to Pearl. 'Mum ended up being exploited by a number of fakes, users and hangers-on – anyone who cared to take advantage of her, in fact. If she'd only stayed here and managed the dance school—'

'Then you might never have been born,' said Irene, breaking in. 'She met your father in the States and you're half American, remember? The child of two parents.'

'Don't you mean orphan?' said Tanya. 'My parents are dead. "Live fast – die young – and leave a good-looking corpse."'

Irene appeared to flinch at the harsh truth of this, but Tanya remained defensive. 'That was the maxim they quoted often enough.'

She blinked several times then seemed to remember herself and looked back at Pearl. 'I'm sorry,' she said gently, 'I didn't mean to make you feel awkward – especially about my family life.' She glanced now at Irene and took her aunt's hand. 'I'm incredibly lucky to have you, Aunt Irene,' she said tenderly. 'You've always been the sane one in the family. The voice of reason. I really don't know what I'd do without you.'

Irene returned her niece's smile and placed her own hand over Tanya's before patting it affectionately. 'Come on,' she said, 'let's get those accounts looked over.'

Tanya nodded, got to her feet and raised a smile for Pearl. 'See you before too long,' she said.

After the pair left the restaurant, Pearl found herself staring down at Tanya Ballard's business card in her hand – no longer jealous, but now feeling strangely sorry for the woman.

Chapter Eight

It was after five that afternoon before McGuire managed to extricate himself from a meeting in the Incident Room at Canterbury Police Station. Most of his fellow officers were heading straight to the pub for a pint and a game of pool, but McGuire returned to his office in need of some peace and quiet. Closing the door behind himself, he crossed the room to the window. It was grimy from the traffic that flowed as constantly on the main route below as did the Great River Stour, which wended its way through Canterbury itself. Above the old city walls on the opposite side of the road, the cathedral spires rose against the backdrop of a blue summer sky. In almost three years of living here in Canterbury, McGuire had yet to enter the cathedral, put off by the tourists queueing in the Buttermarket square outside the cathedral gates and by an admission fee that made it seem as if he was buying a ticket to a ride in a theme park. Entrance to the cathedral services was free, but McGuire was not religious; though there had been times in his life when, for want of something else to turn to, and as an indication of his desperation, he had resorted to prayer – never in his personal life, but sometimes in his job.

Twenty years in the force had taught McGuire to keep a professional distance from his cases but it wasn't always easy when they were dropped by the CPS for want of sufficient evidence. And yet, in spite of all the heinous crimes – the muggings, murders, domestic violence, gang rapes, blackmail and racketeering – there was still enough to keep him in his profession. A vocation? Or was it simply that he had ploughed the same furrow for so many years that he felt unable or incapable of doing anything else? Sometimes, while walking within the green open space of Dane John Gardens across the road he would observe the inbred nature of various dogs – a retriever retrieving, a terrier yapping at squirrels and a spaniel digging among the roots of a tree – only for the animals to pause for a moment, looking up as if suddenly questioning why they felt the need to do such things. McGuire reasoned it was the breed – each had their particular role to play – and McGuire had his, too. He was a pedigree policeman. He could do nothing else.

Perhaps that's why he had so much respect for Pearl and her ability to adapt and survive. She had worked hard to become a successful businesswoman, using her cookery skills to create a popular restaurant – so distinct and unlike all the others in Whitstable that relied on swanky beachfront locations and menus featuring 'international cuisine' to compensate for a lack of character, atmosphere and plain good cooking. In contrast, The Whitstable Pearl remained a small but precious gem, full of charm and with a reputation for providing some of the best seafood in town. Fresh oysters, crab, shrimps and prawns were always available at the bar, but Pearl also offered a selection of signature dishes, each one created with the finest ingredients. Her menu had been perfected over time, which meant that while Pearl's presence wasn't always needed at the restaurant, the quality of her food remained constant and guaranteed a steady if not growing trade. Not content with all that, she had then gone on to start up the detective agency, which had ultimately thrown her together with McGuire.

He had to admit she was a good private eye – though her methods were unconventional and she relied too much for his liking on following her gut instincts. Nevertheless, McGuire also had to admit that, for the most part, Pearl's instincts were sound. She was a natural detective – a 'people person' – and combined with her connections and status within the town, Pearl's help had often proved invaluable in McGuire's investigations. In spite of that, the police detective felt conflicted, wishing Pearl could leave the police work to him – not least because she had put herself in danger too many times. So far, she had been lucky in extricating herself from it, but McGuire couldn't help feeling that one day Pearl's luck might run out . . .

Moreover, McGuire's initial move from London to Kent had followed only months after the death of his fiancée, Donna, and although he hadn't recognised it at the time, he knew now that he had been taking flight from that single event and all the raw emotions associated with it. Two things had initially helped him through the first shock of grief: a taste for Bourbon and a reliance on gambling – though he had soon recognised he had to put a curb on both in order to keep his job. These were short-term coping strategies to deal with his loss and the memory of a senseless incident that had robbed him of someone he loved; two drugged-up kids in a stolen car mowing Donna down one cold and rainy night on the streets of Peckham. From that moment on, life had never been the same, but time had moved on and McGuire had managed to do the same, though the itch to gamble was still there to scratch: the desire to play a hand of poker, to place a bet, to engage in a game of pitch and toss merely to see which way the dice would fall, perhaps in the simple hope that luck might come his way once more – as it had always seemed to do when Donna was alive. McGuire now recognised that gambling had been his way of exploring how much influence he, or anyone, might have over events, and as such it represented an analogy for the greater game of life itself. Up to that point, McGuire had been a winner, easing his way up the ranks: collecting plaudits and promotion on the way, while making steady progress and plans for the future. But on that fateful night on a street in Peckham, his future had been snatched from him, together with the luck he had always felt he carried with him. Since then, events seemed increasingly random, including how Pearl had crossed his path – not in the capital where he felt caged by memories, but in the kind of place where crime statistics consisted mainly of stolen bicycles or Saturday-night brawls. Here, in refuge on the North Kent coast, McGuire had found himself involved in a murder case with a woman called Pearl Nolan – a woman who was everything McGuire had least expected to encounter at that time: a restaurateur, a mother, a beautiful headstrong woman who belonged to no one but herself. She and McGuire were opposites but drawn to one another by an indefinable force. Sun and moon, light and dark, yin and yang – they even looked as though they might have sprung from different tribes: Pearl was a dark-haired Whitstable native while McGuire was the tall blond stranger who had entered her life – and failed to leave it. Just a few years on and he was still here, in Canterbury, anchored to the area by his feelings for Pearl – and by crime – but without having moved forward with his relationship with Pearl or his job.

Welch had a lot to do with the latter: McGuire's superior had always shown an instinctive dislike for having a DFL on his force and so he had overlooked and sidelined McGuire in favour of his local team. This served to highlight Welch's own inadequacy, but it also made McGuire increasingly uneasy, as he was reluctant for his relationship with Pearl to become fully known to his churlish superintendent – especially as Welch had been seeking a reason to get rid of the DFL ever since McGuire's temporary secondment from the Met had become a permanent transfer. McGuire knew he could always pass Pearl off as a local informant, something that would appear even more feasible with further budget cuts leading to more staff shortages, but he had never much liked the idea of relying on informants, particularly during his time at the Met. Many of them volunteered their services to even up an old score, while others enjoyed having a level of power from possessing crucial information. McGuire knew the importance of maintaining control of a case, and informants often jeopardised that. Moreover, the use of any informant had to be properly registered by a police officer so that the relationship between the two could be strictly monitored. McGuire had never registered his relationship with Pearl, but there again, she had always volunteered her services with no need for payment – and that had remained McGuire's loophole. Increasingly, McGuire now began to think that Pearl could be kept safe, along with his own job, if she could only be persuaded to give up Nolan's Detective Agency and concentrate solely on The Whitstable Pearl – a view that had become even more apparent while McGuire had been away in Hampshire. But there again, McGuire knew only too well that Pearl wasn't likely to do anything she didn't want to, simply to please a man. With that thought in mind, he picked up his phone and dialled . . .

Pearl had just stepped out of the shower at Seaspray Cottage when she heard her landline ringing. Wrapping a towel around her body she quickly entered her bedroom and picked up the receiver beside her bed.

'Sorry to get back to you so late.'

Pearl smiled at the sound of McGuire's voice and sat down on her bed. 'No problem. I knew you'd have a busy day.'

'And you were right – as usual.'

Pearl eyed the red rose still in the glass beside her bed, as she said: 'I was pretty busy, too. Seems you made quite an impression last night.'

'Oh?'

'Tanya Ballard came into the restaurant today and left her card. For you.'

Pearl took it from her bag and turned it over in her hand as she considered this.

'She wondered if you'd be joining the class next week. Seeing as she's still short of a partner.'

'I'm already taken.'

'Are you?'

'You know I am,' said McGuire softly but with conviction. 'Still driving the girls to Canterbury?'

'They have to be there in an hour.'

'Good. Because I've managed to book a table at the little Italian place by the river.'

'The one right across from your flat?'

In all the time McGuire had lived in his riverside apartment in Best Lane, he had yet to enjoy an evening with Pearl at the Italian bistro on the river's opposite bank, with its pretty alfresco dining area above which climbed a well-established vine. At this time of year, the restaurant's terracotta pots were filled with flowering geraniums to match the red-and-white gingham tablecloths and with McGuire's living-room window swung wide open, he had an uninterrupted view of the couples who sat at the tables sipping glasses of chilled white wine in the warm evening sun, chatting and laughing together or simply gazing into one another's eyes. McGuire had always imagined that, one evening, he and Pearl would get to do the same. Now it looked as though they would. Perhaps things were finally going his way. Perhaps he would even get a chance to persuade Pearl to see things from his point of view about the agency – and their future.

'That's the one,' he said.

'Lovely,' said Pearl finally. 'As soon as I drop the girls off, I'll be with you.'

'I'll be waiting,' said McGuire.

Hearing Pearl disappear from the line, McGuire smiled to himself and stared again out of his office window towards the cathedral. Maybe he wasn't an atheist at all. Maybe one prayer, at least, had just been answered.

Half an hour later, Pearl drew up in her Fiat outside Ballard's School of Dance and turned to Ruby sitting beside her in the passenger seat, dressed in a pretty pink shift dress. It wasn't often that Pearl saw her young waitress out of her usual restaurant uniform of white top, black trousers or skirt and starched *Whitstable Pearl* apron. In fact, Ruby was quite transformed from the pale, wisp-thin teenager who had lived with her grandmother, Mary Hill, in Whitstable's only tower block, Windsor House.

Following Mary's death, Ruby had taken on the flat, and she lived there still, no longer a child – but a young woman with her own life and friends like Florrie Johnson.

'D'you think Florrie will be finished soon?' asked Pearl.

Ruby checked her watch and nodded. 'Should be. It's just gone six.' She gazed out of the car window towards the school.

'Have you known her long?' asked Pearl. 'Florrie, I mean?'

'A couple of years,' Ruby replied. 'She's a good mate and she really enjoys working at the school.' She looked back at Pearl and smiled. 'It's her first job. She loves it now that Tanya and Tony are here. It's been like a real boost for her.'

'Boost?'

'Yeah,' said Ruby, her smile fading as she became thoughtful. 'A year ago she was really down. Depressed. She'd put on loads of weight and didn't want to go anywhere. Now she's lost it all. She looks great, doesn't she?'

'Yes,' said Pearl. 'She looked lovely last night. You both did.' Pearl offered a smile before her own gaze drifted towards the school as she mused on how celebrities like Tanya and Tony Ballard might capture the imagination of young women like Florrie and Ruby – as well as that of many others in a small town like Whitstable.

Ruby took Pearl's silence for impatience and opened the car door as she explained: 'I'll go and see what's keeping her.'

She jumped out of the car, her fair hair bouncing on her shoulders as she hurried towards the school. Pearl looked on as Ruby rang the school's bell then waited patiently. A moment later, she rang the bell again. When nobody appeared, Ruby glanced back towards Pearl and shrugged before calling out: 'I'll go round the back. She's probably in the wardrobe department.'

Pearl nodded and continued to watch as Ruby disappeared around the side of the building. Once she was out of sight, Pearl switched on her car radio and listened idly to the end of the local news as it segued into a long-range weather report. High temperatures were forecast, which would surely result in more busy days for The Whitstable Pearl. At the weekends, Locals and DFLs would emerge – identifying themselves by their preferred activities: locals heading to their beach huts or taking to the water with dinghies, paddleboards and kayaks, while DFLs would flood the shops, renting noisy jet skis or windsurf equipment before taking to the local pubs and eateries for a boozy lunch, followed by a siesta on the beach or on the balconies of local hotels. The evening would finally bring everyone out on to the streets to mingle in the bars and music venues. Pearl sighed to herself and switched off the radio, wondering if McGuire would be free on Sunday afternoon and, if so, whether she could perhaps tempt him to join her for a sail in her dinghy – out towards the west – to the neighbouring coastal village of Seasalter, where a fine Michelin-starred restaurant stood on the old salt marshes. Here, the tide would retreat far out, exposing sand and river silt from a sea channel, the Swale, which ran between the Isle of Sheppey and the mainland. Apart from the restaurant and a few holiday parks, the area was a complete contrast to the summer frenzy of Whitstable – its marshy land crossed only by sheep and the railway line. Pearl thought it was the perfect place for a weekend getaway, during which she and McGuire could sample the restaurant's new tasting menu before perhaps renting one of the beach huts that stood on land at the back of the restaurant in this beautifully desolate retreat.

But for now, she looked forward to their evening in Canterbury, at the little Italian bistro that sat on the opposite bank to McGuire's apartment . . . Smiling to herself at the thought, Pearl turned the volume down on the radio, only to hear the presenter's voice fading into another sound: a loud incongruous scream. For a second Pearl wondered whether she had imagined it, but quickly switching off the radio, she heard another louder wail issuing from the school and knew she wasn't mistaken.

Pearl sprang from her car, heading directly for the rear of the dance school, following Ruby's route. She found the back door unlocked and stepped inside the building, calling out loudly: 'Ruby?'

Silence followed before the door slammed shut behind her. Pearl found herself staring around blindly in the semi-darkness of a narrow corridor, off which several rooms branched. Moving forward, she opened each door in turn, finding nothing but rails of costumes and props. She called out again: 'Ruby, where are you?' Again, only silence.

Staring around helplessly, Pearl's eyes slowly adjusted to the darkness before she heard something more, this time not another scream, but a gentle whimpering.

Steeling herself, Pearl followed the sound to another room further down the corridor. Its door was ajar, and Pearl made out rails of tutus, feathered headdresses and what looked like the front end of a pantomime horse. The heavy scent of naphthalene hung in the air, suggesting years of mothball treatments. At the end of an aisle, Pearl glimpsed a shadow: the silhouette of Ruby's slight frame.

Stepping forward, Pearl could now see that in spite of the stuffy heat of the building, the girl was shivering, one of her tiny hands clenched between her teeth as if to prevent it from trembling.

Pearl's voice dropped to a whisper. 'What is it?' she asked, taking a few more steps forward to see Ruby's gaze finally shift towards her, as if for reassurance, before she looked slowly back again towards something concealed by a rail of costumes. Another step forward revealed to Pearl what Ruby seemed transfixed by. In the harsh light of a stage make-up mirror, framed by several bulbs, a woman was seated in a chair, wearing a tango dress – scarlet with a black frill – the same dress Tanya had worn to give her tango demonstration. Her arms hung down at her sides and her head leaned fully back so that her long dark hair flowed straight down as if drawn to the floor. As Pearl approached she saw a red trail of blood was running down to meet it, issuing from the front of Tanya Ballard's skull into which was impaled the stiletto heel of one of her dance shoes which partially concealed her face. Pearl reached out for Ruby, instinctively drawing the girl into her arms, comforting her, feeling the young waitress sobbing against her chest before Pearl glanced once more at the body in the chair and suddenly registered something else: a small tattoo on the inside wrist of the dead body – a tiny strike of lightning . . .

Stepping away from Ruby, Pearl investigated the corpse, checking for a carotid pulse as the realisation dawned that this wasn't Tanya Ballard at all . . . It was young Florrie Johnson, staring back at Pearl through one of her lifeless baby-blue eyes.

Chapter Nine

Pearl lost herself in McGuire's strong embrace, before they finally broke apart, standing together in Pearl's garden as the early-morning sun spread across the coastline. It had just gone 6 a.m. and McGuire had arrived straight from Canterbury Police Station, a light stubble on his jaw telling Pearl that he had been there all night. Pearl was wearing her crimson silk dressing gown, which she wrapped more tightly about her body as the bells of St Alfred's Church began to ring out for the Sunday service. McGuire set a folder down on the bistro table and looked at Pearl with concern.

'So, you got back okay?' he asked gently.

Pearl nodded. 'One of your DCs drove us home after we gave our statements.'

McGuire lowered his voice as he asked: 'How's Ruby?'

'Asleep in Charlie's room. To be honest, I think she may still be in shock.'

McGuire nodded. 'Thank God she wasn't alone.'

At this, Pearl remembered how tightly Ruby had clutched Pearl's hand as they had been driven to Canterbury Police Station, notified of their rights, fingerprinted, photographed, swabbed for DNA; she'd even had to surrender her clothes for forensic analysis. It was all standard police procedure, but a frightening experience for a young woman who had already suffered the trauma of discovering her friend's dead body.

'How about you?' asked Pearl. 'Have you managed to get any sleep?'

McGuire shook his head and then rubbed his brow. 'I'll grab a few hours in a while but I'm on my way to the dance school – meeting Forensics there.' He nodded towards the folder on the table. 'I went through your statements, Pearl. You understand I couldn't take them myself – knowing you both?'

'Of course,' said Pearl, 'procedure.' She sat down at the patio table and noted McGuire's tension. 'What is it?'

McGuire paused before sitting down beside her and framing a question. 'You told the DS that when you first saw the body you thought it was Tanya Ballard?'

Pearl nodded. 'I couldn't see her face but I recognised the dress – the same one Tanya wore for the class . . . red with black frills at the hip?'

McGuire gave a nod and Pearl continued: 'And the hair was dark – just like Tanya's – but Florrie Johnson's real hair colour was a mousy brown.'

'Seems she dyed it,' said McGuire, taking a photo from his folder that showed Florrie smiling for the camera, her tow-coloured hair pulled back into a ponytail.

Pearl studied the image as McGuire asked, 'Why would she do that?'

'Dye her hair?' asked Pearl. She shrugged. 'I don't know, except that . . . it was a special occasion – her birthday – that's why she and Ruby were going out to celebrate. I was giving them a lift into Canterbury, remember?'

McGuire thought of his restaurant date with Pearl, thwarted by a young woman's murder. He set the photo on the table. 'Even without a murder you'd never have made it on time.'

Pearl frowned. 'Why not?'

'A lorry jack-knifed on Whitstable Road last night,' he explained. 'It took some time to clear and the roads into Canterbury were a complete mess.' He fell silent, remembering how Pearl's call had alerted him to her grim discovery at the dance school. He stared down at Pearl's statement and the photograph of Florrie Johnson, whose body now lay in a chilled drawer of the police morgue awaiting an autopsy.

'How the hell did this happen?' he murmured almost to himself, before he stared away towards the sea, as if for an answer.

'I don't know.' Pearl shook her head, pained. 'From what Ruby told me, Florrie was enjoying her work and had her whole life ahead of her.'

'Why would anyone would want to kill her?'

'Maybe . . . they didn't want to?'

McGuire looked back at Pearl as she explained: 'Have you thought this could be a case of mistaken identity? Florrie was sitting in a chair with her back to the door, so if the killer came up behind her and saw a woman dressed in Tanya's clothes . . .'

'With long dark hair . . .'

'They could easily have assumed it was Tanya Ballard.'

McGuire considered this. 'It's possible,' he agreed. 'There were no defensive wounds.'

'So Florrie didn't try to fight back . . .' Pearl trailed off and frowned again as she reorganised her thoughts. 'She was in front of the make-up mirror. It was lined with light bulbs. They were all on . . . all working . . .'

'So if someone had crept up on her—'

'She would have seen them in the mirror.' She turned to McGuire. 'It must have been someone she knew, someone she trusted.'

'Someone,' said McGuire, 'she wouldn't have been surprised to see.'

'A member of staff . . .'

'Or a friend,' said McGuire, pausing for a moment before: 'Ruby?'

Pearl recoiled, shocked at the suggestion. 'How can you even think—'

'I'm just considering the facts.'

'That Ruby might have done this?' she said in an urgent whisper. 'It isn't possible.'

'Why not?'

'Because I know Ruby, and the two girls were friends. She had no reason to kill Florrie.'

'That you're aware of.' McGuire held Pearl's gaze and began again. 'Look, I know Ruby too,' he went on softly, 'and I also know, as do you, that the first person on the scene of a murder is often the killer. Ruby can't be ruled out as a suspect, Pearl. Not yet.'

Pearl knew McGuire was right, but she said nothing, allowing his words to be erased by the sound of waves washing up on the shore.

'Forensics will rule her out,' she said finally and with conviction.

McGuire nodded slowly. 'But until then everything remains a possibility.'

Pearl took a deep breath to calm herself then closed her eyes and tried to think straight. 'There are many ways to kill someone,' she said. 'Why would anyone choose this?' Though her eyes remained closed, she failed to blot out the image etched indelibly on her memory: the sight of Florrie Johnson with a stiletto heel impaled in the front of her skull.

'I don't know. Yet,' said McGuire. 'But I will.'

His hand reached for Pearl's and held it tightly – an act of assurance and reassurance – before his mobile sounded an incoming text. He checked it quickly then closed his phone.

'Forensics?' asked Pearl.

McGuire nodded. 'They're at the school now. I have to go.'

He got to his feet and Pearl followed. McGuire laid his hands on her shoulders and gently kissed her forehead before holding her tight in his arms.

'Let me know what Forensics find, won't you?' she whispered. 'I'll do what I can with everything else: contacts, local knowledge—' She broke off for a moment then decided to add a coda: 'And I promise I'll share whatever I come up with.'

McGuire broke away from her but his eyes remained locked with hers. 'Be careful, Pearl,' he warned. Picking up his folder, and feeling torn by conflicting loyalties, McGuire finally moved off towards the promenade, where he looked back once before heading on purposefully, leaving Pearl staring after him.

After a moment, she moved into the cottage and picked up the phone, intent on calling Dolly – to ask for Irene Taylor's number.

Later that morning, Pearl drew up in her Fiat on Marine Parade, a long coastal road that began just after Whitstable Castle – 'castle' being a misnomer since the building was actually a nineteenth-century folly built to house a businessman's mistress and now managed by a local trust. Pearl parked just ahead of two replica cannons that stood on the crest of grassy slopes leading down to the sea. Clouds were gathering on the horizon and Pearl took a deep breath of sea air as she tried to clear from her mind the notion that a premonition she had shared with Nathan, over a glass of Limoncello on a hot summer's evening, could possibly have prompted this brutal murder. It was true Pearl had sensed a 'calm before the storm', but there was no way she could have known the 'storm' might result in a young woman's death, especially coming so soon after something as innocent as a dance class. Staring down towards the beach, her gaze fell on the parade of beach huts whose brightly painted decks and porches pointed straight out to sea. They were laid out in three well-defined rows, separated at intervals by paths leading down to the promenade. Although no bigger than eight feet by ten, the huts had become sought after by Londoners as daytrip boltholes, their value driven up tenfold in as many years. Many had been personalised, bearing names like 'She Shed' or 'Copa Cabana', but all seemed to be unoccupied at this early hour. Summer was beginning to fade, but Pearl was well aware that in a week's time, the smell of barbecue coals would be hanging in the air, wine corks popping as hut owners enjoyed the August Bank Holiday. Continuing on, Pearl found Irene Taylor's bungalow with its well-kept front garden filled with mahonia and lacecap hydrangea. After making her way up an old stone path to the front door, Pearl had no need to ring the bell: Irene was there to greet her before she had even reached the front step.

'Thank you for your call,' she said. 'It was very good of you to check how we are.' She welcomed Pearl inside and then, after glancing left and right down the street, closed the front door securely. Managing a tense smile, she gestured for Pearl to follow her through the hallway and into a tidy kitchen that led out into a pretty country garden. On a table near the garden door, a tray was already set with a jug of iced tea for two. Irene indicated a chair and Pearl sat down, taking in the well-tended flowerbeds filled with bright red poppies, phlox, delphinium and foxgloves. Bees hovered on the warm air. Birds sang in the tall fruit trees. In such a bucolic scene, it seemed almost impossible to Pearl that they were about to discuss the murder of a young girl who had been one of Irene's employees. Perhaps Irene Taylor felt exactly the same way because she frowned for a moment before pouring two cups of tea. 'I've been trying to come to terms with this,' she said finally. 'I could hardly believe it when the police broke the news last night. It must have been such a terrible shock for you – finding poor Florrie's body like that.' She paused for a moment as she pushed a cup and saucer towards Pearl and indicated for her to help herself to sugar.

Pearl chose her words carefully. 'It was actually Ruby, my waitress, who found Florrie. She was on the scene first. I heard her scream.'

Irene nodded once more as she took this in.

'Florrie had been working yesterday afternoon?' asked Pearl.

'Logging wardrobe items,' Irene replied, taking a sip of her iced tea. 'She loved working with our costumes; it was one of her favourite jobs, so Tanya had asked her to make a proper inventory – a list of everything we have.'

'You don't have one already?'

Irene looked pained. 'I have a mental list of what there

is, but we need to itemise all the school's stock for our accountant. It all has a financial value – and what with Tanya taking over . . .'

'And Tony,' said Pearl. 'They're husband and wife, so this is presumably a joint venture?'

Irene nodded. 'Of course.' She paused then collected her thoughts. 'Florrie was going to work from one o'clock until six, and then lock up. A simple operation. She'd done it many times before. All she had to do was check that the lights were off and set the alarm before leaving.'

'By the back door?' asked Pearl. 'That's how Ruby and I came in,' she explained. 'It was unlocked.'

'Yes,' said Irene, pensive. 'That's probably how Florrie planned to leave. It's nearer to the dressing rooms.' She broke off and thought for a moment before continuing. 'When we learned what had happened . . .' She trailed off and composed herself again before continuing. 'As I say, it seems impossible to believe. Such a terrible way to die.' She closed her eyes.

'Yes,' said Pearl softly. 'And on her birthday, too.'

Irene looked up at Pearl, shocked into silence.

'It's true,' said Pearl. 'She was going to celebrate in the evening with Ruby. I'd promised the girls a lift into Canterbury.'

Irene looked bereft. 'I'm sorry,' she said. 'I had no idea. She . . . didn't mention a thing to me – or to Tanya, as far as I know.'

'Tanya?'

Irene nodded. 'Neither of us saw Florrie yesterday as she would have let herself in with her own key. Tanya was having to look after Tony. He's been in pain since the class, and to be perfectly honest, Tanya felt responsible because she'd encouraged him to join her in the demonstration.' She looked at Pearl. 'She can be hard on herself, but I told her it wasn't her fault. Tony is half the partnership – Tanya and Tony – so of course people expected to see them both . . . and to see them dance.' Irene's expression clouded for a moment before she looked directly at Pearl. 'But when I learned that Florrie had dyed her hair, dark, like Tanya's? And that she was wearing . . .'

'Tanya's dress.'

Irene nodded slowly. 'I identified it. And I couldn't help but think . . .' She trailed off once more.

'What?' Pearl prompted.

'Well, Florrie admired Tanya so much. She adored her – looked up to her – so it was only natural, I suppose, that she would want to . . . to copy how Tanya looks. Young girls so often seek role models.'

'True,' said Pearl pensively, recognising that although Florrie Johnson was no adolescent, she was barely beyond a teenager. Irene fixed Pearl with her gaze.

'I'm scared.'

'Scared?'

'I can't help but suspect that my niece may have been the intended victim.'

Pearl remained silent. Irene's concern rose. 'It's perfectly possible, isn't it?' she asked. 'Someone came to the school . . . saw Florrie in the dressing room, and with her dark hair and wearing Tanya's dress, thought—' She broke off, as if unable to articulate any other thoughts.

'You think Florrie was murdered by mistake,' said Pearl, 'by someone who believed her to be Tanya?'

Irene stared at Pearl for a moment then blinked several times. Finally she nodded.

Pearl took a deep breath and began to reorganise her own thoughts. 'If that was the case,' she began, 'with Florrie sitting at the dressing table, and the mirror fully lit, why wouldn't the killer have recognised Florrie in the reflection?'

Irene looked suddenly lost for a response so Pearl went on: 'There's an ongoing police investigation. There'll be forensic tests to be concluded and an autopsy to be performed—'

'Of course,' said Irene, breaking in, still troubled. 'Nevertheless, if my fears are justified, it would mean that Tanya is still at risk.' She held Pearl's gaze then went on: 'Florrie's murder is a terrible tragedy, but *if* the real victim was meant to have been Tanya,' her voice lowered to a whisper, 'then my niece is in grave danger.' She paused, then: 'I know the police will do their job. The . . . inspector, McGuire, seems thorough.' She indicated her mobile phone on the table. 'He's given me his number so I can call him if I think of anything that might help, but there can't be any delay in finding Florrie's killer. Do you understand?' She stared beseechingly at Pearl. 'I know your mother well, and I also know you're respected in this town for everything you do. If you find Florrie's killer you'll be protecting my niece.'

Pearl allowed herself a moment to absorb this, then she stared away towards Irene's beautiful garden and the manicured lawn on which starlings were fluttering down to feed. Somewhere in this small seaside town, perhaps even in a home as peaceful and genteel as Irene Taylor's bungalow, the murderer of a young girl remained undiscovered and, perhaps, poised to strike again.

'Well?' asked Irene, a degree of impatience, or perhaps even desperation, sounding in her tone.

'Of course,' said Pearl finally. 'I'll do whatever I can, but I need you to keep me informed. If you think of anything that might be connected to this murder . . .'

Irene nodded quickly and reached out a hand, which she laid on Pearl's. 'I will. I promise,' she said gratefully.

At that moment, Pearl looked up and noticed a photograph on the wall near the table, showing two young teenagers posed together on a summer's day: one plain and plump, the other petite and pretty. Pearl remembered Dolly's comment about Susanne Taylor resembling a 'little sylph'; certainly the dark-haired girl in the photograph fitted that description, with the diaphanous skirt she wore and a trailing paisley scarf tied around her forehead.

Pearl looked back at Irene, who took in Pearl's view of the photograph. 'My sister, Susanne,' she explained. 'So long ago,' she added, 'though it seems like only yesterday. There was something magical about her,' she went on, 'even as a child. I always felt like such a clumsy lump beside her.' She raised a sad smile. 'That wasn't Susie's fault – but mine. I lacked my sister's grace, her talent.' She paused, still focusing on the photograph. 'I so wish she was still here, but I honestly believe she was too precious, too special, for this world. Some people are, don't you think? Like . . . angels. Perhaps their purpose is to leave us with a message.' She looked to Pearl for a response.

'And what would Susanne's message be?' asked Pearl.

Irene considered this. 'To take care of those we love,' she said softly, immediately casting her eyes down as though she was ashamed. 'I only wish I could have protected Susie.'

In the next moment, Pearl became aware of a great weight of sadness that Irene Taylor seemed to carry with her concerning her dead sister. Perhaps it was unresolved grief or, thought Pearl, a burden of guilt for not having taken greater care of her. Pearl remained silent for a time before asking: 'Why would anyone want to kill Tanya?'

Irene took on a pained expression, as though she had been asked to betray an important secret. Finally she responded: 'I think it's best if you asked my niece that question.'

Before Pearl could reply, her smartphone sounded. She took it from her pocket and excused herself to Irene before she noted that the caller was Peter Radcliffe. Although she would have preferred to let his call go to voicemail, Pearl decided instead to answer it and Radcliffe immediately sounded off in her ear.

'I realise with a murderer in our midst, you are no doubt very busy,' he began. 'Nevertheless, you are still acting for me at the moment, and I really do not want to have to turn my case over to the police – especially as, with a murder case to solve, Hilary's lingerie will only sink to the bottom of the pile. But you should know,' Radcliffe paused for a moment, as if for great effect, before announcing, 'the thief has struck again.'

Chapter Ten

Pearl drove quickly back into town and managed to find a space in the Gorrell Tank car park opposite the harbour. The area, commonly known as the 'Tank', was actually a reservoir, formerly a backwater constructed by the railways to flush out silt at low tide. These days, water was still pumped out from it, but a host of parked cars now sat on its surface. Pearl locked her Fiat and walked the few hundred metres or so towards the busiest section of Harbour Street that was lined with shops selling everything from English cheese to vintage vinyl. She couldn't help wishing she had taken Dolly's advice never to get involved with the Radcliffes – not least because discovering the identity of an underwear thief now seemed such a trifling matter when compared to Florrie's murder. Peter Radcliffe had made it clear that he knew about the incident – police tape would surely be surrounding the building until the Forensics team had finished their work – and yet he had still seen fit to lay claim to Pearl's time, as though missing lingerie could possibly compete with a young girl's death. One thing was certain: if the Radcliffes had got wind of the murder, then so would many others . . .

In a small town like Whitstable, the jungle telegraph would be sounding with dispatches being broadcast like soundwaves from a radio transmitter – gory details relayed across shop counters and garden fences – by phone, email and social media. Many of those details would become garbled in transmission – elaborated upon, embellished and exaggerated, customised for the teller's own purpose, all of which would make it increasingly difficult for McGuire to be sure of what was – and wasn't – true. He and his team would have the task of sifting truth from fantasy – like wheat from chaff – a time-consuming process, which was why Pearl's statement had been taken separately from Ruby's: reducing the risk of either witness influencing the other's recollection of events. A violent crime like this would impact the whole town. For visitors, that might only result in an anecdote or two to relay once they had returned home; but for locals, like Pearl, a brutal murder was viewed as an assault on the whole community, and the reason why, after Pearl's meeting with Irene Taylor, she now felt a weight of responsibility about bringing Florrie's killer to justice.

As she approached the Old Captain's House, Pearl could see the Sunday crowds of DFLs were already shuffling their way along the narrow pavements. Traffic was crawling down the road – mainly SUVs filled with restless children, and overheated dogs panting from windows. For a moment Pearl allowed herself to consider that there would be few local residents, apart from Hilary Radcliffe, who would wish for a pedestrianised area in this bottle-neck between the harbour and the High Street – certainly not the many shopkeepers in other parts of the town who would suffer a lack of trade from a one-way system and its resulting parking restrictions. Road surfaces would need reinforcement to bear extra traffic in other areas, costing money the local council did not have, and yet, possibly with Radcliffe's influence, such a madcap scheme might yet be put in place. Pearl sighed and was about to ring the Radcliffes' bell when she caught sight of something across the road. A familiar figure was stepping out of an impres-sive castellated building set on a triangular piece of land at the end of Harbour Street. It was Jack Harper who had just exited the front door to Harbour Buildings. Looking both right and left, he failed to notice Pearl, who, at that moment was obscured by a group of French teenagers passing by on the pavement. An anxious expression on his face, Jack slung a navy-blue backpack over one shoul-der and set off towards the High Street. For a moment, Pearl remained rooted to the spot, bothered by something, though at that moment she wasn't quite sure what that was. Deciding to abandon her meeting with the Radcliffes, she followed Jack Harper instead, keeping her distance on the crowded pavements so the young man wouldn't suspect he was being tailed. Jack continued at a pace, weaving his way through pockets of tourists and shoppers, until he finally made a sharp right turn off the High Street and disappeared out of view.

Hurrying on, Pearl reached the same corner just in time to see Jack, now some way ahead of her, turning left on to West Cliff – a residential road lined with large Edwardian houses, most of which enjoyed a spectacular view of the local golf course – Whitstable and Seasalter Golf Club – which lay nestled in the heart of the town with stunning views across the Old Salts Flats towards the estuary. Jack, however, appeared to be making his way towards a path that began at the end of the road. Beyond some tall trees lining the golf course he was heading towards a short flight of steps that led up to a bridge spanning the railway line. Pearl waited a few moments before following, noting the young man was hurrying down the other side of the bridge towards another path that ran alongside the embankment. Sticking to Jack's trail, Pearl continued to keep her distance on the same path, which soon became overgrown with shrubs on one side and sycamores meeting in the centre to create a dark glade. Still Jack headed on purposefully, unaware of Pearl holding back as she kept him in sight, using the undergrowth as cover. After a few hundred metres, Pearl realised that Harper was approaching an area known as Prospect Field – four acres of scrub and grassland that, when added to neighbouring allotments, gardens, railway embankment and the golf course itself, provided a precious wildlife corridor for local species, including butterflies, woodpeckers, grass snakes and lizards, not to mention other birds and foxes. A group of dedicated volunteers managed the area, which also provided space for local people to sit and enjoy the view of the coastline across the Swale Estuary. Pearl remembered having once brought McGuire here, explaining that on a clear day he might even be able to smell the candyfloss from Southend. McGuire had stood close beside her, sharing the same view of the coast beyond the railway lines that greeted her now, with a border comprised of pastel-coloured beach huts. A few benches were set on a grassy plain but as Pearl approached, she saw that Jack Harper was staring out towards the sea with a lost expression on his face. It was a fine day and a peaceful spot. A few wild rabbits were scampering across the embankment and the bells of St Alfred's Church could be heard chiming – a reminder that the centre of town wasn't far away. In this haven it was possible to find some tranquillity and calm, watching the waves creeping up on to the shore with the certainty of each new tide, but Jack Harper was now looking down at the grass beneath his feet. Then he seemed to steel himself and glance back towards a wooden picnic table and a few surrounding benches that were carved in the shape of caterpillars. Jack approached and sat down, then took off his backpack. Searching inside it, he produced what appeared to be several sheets of paper which he laid on the table and gave his attention to. Some moments later, he looked up and closed his eyes, perhaps to shut out an image he found too difficult to bear, but it was an image visible only to Harper in that moment, for Pearl saw nothing but the empty picnic area and the scrubland beyond. The young man now quickly gathered up the sheets of paper from the table, ripping them into shreds before stuffing them back into the backpack. Getting quickly to his feet he then headed on along the path, while Pearl followed, hanging back once more as Harper mounted another bridge across the railway tracks.

Pearl kept Jack in sight as he began to cross the bridge, but the young man's pace finally slowed and he seemed to need a moment to catch his breath, pausing at the centre of the bridge to stare down at the rails below. From Pearl's vantage point behind some trees, she saw Jack's face take on a troubled expression – a mixture of pain and great confusion. In the distance, a train could be heard approaching on the lines as it transported passengers westwards. The train remained out of sight but the rhythm of its wheels tapped out on the tracks like an urgent drumbeat. Up on the centre of the bridge, Jack Harper was now staring ahead, as though waiting patiently for this train – perhaps, thought Pearl, he might even have timed his arrival at this point for it. He stood completely still, a lifeless statue, staring into the distance as though preparing himself to meet something that still remained invisible to Pearl – until she saw the grey shadow of the London-bound train snaking its way towards them. The pulsing of wheels continued to sound on the track, growing faster as it signalled the train's imminent arrival. Then a flock of birds suddenly flew up, and out, from the surrounding trees, blanking Pearl's view for a moment as the train finally appeared, thundering past while sounding a loud horn. As quickly as it had arrived, the train disappeared. The leaves of the trees settled down with a soft breeze, sparrows returned to the branches and silence was restored.

Staring across at the old railway bridge, Pearl saw that Jack Harper was still there. Reaching into her bag, Pearl took her smartphone from it and focused its camera lens on Jack. As though waking from a dream, the young man suddenly leaned back before coming to his senses and hurrying across to the other side of the bridge – out of Pearl's line of vision. Pearl followed, noting as she crossed the bridge that Jack was already some distance away, cutting a path across the golf course in the direction of the beach. This time, he carried no backpack.

Frowning to herself, Pearl slipped her phone back into her bag and raced down the steps of the railway bridge. Looking around on the path, she suddenly paused as she noticed a large municipal bin positioned against the boundary fence of the golf course. Hesitating for only a moment, Pearl opened the lid to find, resting on a bed of dry leaves, a navy blue backpack. She grabbed it, opened it and found inside the torn sheets of paper. Each fragment formed part of several pages that were filled with bold handwriting not unlike a child's – large curling letters which, when placed back together, spelled out a number of love poems – with a signature at the foot of each of them. *Florrie Johnson*.

Chapter Eleven

Two hours later, Pearl was sitting in McGuire's office at Canterbury Police Station, waiting for his return. In front of her, the desk was strewn with paperwork, a few unsharpened pencils, a ball made from rubber bands – and some crumbs from what Pearl assumed must have been a hastily consumed breakfast. There was also McGuire's laptop, the lid of which was open. The screen was black, but Pearl knew from the flashing light on its keyboard that it was only in sleep mode – all she needed to do, to bring it to life, would be to tap a single key . . .

In that moment, Pearl viewed the laptop like a half-open door leading into an undiscovered room – one she suspected might be littered with clues gleaned from McGuire's team following their door-to-door inquiries. All those vital pieces of the jigsaw would, when finally gathered together and added to the fine details of forensic reports, form a picture showing exactly what had occurred on the night Florrie Johnson was murdered. For now, however, that remained a mystery, along with whatever Jack Harper had been telling McGuire. The young man had been brought in for questioning following Pearl's discovery that morning – Harper's backpack, containing torn sheets of paper which, when put together, formed a total of three love poems signed with Florrie Johnson's name. They were no great works of literature, just simple adolescent offerings with predictable 'moon in June' rhymes, but in the light of the young woman's horrific murder, they seemed especially poignant.

Pearl glanced at the clock on the wall, watching the minute hand clicking closer to midday. Chef Dean would be coping at The Whitstable Pearl – but without Ruby, who was still at Seaspray Cottage recovering from her ordeal, or Dolly, who was still resting her back. Part-time staff would be filling in, but Pearl wished McGuire would hurry back to her so she could return to help during the busiest part of the Sunday-lunchtime shift. She looked around and heaved a sigh before killing some time by imagining that this was her own office with the plaque on the door showing Pearl's name and not McGuire's. She leaned back in his office chair, then tidied up the paperwork, sharpened a few pencils, brushed the breakfast crumbs into the bin and picked up the rubber-band ball, wondering what McGuire might use it for – apart from storing rubber bands. She imagined him squeezing it tightly in his strong grip to rid himself of stress after a meeting with his despised superintendent, or perhaps hurling it towards the opposite wall whenever he received news that the CPS had decided not to proceed with a case. Setting the ball down again, she eyed the laptop once more . . . Irresistibly drawn to its keys, she reached out towards it, then hesitated, drumming her fingers on the desk as she weighed up her options. But temptation proved too great. Reaching out again, this time she tapped the keyboard's space bar – and the door suddenly opened . . .

Seeing McGuire in its frame, Pearl jumped up and put some distance between herself and the desk.

'What did he have to say?' she asked quickly.

McGuire shook his head in frustration and closed the office door behind him, before tossing a large manila envelope onto his desk.

'Not much,' he replied. 'The only thing he's admitted to so far is wanting the contents of that backpack off the property.'

'His home, you mean? Harbour Buildings?'

McGuire nodded. 'It's pretty clear he dumped the bag and those poems because he knew they implicated him in Florrie's murder.'

Pearl considered this, adding: '*And* he wouldn't want his wife to find them.'

McGuire looked at her. Pearl explained: 'Think about it, if it was just a case of disposing of those poems, he could have thrown them away at home. But that would have meant there was a chance Laura might find them in the rubbish or recycling bins,' she paused for a moment, 'so he had to dispose of them elsewhere.'

McGuire reflected on this before moving across to his office window. 'Maybe he thought he was being smart using that municipal bin, but he didn't count on you following him.' He turned the plastic rod on his Venetian blinds and the glaring sun disappeared from the room, leaving slats of shade striping the surface of his desk. 'What made you do that?' he asked, coming close to her.

Pearl shrugged. 'Instinct. A hunch? Something bothered me when I saw him; it was hot this morning, but he was wearing gloves – though I only clocked that subconsciously, until I saw him take the sheets of paper from his backpack and spread them on the picnic table. He never took his gloves off.' She produced her smartphone from her pocket and brought up the photo she had taken of Jack Harper, then handed it to McGuire, who saw Jack, wearing gloves, as he leaned over the railway bridge, staring down at the tracks.

'He stood there for some time,' Pearl went on, 'and I honestly thought that he . . .'

'What?' McGuire prompted.

'I thought he might be considering . . .' She trailed off.

'Throwing himself under a train?'

Pearl remained silent.

'But he didn't,' said McGuire, handing back her phone. 'You said he crossed the bridge over the tracks and disposed of the backpack – containing these.' McGuire picked up the manila envelope from his desk and pulled out a plastic evidence bag. Inside, Pearl recognised the torn sheets of paper she had found – each now carefully stuck together.

'Love poems,' she said. 'All signed by Florrie Johnson.'

'And a note from the girl to Harper,' said McGuire.

Pearl read it through the evidence bag. 'Thanking him for the time he spent with her . . . at Prospect Field.'

Pearl slipped her smartphone back into her pocket and continued to give her full attention to the evidence bag, through which she eyed Florrie's sentimental verses, feeling uncomfortable as she did so – as though she was snooping in a teenage girl's diary. McGuire watched her, waiting for her reaction.

'And this is definitely Florrie's handwriting?' she asked.

'It matches a specimen sample,' said McGuire, turning the bag around to check it himself. 'And Harper hasn't denied it either,' he added. 'Or anything else – yet. Since the duty solicitor arrived, he's gone down the "No Comment" route.'

Pearl frowned. 'So, what do you think?'

'What I think is less important than what I know,' said McGuire. 'And I *know* that I have a murder suspect, caught on camera, trying to dispose of evidence after a young woman was found with a metal stiletto through her skull. If Harper doesn't come up with something more enlightening than "No comment", he'll soon find himself on a murder charge.'

Pearl frowned. 'But . . . what you have on him so far is only circumstantial. I caught him on camera on the bridge, but I didn't actually see him dump the backpack in the bin.'

'You've no doubt that he did, though?' said McGuire. 'You said there was no one else around.'

'True,' said Pearl. 'But I'm thinking ahead to what a defence brief might ask in court.'

'Thanks for reminding me,' said McGuire with irony.

Pearl reached for his hand and squeezed it gently. 'You'll need a lot more to make a murder charge stick.'

McGuire looked back at her and admitted: 'I know. And my time's running out like sand in a bottle. You know I can only keep him in custody for thirty-six hours without charging him.'

Before Pearl could respond to this, McGuire's phone rang. He kept his eyes on Pearl as he picked up the receiver and answered only with his name. Listening to the caller, he then selected one of the recently sharpened pencils and began tapping it idly on the desk's surface, until the tip broke. 'Okay,' he said finally, 'I'll be right there.' Ending the call he tossed the pencil back on to his desk. 'Welch,' he explained. 'I have to report to him.'

Seeing McGuire was torn, Pearl nodded. 'I'd better go,' she said, getting to her feet. 'Ruby's on her own at home and I need to check in at the restaurant too.' She moved to go but McGuire gently took her arm.

'Pearl?'

Turning to face him, she smiled, anticipating what he was about to say.

'Don't worry,' she said. 'I'll be careful.' Leaning in, she gently kissed him, then moved to the door, where she turned back to add: 'But I'll also see what else I can find out.'

Before McGuire could protest, Pearl gave him a wink

and left the room while McGuire stared down at his desk, noticing for the first time that his paperwork was now in neat piles . . .

Pearl returned to Whitstable to find her restaurant packed. In twenty years of observing her customers, Pearl had learned she could judge their moods from the way they might sit or from what they chose to eat. For instance, strawberries and melted chocolate was the dessert of lovers, while a sizzling dish like Pearl's Spicy Teriyaki Squid and Shrimp could disguise the awkward silence between a couple who had run out of things to say to one another. For 'first-daters' or those engaged in a business lunch, the extensive taster menu offered time for trust to be established. Considering the recent murder at the Ballards' school, Pearl found herself brought up short to see Max Sanchez and Vivian Gleaves sitting together at the rear of the restaurant in an intimate spot Pearl usually reserved for couples. Viewed from a distance, the pair seemed somewhat out of sync: Max wore an anxious frown, looking edgy as he toyed with the corner of his linen napkin, while Vivian seemed altogether more relaxed and engrossed in her meal. Pearl headed straight across to them and immediately offered her condolences on the tragic death of their fellow staff member.

'A terrible thing,' Vivian agreed, issuing a long sigh before sipping a glass of Muscadet.

'Yes,' said Pearl. 'And I'm sorry I wasn't here to welcome you. If I'd known you were coming—'

'We've been well looked after.' Vivian smiled. 'Haven't we, Max?'

'Sure,' he said, failing to conceal some tension. 'It was a spur-of-the-moment thing,' he added quickly.

'My idea,' said Vivian, 'Max's treat.' She turned to him. 'And very kind of you,' she added. 'It's nice to seek solace in each other's company.' She looked again at Pearl. 'And the lobster Thermidor was superb.' She pressed a napkin to her lips while Max saw Pearl eyeing the empty salad bowl in front of him.

'I can't say I have much of an appetite today,' he explained. With that, he reached quickly for the bill that was sitting on a saucer on the table and took out his wallet.

'Poor Florrie,' said Vivian. 'What a terrible tragedy.'

Max laid cash on top of the bill and asked: 'How are the police getting on? Any clues to go on?'

Pearl shook her head, knowing better than to share what she'd discussed with McGuire.

'Well,' said Vivian, 'I'm sure they'll come up with an answer soon.'

'I'm sure they will,' said Pearl. 'I always say that clues to a crime are like the ingredients of a meal: put them together in the right way, and the results can be very satisfying.'

'You're right!' said Vivian. 'It's just the same with choreography, isn't that so, Max?' She gave another smile. 'Sooner or later, I'm sure someone will come forward with exactly the right piece of information to help the police. That's what often happens, isn't it? After a while, someone realises that something seemingly trivial is really quite significant and everything then looks quite clear?'

'Yes,' said Pearl. 'I'm sure that's what the investigating officer hopes for.'

Pearl allowed herself to hope that such a break might soon come McGuire's way.

'Are you sure I can't get you some dessert?' she asked. 'On the house? There's syllabub, pastries and homemade vanilla and honeycomb ice-cream?'

Vivian looked tempted but Max answered swiftly: 'I'm afraid I don't have the time.' He handed his payment to Pearl and then turned to Vivian. 'I'm really sorry, Vivian, I have to go.'

'Of course,' said Vivian, 'I understand.' A smile seemed painted on her face as she looked back at Pearl. 'I'm sure we'll come again.'

Pearl nodded and moved off to the till with Max's payment. Once she had processed it, she turned to see Max handing Vivian her jacket. Vivian took it without another word, the smile now erased from her face, and the pair headed for the door, which Max opened. After allowing his companion to exit first, he gave a look back towards Pearl and tried to summon a smile – but the effort proved too great – which was understandable, thought Pearl, in the light of young Florrie Johnson's death.

As soon as the busy lunchtime session was over, Pearl headed back to Seaspray Cottage to find Ruby waiting patiently for her, ready to leave. Pearl knew the girl was putting on a brave face but she could see through this to Ruby's anxiety. With her pale complexion there were times when Ruby Hill could sometimes look drained and undernourished – some days her skin seemed almost translucent, allowing tiny blue veins to shine through it like threads; but this afternoon, her pallor was emphasised by the fact that her eyes were still red from crying. Pearl insisted on driving her home rather than allowing Ruby to walk, but at the front door, she turned to the girl and asked: 'Are you sure you wouldn't rather stay? You're welcome to – for as long as you want?'

'I know,' Ruby replied. 'And I appreciate it, Pearl. But I'll feel better once I'm home.'

Pearl nodded. 'All right, I understand, but you will let me know if you change your mind, won't you?'

'I promise.'

Ruby got into the passenger seat of the Fiat and Pearl closed the car door after her, before heading to the driver's side and setting a bag on the back seat. Despite the scorching heat, the streets were still filled with people, going about their business as though nothing had happened – something which Pearl knew Ruby would find as disconcerting as she herself did. Offering the girl a reassuring smile, Pearl drove off along Island Wall, pausing at traffic lights in the High Street just as Ruby asked: 'Has he found out anything yet? Any clues?'

'McGuire, you mean?'

Ruby nodded.

Pearl paused, deciding to keep quiet about Jack Harper's arrest for fear of upsetting Ruby any further.

'Not yet,' said Pearl. 'But he will,' she added confidently. 'There'll be forensic results to come through, more interviews to be done, statements to be taken . . .'

'A post-mortem,' said Ruby. She turned to Pearl. 'That's what they call it, don't they?' Pearl nodded. Ruby frowned as she went on: 'But we know what killed Florrie. We just don't know who did it.'

'We will,' said Pearl, with certainty.

She pressed the girl's hand before the traffic lights changed to amber. Slipping the car into gear, she then followed slow traffic up the High Street and towards the entrance to town, where Ruby spoke again. 'She loved that job,' she said. 'Working at the school. She was so excited – all week – about the classes starting up and having Tanya and Tony there.'

'And her birthday?'

'Yeah.' Ruby lowered her head, fighting back sadness.

'But she didn't tell anyone else about it,' said Pearl gently. 'Only you?'

Ruby nodded.

'Why was that?'

Ruby shrugged her shoulders. 'I don't know. Maybe she just didn't want any fuss. Earlier in the week, she'd said not to get her a present because, well . . .' She trailed off for a moment as though confused.

'Because of what?'

Ruby looked at Pearl and continued: 'She told me she had everything she'd ever wanted – even a partner.' Ruby gave a puzzled smile. 'Funny that. I didn't think much about it at the time because it was the day everyone came for lunch at the restaurant and I was working. I just thought she meant a partner for the dance class, but—' She broke off.

'What is it?'

'Well, maybe she didn't mean the dance class after all. Maybe she meant . . .' She trailed off again and Pearl stopped the car.

'A boyfriend?' she asked, her thoughts still on Jack Harper and a backpack of love poems. 'Did you mention this to the police last night, Ruby?'

The girl shook her head. 'The woman sergeant I talked to only asked me to describe what happened when I found Florrie. I was upset. I hadn't even thought about this until now – when you asked me.'

Pearl read concern on the girl's face. 'Don't worry,' she said gently. 'I'll tell McGuire. He'll have more questions for us soon, I'm sure.'

'Questions?' Ruby looked even more concerned.

'Just routine.'

Ruby nodded, reassured, and Pearl asked tentatively: 'Did . . . Florrie ever mention having a boyfriend?'

Ruby frowned once more, this time as though she was deep in thought. Finally she shook her head.

'Not that I remember. She was a bit like me – finding her feet? Maybe that's why we got on. Since she came out of foster care, she'd been all on her own, so she used to ask me how I coped, you know, after Gran died?' She paused. 'I . . . told Florrie how you'd helped me.'

'Me?' asked Pearl, glancing at her.

Ruby nodded. 'Yeah. With the council and getting Gran's flat put in my name. And giving me the job at the restaurant? That was like having family again.' She looked directly at Pearl and went on. 'I think Florrie felt the same about the dance school.' She turned now to look out of her passenger window, across a well-tended lawn towards a tower block known as Windsor House – the social housing unit that was looked on by so many in the town as a blot on the landscape – an architectural eyesore – though it was home to Ruby and her neighbours.

'I'd better go,' she said quickly.

'Hold on.' Pearl reached into the back seat for the bag she had placed there. 'Mustn't forget this.'

'What is it?'

'Supper,' said Pearl. 'Salmon quiche and salad – and there's some trifle too.'

Ruby's sad features broke into a smile. 'My favourite.'

'I know,' said Pearl softly.

The two women got out of the car and Pearl slipped the strap of the bag on to Ruby's shoulder before she held out her arms to her. Ruby came closer, allowing Pearl to envelope her in an embrace. For a moment, neither spoke, recalling the last dreadful moment Pearl had comforted Ruby in this way.

Finally the girl whispered: 'It's true – what I said? You are just like family.' Gently breaking away, she managed a smile for Pearl, before hitching the bag higher on to her shoulder and setting off across the lawn. As Pearl watched her go, she heard a triumphant cheer sounding from the nearby football ground as a goal was scored, although Pearl liked to think it was for Ruby, striding out confidently across the lawn to her home. At the entrance to Windsor House, Ruby turned back and gave a wave before finally disappearing inside.

On her drive back to Island Wall, Pearl reflected on everything Ruby had told her about Florrie. It didn't amount to much – a young woman finding her feet in a job she loved, a job that had brought her into contact with two celebrities in the world of dance. Florrie might well have been simply referring to a dance partner on the night of the first tango class and nothing whatsoever to do with any boyfriend, with Jack Harper or love. Pearl thought back to the night at Ballard's, remembering how it had been Florrie's job to deal with the reception while Jack Harper had cued the music and his wife had dealt with the lights. Tony's knee had given out just after the tango demonstration had begun and McGuire had arrived shortly after – nothing appeared to have gone to plan at all – but then Pearl remembered something Max Sanchez had said shortly after Pearl's own arrival in the studio: something about partners . . .

Drawing up a short way from Seaspray Cottage, Pearl sat quietly in her car as she tried to remember what it was. Looking across the room that night, she had seen Laura Harper standing with her husband as Max had explained: *Laura's been drafted in too. Though I can't say any of us had much choice in the matter. Tanya's arranged everything – including who we partner . . .*

Pearl considered his words – recalling, too, something Ruby had told her at reception: Dolly had been expecting to partner Ruby, but on the night she had danced instead with Irene Taylor, and as Florrie had explained: *Jack will be dancing with his wife, Laura . . . Tanya's put me with Max.*

So, in fact, Florrie had had no choice in the matter either. As Max had pointed out, Tanya had arranged everything – apart, thought Pearl, from Tanya Ballard dancing with McGuire, because there was no way Tanya could have known that McGuire would come walking through the door that evening, summoned by Pearl's text, just as Tanya had been seeking a replacement partner for this important occasion. That had been a piece of sheer synchronicity. So, thought Pearl, perhaps Florrie had been talking about a partner in a romantic sense, after all. Why else would Jack Harper have needed to dispose of the girl's poems and her note to him if he hadn't been involved with her? And if he had nothing to hide, why was he refusing to answer McGuire's questions?

Pearl got out of the Fiat, locked the car and approached Seaspray Cottage, which was aptly named as its garden backed on to the beach, with an old oyster yawl, *The Favourite*, permanently moored alongside the cottage on Starboard Light Alley. Rescued by enthusiasts, the boat was a reminder of another time, when ship construction had dominated Whitstable's shores and tall three-masted schooners had towered over the roofline of fishermen's cottages like Pearl's. A century or more ago, over a hundred master mariners had been listed in the town, and the trade in oysters had flourished. These days, yawls were only to be seen during the town's Regatta, though the local oyster tradition continued in the form of an annual festival as well as on the menu of Pearl's restaurant.

The tide was out – but returning – and the air was filled with the briny smell of seaweed. Opening the gate to her garden, Pearl stepped down on to her small patch of lawn and was just rounding her lilac-timbered beach hut when a figure suddenly stepped out in front of her. Pearl started in fear, then recognised who it was.

'I need to talk to you,' said Laura Harper.

Chapter Twelve

A few moments later, Laura Harper was standing in the middle of Pearl's living room, toying nervously with one of the straps of her leather shoulder bag. Pearl felt for the woman and offered a reassuring smile.

'You said you wanted to talk?'

Jack Harper's wife gave a quick nod of her head, looking in that moment as though she was in need of great comfort. Her pretty features underscored a sense of vulnerability, making her appear more like a little girl than a woman in her thirties.

'Can I get you a drink?' Pearl added. 'Tea? Coffee?'

Laura shook her head, so Pearl invited her to take a seat on the sofa and joined her there. After a few moments, Laura spoke.

'Jack's been arrested,' she said softly. 'Just for questioning,' she added quickly. 'He hasn't been charged with anything.'

Pearl sensed Laura Harper was using that fact as a lifeline. 'I know,' she replied, feeling conflicted now about her own part in Jack's arrest.

Laura looked surprised but Pearl explained: 'I talked to DCI McGuire.'

Laura nodded, then frowned as she went on: 'The duty solicitor said Jack was seen dumping a bag near the golf course. It . . . had some sort of papers in it . . . with Florrie's name on them. I don't understand. Do you?'

Pearl took a deep breath but remained silent. Laura edged closer to Pearl and pleaded, 'If you know anything, please tell me. You're not a police officer – just a private detective – so you wouldn't be breaking any rules?'

Pearl reflected on this for a moment, recognising Laura was right, but said only: 'I think you should ask Jack. He really needs to cooperate with the police.'

Laura remained quite still, as though she required every sinew of her delicate frame to absorb what Pearl was telling her. Finally, she swallowed hard and looked at Pearl, resolved.

'My husband didn't kill that girl,' she said resolutely. 'I know because Jack isn't capable of murder. The detective, Inspector McGuire? He's a friend of yours, isn't he? If he believes Jack was involved with Florrie . . . he's wrong.'

Silence fell, broken only by the sound of seagulls shrieking beyond Pearl's open windows. In that moment, it seemed to Pearl as though the gulls might be laughing, perhaps ridiculing Laura Harper's blind faith in her husband.

'You seem very sure of that,' said Pearl.

'I am,' said Laura. 'I know Jack better than anyone. We've been through a lot and we've come through it together. There's no way he'd throw all that away for . . . a young girl like Florrie.'

'Why doesn't he tell the police that?'

Laura turned away at this, but Pearl tried to reason with her.

'Laura, Jack's been arrested for questioning – under caution. Anything he says during his interviews can be used against him in evidence but . . . the duty solicitor is with him and I believe he's been advised not to answer any questions from the police?'

Laura looked back defensively at Pearl. 'He has a right to remain silent.'

Pearl nodded. 'Yes, he does. But I have to ask why he wouldn't want to help the police with their inquiries? This is a serious crime.'

'I've told you,' Laura insisted, 'all he did was dump a backpack into a bin.'

'Containing "papers" belonging to Florrie Johnson.'

Laura frowned. 'So?'

'Florrie was murdered less than twenty-four hours ago.'

'Not by Jack.'

'Then why won't he tell the police that?'

Laura turned away from Pearl's gaze and took a moment to think before she replied. 'Like you said, he's taking advice from the solicitor . . . he's been warned not to incriminate himself.'

'By telling the truth?' asked Pearl gently. On Laura's silence, Pearl took a deep breath and continued calmly. 'You can't speak for him, Laura, no matter how sure you are that he wasn't involved with Florrie's death.' She paused before continuing: 'Jack's your husband. You love him and you trust him. But there are questions you can't answer for him. Why did he try to dispose of those papers rather than handing them to the police?'

Laura spun round to face Pearl – but failed to respond – so Pearl went on, 'Jack has a responsibility to help the police find Florrie's killer, but instead he's actually obstructed the police by trying to get rid of evidence.'

Laura got up and walked away to face the wall. Pearl left her alone for a moment before she joined her, placing a hand gently on the woman's shoulder.

'Are you sure I can't get you a drink? A brandy, perhaps? It might help to calm your nerves.'

Laura shook her head and turned again to face Pearl, looking as though she was weighing up whether to divulge anything more. Then she made her decision and said starkly: 'I'm pregnant.'

It took a few moments for the news to sink in, but as Pearl withdrew her hand from Laura's shoulder, she suddenly understood the woman's overwhelming need to believe in her husband.

'I . . . haven't told anyone yet,' Laura explained. 'Only Jack knows. We were waiting a bit longer until my next appointment, my scan, before breaking the news to anyone.' She frowned as though she was trying to make sense of this, then: 'We've tried for so long, for a family? It was all my fault,' she went on quickly, 'not Jack's. He was so patient, so . . . understanding. He never once blamed me or reproached me in any way.'

'Laura,' said Pearl, feeling a weight of responsibility for Jack Harper's wife to unburden herself in this way.

'No,' Laura cut in quickly. 'You have to listen. You need to understand. Jack has a real talent. It's one of the things that first attracted me to him: seeing him on stage, performing. That's how we met – at a theatre in Margate. I was helping with the costumes for a production and Jack was brought in to write some songs. Seeing him work with the cast, I was . . . spellbound. He's young but he has a special gift. His songs . . . they touch you. Hearing them, you feel as though he's written them just for you – as though he really understands you? He's a gentle man . . . a gentleman. So creative . . . so . . . incapable of harming anyone. Not Florrie. Nor me.' She paused. 'Jack had some money from an inheritance,' she explained. 'It was meant to be used to allow him time to write more songs – for a musical of his own. A company was interested – there was a chance they would back him – if only he could write the score in time, but—' She broke off.

'What happened?'

Laura took a deep breath and continued. 'We'd been seeing a specialist. About fertility. My test results came back.' She paused, then: 'There was nothing we could try but IVF.' She shook her head. 'So we did. And I . . . found it very difficult – failing all over again? We went through the three cycles we were offered. My birthday was coming up – I'm ten years older than Jack, if you haven't already guessed? I was going to be thirty-five and I just knew that things would only get harder—' She broke off for a moment, then went on: 'It suddenly felt as though I was disappearing into a black hole. Jack said it would all be okay, that we would get through it – like so many other couples. He said that perhaps if I didn't worry so much, it might just happen – a kind of . . . miracle. And it's true,' she went on. 'It can happen like that – for some people?'

'Yes,' whispered Pearl gently.

'For some people,' Laura repeated. 'But not for us.' She looked away, out of the window. 'It's so hard,' she said, 'to wake up every day and find no joy in life because . . . there's this void inside you . . . one you're sure can never be filled.' She looked back at Pearl as she went on, 'That vacuum, it . . . ate us both up. Jack found it hard to write and I . . . well, I just couldn't give up wanting what I always thought I would have – a family.' She paused again before explaining: 'I'm an only child. My parents didn't get on. All I ever knew was their arguments, fights . . . trying to hide from them both when they were together like that? Finally, they divorced, and I swore that when I had a family of my own things would be different, that I'd create a happy, perfect family. It was my dream. I couldn't give up on that,' she said. 'So Jack gave up on his.'

'What do you mean?' asked Pearl.

Laura looked pained. 'We spent all of Jack's inheritance on more rounds of IVF.' She hung her head, then went on, 'Jack stopped writing music and began playing wherever he could – mainly as a cocktail pianist in a hotel in Canterbury – The Pilgrims Rest. He's still having to do that,' she added. 'And he took the job at the dance school, too. Music consultant?' She shrugged derisively. 'Half the time it consists of him cueing tracks on the music system or playing the same section over and over again on the piano, until a class finally gets their steps right?' She took a deep breath. 'And all because of me,' she added ruefully.

Pearl allowed herself a moment to absorb this. 'But it worked,' she said. 'The IVF. You . . . said you're pregnant?'

Laura nodded. 'Yes. Finally, I'm pregnant. I have everything I've ever wanted.' She paused. 'Except Jack.'

Pearl glanced towards the window and saw dark clouds were blowing in with the new tide. A spray of light rain suddenly splashed against the leaded pane, obscuring Pearl's view, and she thought to herself for a moment, trying to make sense of what she had just heard. It seemed entirely possible that if Laura Harper had blinkered herself to accept only the possibility of her happy-ever-after family life, she was now incapable of seeing that the father of her unborn child might have responded to the flattery and attention of a young girl like Florrie – especially as an escape from any tensions at home. Pearl, however, didn't have the heart to articulate this and by doing so, shatter Laura Harper's precious dream. Nor did she feel able to voice the suggestion that if Jack Harper was indeed the 'partner' Florrie had mentioned to Ruby, he might not have trusted such a vulnerable young girl to keep quiet. Was it possible that he could have killed Florrie and tried to dispose of evidence linked to their relationship? Why else would he be in possession of love poems written by the girl and a note from Florrie mentioning their time spent together at Prospect Field?

Pearl turned back to Laura Harper, still wishing she could gain answers to these questions, but knowing this was not the time. Feeling for the woman in front of her, she said reassuringly: 'The most important thing right now is that you take care of yourself and the baby. The police have a job to do and McGuire is a good detective. He'll get to the bottom of this and find the truth – one way or another.'

Laura fixed Pearl with her gaze then simply nodded while Pearl picked up the woman's shoulder bag and handed it to her. As Laura took it, Pearl asked, 'Where were you last night when Florrie was murdered?'

'At home,' said Laura, as she slipped the bag's strap over her shoulder. 'Like I said, Jack plays at The Pilgrims Rest three times a week – Wednesdays, Thursdays and Saturdays. He said I was looking tired and that I should rest so . . . I took a nap just before he left and I woke up shortly before he got home, at around eight.'

'And . . . what time did Jack leave?'

'He has to begin playing at six. It's entertainment for the pre-theatre crowd, so he always leaves home by five thirty in order to get there on time.'

'But you didn't actually see him leave?'

'I just told you,' said Laura with some impatience, 'I fell asleep before he left. But he played at the hotel and he always stays for a beer after he finishes. Like I said, he was home by eight – as usual.' Laura fixed Pearl with a determined look. 'So there's no way he could have murdered that girl.'

For a moment, Laura Harper stared resolutely at Pearl then she turned for the door and exited. Pearl realised she had been left with more questions than answers, and had just begun to organise her thoughts around what she had learned when the landline suddenly rang. Registering McGuire's number she quickly grabbed the receiver.

'I'm still at the station,' he explained before Pearl could utter a word.

'Any news?'

'Yes. Welch is threatening a transfer.'

Pearl slumped on to the sofa. 'He's what?'

'He's using the need for staff cuts as an excuse to shunt me off elsewhere.'

'Where to?'

'The south-west.'

'London?'

McGuire paused, then: 'Cornwall.'

Shocked, Pearl hesitated before asking: 'Can he do that?'

'If I don't come up with the goods.'

'You mean . . . this case.'

'Exactly,' said McGuire, adding: 'I can't afford to put a foot wrong, Pearl.'

Chapter Thirteen

'Are you sure you should be up?' asked Pearl the next morning as she watched her mother mincing around her garden wearing her favourite artist's smock. Made from patchwork squares of material featuring various species of plant life ranging from cactus to anemone, it had the effect of merging Dolly into the backdrop of her own horticultural space so that only her head was visible – a bright turquoise fringe appearing vivid in the strong sunlight. Ignoring Pearl, she bellowed: 'Mojo!'

Dolly's voice sounded so thunderously Pearl felt sure that anyone within a mile of Harbour Street would have heard – including her mother's errant 'familiar' – the moggy that had still not deigned to appear.

'You were saying?' said Dolly as she finally turned to her daughter.

'Your back,' Pearl reminded her. 'Shouldn't you be resting?'

'I am resting,' said Dolly. 'My attic guests don't need my attention. They're quite happy exploring the beach every day, not to mention the castle grounds and the museum. I haven't opened the shop,' she went on, 'and I haven't helped out at the restaurant either, so I'm hardly overdoing things,' she pointed out. 'A gentle stroll around my garden won't do me any harm.'

'And fretting about Mojo?' said Pearl knowingly. At this, Dolly joined Pearl and sat down at her garden table beneath a large canvas parasol.

'You'd be fretting too if it was Pilchard or Sprat who'd gone missing.' Dolly poured herself a glass of the fresh lemonade Pearl had made for them, and after sipping it, she gave a long sigh.

'Any progress from McGuire about that poor girl's murder?'

Pearl shook her head and frowned as she considered her last conversation with the police detective. 'He's under pressure with this case,' she said, 'and he only has a limited amount of time to hold Jack Harper for questioning.'

'But you told him about your visit from Laura Harper?'

Pearl nodded and Dolly gave a rueful look. 'Poor woman. Just as she manages to get pregnant, she finds her husband's been involved with a girl almost half her age.' She reached for her sun hat and put it on.

'We don't know that for sure,' said Pearl; 'that Jack was involved with Florrie – romantically, I mean.'

Dolly gave Pearl a look. 'Romance may never have entered into it – for him, at least. Though from what you've told me, the girl must have been quite infatuated with him to write him all those poems. You're sure they were written by her?'

Pearl shrugged. 'Florrie's name was on every one of them, the note too, and McGuire said the handwriting matched a sample.'

'Well then,' said Dolly, raising her hands to show she considered it a fait accompli, 'coupled with the fact that he dumped that backpack rather than handing it over to the police—'

'I know,' said Pearl, breaking in.

Dolly saw Pearl was looking troubled. 'What is it?' she asked, concerned.

Pearl shook her head. 'I can still see the look on Jack Harper's face that day,' she said finally, 'as he stood on the railway bridge? He was there for some time, just staring down at the tracks. And when I heard the train approaching on the lines, I really felt at that moment that he might be there to take his own life.' She looked at Dolly and went on, 'Perhaps he was.'

'Guilt?' asked Dolly.

Pearl frowned. 'It wasn't guilt I saw on his face – it was . . . an overwhelming sadness.'

Dolly reflected on this for a moment. 'So . . . maybe he did love the girl.'

'If he did,' said Pearl, 'why would he kill her? And in such a violent way?' She shook her head slowly. 'Laura Harper didn't paint a picture of a man capable of that kind of rage.'

Dolly shrugged. 'Well, she wouldn't, would she? He's the father of her unborn child, and from what you've told me, a child they've waited a long time for.' A silence followed, during which Pearl had to agree with her mother. Dolly sipped her lemonade and asked: 'What did Irene have to say?'

'Irene?' Lost in thought for a moment, Pearl betrayed some confusion until she gathered her thoughts and explained: 'She's concerned that the murder may have been a case of mistaken identity. If it was, then . . .'

'Tanya may have been the intended victim?'

Pearl's frown was still in place as she replied, 'I can't see any reason why Jack Harper would have wanted Tanya dead. She was his employer – and the Harpers are short of money – especially right now, with a baby on the way.' She paused for a moment, then: 'I'm going to see them both.'

'Good,' said Dolly.

Surprised by such a positive response, Pearl reminded her mother: 'You're always telling me to stay out of McGuire's cases.'

'I know,' said Dolly. 'And you never take my advice. But for what it's worth, I trust Irene Taylor. Her instincts are good, like yours, and she loves her niece as if she was her own daughter. Besides, we owe it to that poor girl to find her killer,' she added. 'After all, she was Ruby's friend.' Dolly closed her eyes now and leaned back in the sun.

'Yes,' said Pearl, as she remembered Ruby's anguish at

finding Florrie's body slumped in the chair of the dance-school dressing room on the evening of the birthday she had failed to celebrate. In the silence that followed, Dolly opened one eye.

'And what about the Radcliffes?'

As Pearl looked up, Dolly caught her daughter's lost expression. 'Your other case?'

Pearl suddenly realised. 'I completely forgot!' she said, jumping up from her chair. 'I was on my way to them yesterday when I ended up trailing Jack Harper. I was meant to inspect the surveillance footage.'

'Well,' said Dolly, unperturbed, 'I wouldn't worry too much. Considering what's happened, there are far more important things to consider than Hilary Radcliffe's missing drawers.'

And with that, she closed her eyes once more and prepared to take a nap.

Half an hour later, after apologising for the delay in re-trieving her surveillance cameras, Pearl stood in the garden of the Old Captain's House as Hilary Radcliffe watched her taking down one of the cameras from the garden wall. 'So,' said Pearl, 'the decoy items *all* disappeared?'

Hilary nodded and gave a deep sigh. 'All that remained on the washing line were a few sparrows.' She gave a disappointed look as Pearl took down the second camera. 'I take my hat off to you,' she went on. 'I wouldn't have a clue how to work all that equipment.'

'It's nothing too sophisticated,' Pearl explained. She

held up one of the cameras. 'You see the little things that look like reflectors around the lens? At night, they throw out an invisible infrared beam that produces a very clear black-and-white image.' She paused as she considered her equipment. 'I put memory cards into both of these cameras and set them up in positions with a good view of the access points to the garden. So, once I get home and insert those cards into my laptop, I can view everything that happened on the night sequences. It's really very simple.'

Hilary Radcliffe, however, looked none the wiser as she asked: 'And . . . you're sure they will have recorded the thief?'

'Absolutely.' Pearl indicated the vantage points she had used. 'From those angles, the cameras would definitely have caught the culprit, because he or she must have entered either by climbing over the garden walls or by entering by the gate somehow.'

'The gate?'

Pearl nodded. 'It's always possible the lock might have been picked.'

Hilary frowned at this. 'How vulnerable we are,' she said, staring around the garden with a hunted look. 'The news of that poor murdered girl should make us all far more security conscious, don't you think?' Hilary watched as Pearl slipped the cameras into her bag and added: 'It's obvious we have a complete psychopath on the prowl. Driving a steel stiletto heel through a girl's skull?' She gave a shudder.

Pearl looked at her sharply and asked: 'How do you know those details?'

Hilary appeared affronted by Pearl's question. 'Oh, come on,' she said, 'you're acting like a TV detective whose prime suspect has just made a glaring error.' She went on. 'You can't possibly suspect me just for knowing what happened. This is Whitstable, and you know as well as I do, nothing can be kept secret in this town. Besides, as a respected local councillor Peter has contacts in the force. There's always someone connected to someone else in the know – just like you,' she added, 'with your own . . . relationship with the police?'

Pearl zipped up her bag to avoid Hilary's gaze and said: 'I run a local detective agency and DCI McGuire is employed by Canterbury CID. Our paths were always likely to cross.'

'Hmm . . . of course they were,' murmured Hilary as she considered this. 'Well, let's hope the inspector can catch this killer – while *you* unmask the person who stole my underwear.' She corrected herself: 'Lingerie, I mean.'

Pearl reflected for a moment on what she had just heard: McGuire was charged with the task of solving a murder case while Pearl, as a local private eye, was left to track down an underwear thief. She managed only a weak smile for Hilary Radcliffe but said, nonetheless: 'I'm sure I will.'

Later that afternoon, Pearl sat at her laptop, a glass of chilled white wine before her, as she prepared to view the last of the surveillance camera footage. So far, all she had noted on it were sycamore branches and other vegetation swaying in the evening breeze in the alley that backed on to the Old Captain's House. Just as she was about to fast-forward, her phone sounded. Picking up the receiver she found it was McGuire.

'I can't talk for long,' he said, as he walked briskly along a busy corridor in Canterbury Police Station. 'Can we meet later?'

Pearl glanced away from the frozen image on her laptop and quickly checked her watch, noting she didn't have long before the meeting she'd arranged with Irene Taylor and Tanya Ballard. 'Sure,' she replied. 'But I have to be somewhere in a while. How about eight?'

'Where?'

'On the beach at Tankerton, just past the castle. Below the cannons?'

'I'll be there,' said McGuire.

Pearl considered the tension she had heard in McGuire's voice – it matched her own at the thought of his possible transfer – then she replaced the phone receiver and returned to her footage, pressing the 'play' button just in time to see Hilary Radcliffe's lace bras disappearing sharply from her washing line, swiftly followed by panties. Pearl frowned and quickly viewed the footage again – and then one more time for luck. It was just as she thought: no one had entered the garden gate or scaled the ivy-clad walls. Instead, the items had been snatched fiercely from below, leaving Pearl clueless as to how the thief had entered the garden – or escaped. Of only one thing she was sure: she didn't relish the idea of having to explain this to Peter and Hilary Radcliffe.

Chapter Fourteen

It was early evening when Pearl found herself in a lift ascending to the penthouse suite of a new apartment block in town. She had passed by the building on foot and by car but had never actually been inside – until now. The property was far removed from 'Old Whitstable' in style – not a plank of weatherboard in sight. Instead, it had a concrete exterior and sleek lines, and the foyer still smelt of fresh paint. Panels of smoked glass lined the walls of the lift as it carried Pearl soundlessly towards the upper floors. The new development could have been anywhere in London, thought Pearl; it would certainly not look out of place among the chic second homes that had sprung up along the Thames, afforded by no one but the super-rich and oligarchs who had earned London the nickname of Moscow-on-Thames in the Russian newspaper *Izvestiya*. A nationwide demand for property, not as homes but as investment commodities, had led to an explosion in prices, which also impacted people in Whitstable. Some streets remained empty throughout the week – a ghost town – until their owners arrived for summer weekends or rented their properties out to staycationers. The second homes could generally be identified by white-shuttered wooden blinds at their windows – which, for most of the time, remained closed – and the use of names like Harbour Hideaway or Oyster Retreat, painted conspicuously in pastel shades on fragments of weatherboard. Pearl's son was one of many young people now unable to afford to rent in his own home town. Instead, he was based in Canterbury – since starting his college courses, Charlie had come to feel at home in a university city filled with tourists, bars, chain stores and restaurants. In contrast, the sea remained in Pearl's DNA, gifted to her by her father, and his before him, from a bloodline of fishermen whose own harvests were not gathered from the land but from the seabed itself. Whitstable's estuary waters still coursed through Pearl's veins, ebbing and flowing with each beat of her heart.

The lift doors finally opened, to reveal Irene Taylor and Tanya Ballard ready to welcome Pearl into the Ballards' penthouse apartment. Before Pearl could utter a word, Tanya pressed a finger to her lips and whispered: 'We have to be quiet. Tony's sleeping and I don't want to disturb him. He's been in pain since the class.' She managed a smile and led the way into the apartment.

Once inside, Irene leaned in to Pearl and said in a hushed tone: 'Thank you for coming.'

Pearl stepped into a large airy room, bordered on two sides by windows offering a breathtaking sea view. From this vantage point, it was possible to appreciate the various shades of colour in the incoming tide – patches of blue melding with grey beneath banks of white cumulus cloud – while the breeze created patterns in the water resembling the shapes formed by murmurations of starlings in the sky.

'Beautiful,' said Pearl softly.

'The view?' said Tanya, taking in Pearl's gaze at the coastline. 'Yes, it is rather special,' she agreed. 'Peaceful, too. I sometimes feel as though I'm in an eyrie.' She glanced around then indicated the way towards some glass-panelled doors. 'Let's sit outside,' she said. 'It's a nice evening and we've less chance of disturbing Tony there.'

Sliding open the doors, she beckoned Pearl on to a balcony that wrapped around the entire apartment. The western side of the building offered an entirely different bird's-eye view, down on to the rooftops of other properties in the area, including into the gardens of homes: Pearl spied sprinkler systems watering emerald-green lawns, their owners relaxing beneath parasols or on sunloungers – a reminder of Hilary Radcliffe's idle existence at The Old Captain's House . . . and the fact that Pearl had yet to explain to her clients that her surveillance cameras had discovered nothing about the identity of the thief. Tanya offered an invitation to sit at a grey metal table that was set for three. 'I made some Pimm's,' she explained, indicating a jug of fruity punch topped with cucumber, orange and mint. Taking her place, Pearl felt the breeze blowing in from the sea, as cool and refreshing as her first sip from the tall iced glass

Tanya handed to her. Irene accepted another and Tanya paused for a moment before speaking.

'Florrie's murder is a truly shocking event,' she began. 'So shocking, I don't think any of us at the school have been able to believe it's really happened . . .' She trailed off, clearly upset.

Irene Taylor took her niece's hand and said: 'But it has, Tanya.' Her tone was soft but resigned. Tanya nodded mutely and Irene turned to Pearl as she went on. 'Tanya knows I've voiced my concerns to you, Pearl, which is why I wanted her to talk to you.' She looked back to her niece, encouraging her to speak. Tanya did so, falteringly.

'My aunt believes . . . it's possible that . . . the killer mistook Florrie for . . . me?' Tanya seemed wounded by this thought and shook her head. 'I can't see why.' Then she gave a bold and defiant look.

Pearl chose her words very carefully. 'When I first saw the body,' she began gently, 'I have to admit . . . I thought it was you.'

Tanya looked quickly away but Pearl went on: 'I saw long dark hair, just like yours, and the same dress you wore on the night of the class.'

Tanya said nothing. Irene prompted her. 'You see what I mean?' she said. 'What I've been trying to warn you about?' Though Irene's tone was urgent, her voice remained low. Nonetheless, Tanya pressed a finger to her lips again as an instruction to keep quiet.

'Please,' she hissed, 'don't wake Tony.' She looked back

at Pearl and continued: 'Are you seriously suggesting that someone could possibly have mistaken Florrie for me?'

'In the circumstances,' said Pearl, 'and in the heat of the moment – yes. It was only when I caught sight of Florrie's tattoo on her wrist that I realised it wasn't you. I'd noticed the tattoo in the restaurant the other day.' She paused, then: 'Did you know Florrie had dyed her hair?'

Tanya shook her head, confused. 'I . . . didn't see Florrie Saturday. I was here – with Tony. I had to call his specialist for advice. Then I went into town, on foot, as our car's been in the garage for repairs all week, and then I met Aunt Irene about the school's accounts. Remember? We saw you in the restaurant in the afternoon?'

Pearl nodded and Irene took up the story. 'I'd picked up the paperwork from our accountant, saw Tanya with you in The Whitstable Pearl – and we then went home to my bungalow. Florrie was expected to start work after lunch. She would have been alone, logging the costumes in the wardrobe department. Our evening ballet class doesn't begin until seven.'

'Vivian's class?'

Irene nodded. 'That's right; her classes at Ballard's are all in the evening. On weekdays she teaches at a nearby school – St Edwards.'

Pearl took this in. 'So . . . in fact, no one saw Florrie at the school on Saturday afternoon?'

Tanya shook her head. 'Not that I know of. Florrie always worked very well on her own. To be honest, she could get distracted by others.'

'Others?'

'Anyone really,' said Irene. 'She was a chatty girl. But she loved working with wardrobe and tidying up the dressing rooms. You saw that the studio is at the front of the building.'

'And the back door was unlocked on the evening of Florrie's murder,' said Pearl.

Irene nodded. 'Yes, it can get very stuffy in the dressing rooms, so in summer the back door is sometimes left open. Florrie was due to work until six and then lock up.'

Tanya continued: 'And then Vivian was due to arrive a little before seven. But as soon as we heard the news about what happened, Aunt Irene called Vivian and the ballet class was cancelled.'

'And Jack Harper wouldn't have been supplying any music for the ballet class?' asked Pearl.

'No,' said Tanya. 'Jack doesn't work at the school on Saturday evenings. Vivian's class has been rehearsing a section of *The Nutcracker* for our Christmas show and she prefers to use orchestral pieces – on the music system.' Tanya broke off then looked troubled before continuing, 'I can only think that Florrie . . .' She trailed off once more.

'What?' asked Pearl. 'That she may have admired you so much she wanted to try to copy your look?'

Tanya gazed down and began toying with the serviette in her hand. 'I . . . think she really did enjoy working at the school.'

'Especially since you came back, Tanya,' said Irene gently. She turned to Pearl. 'Florrie adored Tanya – and the school. She would have worked there for nothing – all day, every day, if we had allowed her to.' Irene sighed. 'She was a lovely girl but in many ways she . . . seemed much younger than her age.'

Pearl considered this, then asked: 'Did you know she had family problems – and that she'd grown up in foster care?'

Irene and Tanya shared a shocked look. 'No,' said Tanya. 'She told me that her mother had died but . . . I assumed that was recently and, to be honest, I didn't like to pry.'

'It was her birthday too,' said Pearl. 'She was planning to go to Canterbury that night with her friend, my waitress Ruby. I was giving them a lift.'

'Poor Florrie,' said Tanya, using the serviette in her hand to dab her tears.

A silence followed, broken by Pearl, who asked: 'Why would anyone want to kill Florrie Johnson?'

'I honestly can't say,' Tanya said firmly. 'And I know from Laura that the police have taken Jack in for questioning – but that has to be a mistake because there's no way he would have killed Florrie.'

'Then perhaps,' said Pearl, 'what we should be asking is: why would anyone want to kill you?'

Tanya looked away, as though stung. Irene reached once more for her niece's hand but this time Tanya withdrew it.

'I have no idea,' Tanya said fiercely.

Irene frowned and turned to Pearl. 'I'm afraid my niece isn't telling the truth—'

'Of course I am,' Tanya insisted. She leaned in to her aunt and snapped: 'You've got it wrong.'

'Have I?' asked Irene, unconvinced. Tanya held Irene's gaze before she said in an urgent whisper: 'Tony loves me.'

'And is that why he left you?' said Irene.

At this, Tanya looked away again but her aunt continued: 'I'm sorry, Tanya, but if you won't tell Pearl – then I will.' Irene Taylor allowed a moment to pass as Tanya steadied herself and finally explained to Pearl.

'All right,' she began, 'Tony and I had problems. It's one reason why we are here, in Whitstable. For me – it was the main reason.' Pearl noted that once Tanya began to explain, the words came faster, as though finding their own momentum.

'For years,' Tanya continued, 'Tony and I have done nothing but work. We had to. In this business, you're lucky if you get one chance and so you have to grasp it. Years of working the circuit finally paid off for us – but they also took their toll on our relationship – and on our bodies,' she added. She glanced quickly towards the lounge, as if to make sure Tony wasn't there, before opening up once more. 'Tony developed a cartilage injury and I pushed him. I shouldn't have done, but at the time, I didn't realise how serious it was. Once his surgery was over, I just wanted him to get better and return to work. I thought it was the best thing. I was wrong. He tired of me nagging him, pushing him—' She broke off suddenly and ran the palm of her hand through her long dark hair. 'He insisted he needed more time to recuperate and he

flew to Retiro – it's a quiet little district in Buenos Aires
– we've danced there many times. Buenos Aires is the
capital of tango.' She looked down and paused. 'I should
have gone with him.'

'It wasn't your fault,' said Irene.

'What wasn't?' asked Pearl.

Tanya remained silent. Irene pressed her once more.
'Tanya?'

'Tony had an affair,' Tanya admitted finally.

Irene seemed to breathe a sigh of relief before adding:
'He must have known it would get back to Tanya.'

'He wasn't thinking of that.'

'He wasn't thinking at all!' said Irene. 'And certainly
not about you.' She put a hand to her mouth, as if to
silence herself, then she lowered her voice as she asked:
'How could you possibly have taken him back?'

'How could I not?' said Tanya, affronted. Turning to
Pearl she tried to explain further: 'Tony and I are . . .
inseparable. The idea of us being without one another
is . . . simply unthinkable. Tony realises that. He was
sorry . . . he begged me to forgive him, to take him back.
And I had to. I'm nothing without him.'

'That's not true,' said Irene firmly. 'You could have
started again – a solo career – or a new life with another
partner, someone who would never be unfaithful to you.
You deserve better, Tanya—'

'Enough!' Tanya Ballard's voice suddenly shattered
the peace of the afternoon as she held her aunt's gaze.
'Tony is my husband,' she said stiffly. 'We have a loving

relationship and a strong marriage. And that's something you'll never understand.' Tanya's eyes shone with a fierce anger, but in the next instant, as she saw her aunt recoil, she looked contrite. 'I'm so sorry,' she said quickly. 'Why do you make me say these things?'

Before Irene Taylor could utter another word, a man's voice rang out.

'Tanya? Is that you?'

Tony Ballard, looking pale and drawn, was leaning against the glass door. Noting Irene sitting with Pearl at the table, he seemed confused.

'What the—'

Before he could say another word, Tanya sprang to her feet and moved quickly to her husband.

'You shouldn't be up, Tony,' she warned. 'Here . . .' Taking his arm, she began leading him away, but Tony looked back with some suspicion at Pearl and Irene.

'What's going on?' he asked.

'Nothing,' said Tanya firmly, glancing just once in Pearl's direction, as she steered her husband back into the apartment.

Once Tanya and Tony had disappeared, Irene Taylor got up from the table and closed the glass doors before she moved back towards Pearl and leaned against the balcony, staring out to sea. 'I'm sorry,' she said softly. 'I didn't feel I could tell you myself. I wanted Tanya to do it because the more she admits to herself what happened, the more she might realise what a fool she's been.' She took a deep breath and went on: 'It was Tanya who got them to where they are now – her talent, her ambition . . . And Tony was ready to throw it all away.' Irene pushed herself from the balcony and turned back to face Pearl. 'I just can't get her to see . . . that she's making the same mistake as her mother.'

'Susanne?' said Pearl.

Irene nodded. 'My poor sister – another special talent – wasted on the wrong choice of men. With Susie, it was the time, I suppose. The sixties? She became just a muse to others. A pretty young thing on the arm of rock stars and charlatans. Losers.' She went on: 'But, in fact, Susie was a loser too,' she whispered sadly. 'She almost lost Tanya, but I flew out to America and brought her back here to live with me until my sister had got some help. Rehab. Tanya's right: I've never married and I'll never know what it's like to have a husband, but for a while . . . I had Tanya. And I missed her so much when she finally went back to her mother. She was only nine years old and a real talent even then.' She gave a broken smile.

Pearl spoke softly: 'And now she's a grown woman.'

Irene Taylor nodded slowly. 'Yes,' she said. 'And so I really shouldn't interfere – is that what you're telling me?'

Pearl paused. 'I'm not sure what any of this has to do with Florrie Johnson's murder,' she said finally.

'Aren't you?' Irene looked back towards the apartment with an ice-cold stare as she went on: 'Why do you think I'm trying to secure Tanya's future with this business? Tony's been used to the high life. Now his career might well be over. If so, he'll want as much as he can get – and however he can lay claim to it. If you're looking for someone who would like to see my niece dead,' she paused for a moment, steeling herself before she continued, 'look no further than her husband, Tony Ballard.'

Irene Taylor stared at Pearl – conviction written on her face.

Chapter Fifteen

By day, the two impressive replica cannons that stood guard on the crest of Tankerton Slopes were clambered over by an army of kids. At dusk, they remained undisturbed, with only the pitch-pot beacon for company. The beacon was also a replica, comprising an iron basket on top of a tall pole into which pitch would be placed and lit – like so many coastal beacons that had been used throughout the centuries to signal danger from the sea. They had once been employed to warn of an approaching Armada and throughout the Napoleonic Wars, but tonight there was only a warm breeze to disturb the waves as Pearl made her way down the slopes. Gulls brawled over scraps of food amongst the long grass as she headed past the rows of brightly coloured beach huts towards the prom. The sky was darkening, a red streak fading on the horizon, and surf rolled up on to the shoreline as she finally stepped down on to the beach where clumps of yellow horned-poppy had somehow managed to find a home amongst the harsh shingle. In the distance, the lights of the wind farm were visible, red and white against the night sky. Other lights were spread across the sea: navigation signals from a few yachts, and a large container ship that was disappearing below the line of the horizon. The local fishing boats would soon set out on the rising tide and return with their catch as it lowered, seeking safe haven once more in the town's muddy-bottomed harbour.

Pearl found herself reflecting on what she had heard at the Ballards' penthouse apartment. It was clear Irene Taylor had little affection, or respect, for her niece's husband, but Pearl couldn't be sure if this had always been the case or whether it was the result of Tony's affair. The couple had been together for some considerable time and maintaining their celebrity status must have put pressure on their marriage – though whether that resulted in sufficient motive for Tony Ballard to want his wife dead was uncertain. And was he even physically capable of murder? Tanya claimed her husband had been at home, sedated, at the time Florrie Johnson was killed, and that she had been with him. That gave the couple mutual alibis – useful for Tanya if, in fact, she had been elsewhere. But if she had been elsewhere, why would she have felt the need to lie about it? To protect her husband, as she had done so well today? Or to protect herself? Was it possible that Tanya had murdered Florrie Johnson – and if so, why?

It was still too early to make sense of all Pearl had gleaned so far, though she was sure McGuire would have more clues for her once his team had concluded their preliminary investigations: checking alibis, conducting house-to-house calls, interviewing residents and slowly piecing together the elements that would make up a more complete picture of what had taken place leading up to the young girl's murder.

Before she was able to reach any further conclusion, the sound of footsteps crunching on the shore behind her caused Pearl to turn quickly – and she saw McGuire approaching, his jacket tucked beneath his arm. Once he had reached her, he tossed the jacket on to a timber groyne before raising both hands to frame Pearl's face with his palms. Without saying a word, his lips met hers in a kiss, before he held her tightly in his arms. As he did so, Pearl sensed the tension of McGuire's day draining from him. She waited until they had broken apart before she looked up into his blue eyes and asked: 'Tell me it isn't true – that you could be transferred?'

'Disposed of is probably a more accurate description.' McGuire ran his hands through his hair and slumped down on to a groyne.

'But you're a good detective,' said Pearl, sitting close beside him. 'You could appeal this.'

McGuire looked at her and gave a sad smile. 'It's nice you still have your dreams intact about the force.'

Pearl frowned, stung by the remark. 'If it's really that bad, why stay?'

'Why?' said McGuire. He looked at her. 'I'm not you, Pearl,' he said gently. 'This is all I know. And I can't just . . . walk away from it.' After a moment, he got to his feet and walked to the water's edge. Pearl followed him there.

'So you'd walk away from me?'

McGuire turned back to her. He failed to reply but his features betrayed his fatigue and his torn emotions as he remained silent.

'Well, it won't come to that,' said Pearl determinedly. 'Solve this case and Welch won't be able to . . . "dispose" of you so easily, will he?'

'No,' said McGuire.

'Then we'll turn this around,' she insisted.

'How?'

'You still have Jack Harper in custody?'

McGuire gave a long sigh. 'He still won't talk and I haven't enough to charge him.'

'What about the autopsy results – they're through?'

McGuire nodded. 'Time of death: no earlier than five thirty.'

Pearl considered this. 'And Ruby and I arrived a minute or two after six. I'd just missed the early-evening news on the car radio and caught the weather forecast. The timing makes sense,' she went on. 'Florrie's body was still warm when I felt for a pulse.'

'And the results confirm she was seated at the time of death.'

'At the make-up mirror.'

'The weapon—'

'The stiletto heel of a dance shoe?'

McGuire nodded. 'Swung at her with such force, it actually pierced the orbital bone at the back of the eye.'

Pearl looked at him in horror. 'And that was the cause of death?'

McGuire took hold of Pearl's hand as he continued gently: 'The shock would have caused her to lose consciousness immediately. Cause of death was actually a brain haemorrhage from the impact.'

Pearl closed her eyes. 'Poor Florrie.'

McGuire paused before he went on. 'Harper has a rock-solid alibi.'

Pearl looked back at him. 'Playing piano at a hotel bar in Canterbury?'

McGuire nodded. Pearl explained: 'I told you, his wife Laura came to see me yesterday.'

'Did you tell her it was you who found the backpack?' McGuire asked.

Pearl shook her head. 'She's absolutely convinced Jack had nothing to do with Florrie's murder.'

'She would be. She's his wife.'

'But she's also having his baby.'

McGuire shrugged. 'Even more reason for her to believe he's innocent.'

'Or reason,' said Pearl, 'for him *not* to have done it.' Pearl held McGuire's gaze. 'Think about it, why would Jack jeopardise his marriage – and his future – with a young girl?'

'He wouldn't be the first.'

'You're right,' said Pearl. 'But like you say, he has an alibi.'

McGuire considered this, still dissatisfied. 'But what about the dumping of the backpack . . . the note . . . the poems?'

'I don't know,' Pearl admitted in frustration. 'But once Jack does start talking—'

'*If* he ever does,' said McGuire, breaking in. He paused, then: 'If he doesn't, I'm going to have to let him go soon.' He looked at her. 'His solicitor knows it as well as I do.' He turned to look out to sea at a line of shipping on the horizon – navigation lights blinking red and green, like so many rubies and emeralds.

'Forensics?' asked Pearl.

McGuire shook his head. 'SOCOS have finished at the school but there's nothing much to go on. My team have been interviewing the staff—'

'Staff,' said Pearl suddenly, turning to McGuire. 'Max Sanchez and Vivian Gleaves came to the restaurant yesterday.'

'And?'

Pearl shrugged as she recalled: 'They seemed unlikely lunch companions to me. Max looked as though he'd rather be elsewhere. Vivian's a queer fish . . . I can't quite make her out. She seemed more interested in enjoying a good meal than mourning a murdered colleague. And what about Tony Ballard?' she asked. 'Have you taken a statement from him yet?'

'Talking to him tomorrow,' said McGuire. 'He's been out of action, sedated with painkillers.'

'Apparently so,' said Pearl. 'Though he did manage to get up out of bed this evening.' On McGuire's look,

Pearl explained. 'I went to the Ballards' apartment. Irene Taylor's concerned her niece might be in danger.'

'The dress?'

Pearl nodded. 'And Florrie's dyed hair means there's still a chance that this was a case of mistaken identity.' She held McGuire's gaze. 'But there's certainly no love lost between Irene and Tony Ballard. She doesn't trust him an inch . . . because he had an affair.'

McGuire considered this as Pearl went on: 'Tanya took him back but if this . . . knee problem of his persists, it's possible Tony's dancing career might be over—' She broke off for a moment and looked at McGuire. 'Maybe Irene Taylor's right and he really is after whatever he can get.'

'The business, you mean?' asked McGuire. 'Just how much would a dance school like that be worth?'

'I don't know,' said Pearl, 'or what the couple have in assets, but the Ballard brand is still worth something right now.'

McGuire took this in, then: 'If Tanya Ballard decides to divorce him . . .'

'For adultery,' said Pearl. 'It's possible he may end up with very little. The school belonged to her mother originally.'

'And if he chose to contest it,' said McGuire, 'maybe only the lawyers would end up in profit.' He paused to reflect on this, then: 'What about Sanchez?'

'Max is an old friend of Nathan's – American – but according to Nathan, his parents were from Cuba. Max is . . . colourful, pretty honest with his views and I gather he's not too impressed with Tanya – or maybe he's just resentful about her return to the school.' She frowned. 'He seemed to . . . foresee Tony's knee causing problems the other night.'

'What do you mean?'

'Just before the dance class began, he said he'd warned Tanya that Tony wasn't up to giving a tango demonstration – but she hadn't listened. He was right, of course, because Tony's knee did give out, just as they had begun, and then a tall blond stranger happened to walk through the door to save the day.' She stepped closer to McGuire and gave him a knowing look. 'Tanya was very impressed – so much so, she left this for you when she stopped by the restaurant. I should have given it to you earlier.' She reached into her pocket and handed Tanya Ballard's business card to McGuire. He glanced at it – then back at Pearl, who explained: 'I think she's hoping you'll partner her again next week?'

'I told you,' said McGuire, 'I've already got a partner.' He held Pearl's gaze.

'She means a dance partner,' said Pearl. 'You clearly don't need lessons in tango.'

McGuire smiled and reminded her: 'You were telling me about Sanchez . . .'

'So I was,' said Pearl, returning to the subject. 'Mum calls him the King of Tap – but I'm guessing your lessons in Streatham didn't stretch to that?'

'Strictly ballroom,' said McGuire.

'Will the dance school be able to carry on with their classes?'

'Like I say, Forensics and SOCO have finished their work,' he explained.

'And I'm sure the Ballards are relieved about that,' said Pearl, adding: 'Tanya and Tony haven't been able to work their usual circuit. They must be hurting for cash, but from what I understand, it's Tanya who has the ambition, and a keen sense of making use of an opportunity before it disappears.' She frowned as she considered: 'Maybe that's something to do with her mother . . .'

McGuire took a step closer. 'Why?'

'Because Susanne Ballard was a dancer too – one who seemed to have ended up a casualty to celebrity. I don't think Tanya wants to turn out the same way.'

McGuire took this in. 'And Vivian Gleaves,' he began, 'what do you know about her?'

Pearl shook her head. 'Hardly anything,' she admitted, 'other than the fact she's fond of lobster. She was once with the Royal Ballet, so maybe she feels she should be doing better than working at Ballard's, although . . .' She trailed off, suddenly thoughtful.

'What?'

'Irene mentioned that Vivian also teaches a dance class at a local school – St Edwards.'

'And?'

'And I might just take a visit there tomorrow.'

'On what pretext?'

'I'll think of something.' She smiled, and for a moment McGuire was held captive in her gaze. 'Pearl . . .' he began, about to tell her something that had been on his mind since his return from Hampshire. But on hearing the low tone of the bell buoy tolling at sea, he scanned her beautiful features and said only: 'It's always murder that comes between us.'

'Yes,' said Pearl, her voice dropping to a whisper. 'And your job.' She paused. 'All the more reason why we have to solve this.'

McGuire failed to argue with her and leaned forward, his lips about to meet Pearl's, when a phone sounded – not the ring of Pearl's smartphone but the intrusive beep of McGuire's mobile. Exasperated, he pulled it from his pocket and answered tersely: 'McGuire.'

Pearl looked on as he paused, listening intently to the caller before he looked away, as though trying to assimilate the news he was receiving.

'To me and no one else?' He paused again then finally nodded his head. 'Okay,' he said. 'I'll be right there.'

Pearl remained silent until McGuire looked back at her. 'What is it?' she asked.

'Jack Harper,' said McGuire. 'Seems he wants to make a full statement.'

As Pearl took this in, McGuire registered her torn feelings – which mirrored his own. 'Good,' Pearl said finally, before turning back to the timber groyne to pick up McGuire's jacket. Reaching up, she gently placed the palm of her hand against his cheek before kissing him, then she handed him the jacket and ran her fingers through his blonde hair.

'Go on,' she said, managing a smile for him. 'And make sure you let me know what Harper has to say.'

McGuire turned to leave, looking back to see Pearl standing so still on the beach she seemed part of the landscape itself. Then she smiled again and nodded to him – a sign of understanding and common purpose. Throwing his jacket over his shoulder, he headed on, away from the beach and up onto the wide prom, towards his parked car.

Pearl continued to watch as his figure retreated into the night, then she stared back, out towards the incoming tide, refusing even to contemplate what her life might be like without McGuire being a part of it.

Chapter Sixteen

Situated on the main road leading from Whitstable to Canterbury, St Edward's School had welcomed pupils through its doors since the mid-nineteenth century. Originally an old charity school, the establishment had evolved and expanded throughout the years to become a fee-paying independent, far removed from the state school Pearl had attended in the centre of Whitstable town itself. As she strolled along a high-ceilinged corridor, Pearl noted its intricately carved oak panelling while the school's deputy head, Helena Lambton, explained to her: 'I'm so sorry you won't be able to join us for our upcoming Open Day, Ms Nolan. I have such limited time today, but you'll have seen from our website that we're a fully co-educational boarding school, proud of our history and also very forward-looking and ambitious for our pupils. We respect our founding ethos and we pride ourselves on nurturing each child's individuality – creating opportunities for pupils to fulfil their own potential and enabling them to become confident, sociable, well-balanced contributors to society.' She smiled. 'In recent years we've made considerable investment in our facilities and I'm sure your relative would find our curriculum both varied and challenging.' She paused for a moment. 'How old did you say she is? Dolly, was it?'

Pearl nodded. 'That's right. A rather precocious ten.' Pearl smiled at the thought of Dolly ever attending such a prestigious school and turning it into something resembling St Trinian's.

The deputy head nodded. 'And is Dolly sporty?'

'Not so much sporty as creative,' Pearl explained. 'She's very keen on dance and I hear you have an excellent ballet class?'

'We most certainly do,' said Helena. 'In fact, our ballet mistress was once a member of the Royal Ballet and is currently working with pupils on our Christmas performance.'

'*The Nutcracker?*'

Helena's smile faded. 'Predictable, I know, but nevertheless a firm favourite with audiences. I understand you'd like to meet Miss Gleaves? If so, the studio is just along—'

Helena broke off as her mobile phone sounded. Looking apologetically at Pearl, she took the phone from her pocket and registered the caller's ID.

'I'm so sorry,' she said to Pearl, pained by the interruption, 'would you mind if I take this?'

'Not at all,' said Pearl.

Helena quickly answered her call just as Vivian Gleaves

entered the corridor from a door up ahead. On seeing her, Helena put her caller on hold and rushed to Vivian to whisper to her: 'I'm afraid I'm needed elsewhere for a moment. Can I possibly leave Ms Nolan in your capable hands?' She indicated to Pearl as she explained: 'She's particularly interested in our dance classes.'

Pointing to the phone in her hand, Helena then moved off along the corridor to finish her call as Pearl strolled to Vivian and waited for her reaction. The ballet mistress eyed Pearl before she finally offered a smile. 'Well, well,' she began, closing the door behind her, 'fancy seeing you here.' She paused before adding: 'That was a lovely lunch on Sunday. Excellent lobster.'

'Thank you,' said Pearl. 'Shame Max didn't have much of an appetite.'

Vivian shrugged. 'Watching his weight. Though he wouldn't want to broadcast the fact. Men can be just as vain as women, don't you think?' She observed Pearl through her smile. 'It's almost too much of a surprise to see you – here of all places?'

'Actually, I came to see you,' Pearl admitted.

'And not about a prospective pupil, I'm guessing?'

Pearl shook her head. Vivian seemed satisfied her instincts were correct and said: 'Irene told me it was you who found Florrie Johnson's body?'

Pearl nodded. 'With my waitress, Ruby. The girls were friends. Ruby's very upset. So I'd just like to talk to you, that's all. It won't take long?'

Vivian considered this for a moment, then gestured

towards a door leading out from the corridor into some cloisters. Once there, Pearl glanced up at the ornate vaulted ceiling before her gaze wandered to white figures playing cricket on the school's extensive playing fields.

'What is it you want to know?' asked Vivian.

'I talked to Tanya Ballard and her aunt yesterday,' Pearl began. 'They tell me they have no idea why anyone might have wanted to kill Florrie Johnson. She was just a young girl—'

'Nineteen,' said Vivian, thoughtful, 'though she seemed much younger. An *ingénue* in many ways.'

Pearl considered this, then went on: 'You had a class at the school that evening.'

Vivian nodded. 'I did – but I didn't get to it. Irene called me with the news of Florrie's murder after she'd been informed of it by the police.' She paused. 'It hardly seems possible . . . even now.'

'A particularly savage killing.'

Vivian looked at Pearl, who explained, 'The stiletto heel of a dance shoe . . . was driven through her skull.'

Vivian stopped in her tracks and paused for breath before speaking. 'A psychopath, surely?' she said. 'A random act of violence.'

'Perhaps,' Pearl conceded. 'But most murders are actually committed by those known to the victim – including family members.'

Vivian frowned as she considered this. 'I don't believe the girl had any family.'

'Florrie told you that?'

'Someone did. I can't remember who. Her mother was a widow and died some years ago, so the girl had gone into foster care.'

'That's right,' said Pearl. 'But she was making her own way, working at the dance school.'

Vivian nodded. 'A good little worker, too,' she said. 'I think she was rather smitten with the idea of Tanya and Tony Ballard returning here to Whitstable to take over.'

Pearl paused before asking: 'How about you?'

Vivian looked sharply back. 'I was told by Irene that my classes would continue. That's all I was concerned about. I'm hoping to retire before too long. I'd like to move to the countryside and enjoy some peace and quiet.'

'Anywhere in particular?'

Vivian paused, as though considering this. 'A bit of countryside would make a nice change to living on Westmeads Road – Blean, or perhaps Chestfield, if I can stretch to that.' Pearl said nothing, allowing Vivian to go on. 'Most dancing careers are short,' she explained. 'A moment in the spotlight before it's time for another to step forward. Ballet is a strict discipline. It's all about attention to detail. But that was always my forte. I've given my life to it, as a prima ballerina . . . and teaching others.'

'How to step into the spotlight?'

'How to be sufficiently worthy to do so,' said Vivian. 'Fame and acclaim used to be a natural corollary to talent – now it's possible to have fame without it. Girls seek celebrity, but they're not always keen to put in the work.'

'And Florrie?' said Pearl. 'Did she have talent?'

'For dance?' Vivian considered this for a moment with a pained expression. 'When she first started at the school she was a little too plump for ballet. Too . . . lacking in grace. But as time went on she managed to lose her puppy fat and she joined other classes. Tap. She had the right physique for a chorus line.' She smiled. 'Max took her under his wing for a time. Florrie joined his class. But when Tanya arrived, the girl spent all her time trying to please her new boss, falling over herself to help, like the other night at the tango class? She'd been desperate to attend that first lesson but ended up having to ferry Tony home. That was Florrie all over: she'd put in the extra hours, unpaid, and follow Tanya around like a moony schoolgirl.'

'And what about Jack Harper?' said Pearl. 'Did Florrie ever seem . . . "moony" about him?'

'Jack?' Vivian frowned before shaking her head. 'Not that I ever witnessed. Why?'

Pearl explained. 'He worked with Florrie and was much closer to her in age than anyone else – a young man—'

'A young *married* man,' Vivian added. 'I heard he's been taken in for questioning by the police, but I think they're wasting their time. As I said, the killer was clearly deranged.'

'A "random act of violence",' Pearl repeated. 'It's possible Florrie may not have been the intended victim.'

Vivian's face clouded with confusion. 'What do you mean?'

'Florrie had dyed her hair dark brown and was wearing the dress Tanya wore on the night of the tango class.'

'I . . . didn't realise . . .' Vivian trailed off as she stared away towards the peaceful cricket scene playing out on the green fields. 'Do you think someone may have wanted to kill Tanya, but killed Florrie instead?'

Pearl nodded. 'If so,' she paused for a moment, 'then Tanya Ballard may be in danger.'

Vivian shook her head. 'Why would anyone want to kill Tanya?'

'I don't know,' said Pearl. 'But if anything occurs to you, anything at all that might help with finding the killer . . .' Pearl reached into her bag and handed a card to Vivian. 'Would you call me?'

Vivian stared down at Pearl's business card. 'A detective?'

'I have a small agency,' said Pearl. 'Local cases. I can guarantee confidentiality.'

Vivian looked back at Pearl with new eyes and nodded slowly.

'Thank you for your time,' said Pearl. She had just begun to move off towards the playing fields when Vivian suddenly spoke again. 'It was Max,' she called out.

Pearl turned quickly. Vivian continued: 'The person who told me . . . about Florrie's family situation. About her having been in foster care?' She paused. 'I just remembered that.' She gave a proud smile before adding: 'I told you – I'm good at detail.'

Pearl took this in. 'Thank you.'

Pearl walked back to her Fiat and had just got into the car when she realised her smartphone was still switched off from her visit to the school. Switching it back on, a number of messages flashed up – all of them from a single source. She listened to the first. Peter Radcliffe's voice boomed out: 'I honestly don't know what I need to do to get your attention, Pearl, but I'd be grateful if you could call me as soon as possible.'

Then the second: 'Did you get my message? Call me.'

And the third: 'To say I am disappointed with the level of service would be an understatement. Please let me know what you discovered from the footage!'

Pearl stared out of the car window at the spires of St Edwards' chapel and at the figures still playing cricket on the emerald playing field. The sound of children's voices carried across the air from a school music class as they sang the opening lines of 'Jerusalem'. Pearl heaved a sigh and shifted her car into gear in order to return to Whitstable – and her insufferable clients.

Chapter Seventeen

'So,' said Peter Radcliffe, his face quite puce from frustration, and the added discomfort of wearing a toupee on one of the most humid days of the year, 'you're telling me that your specialist surveillance cameras came up with precisely zero in identifying the thief?'

Pearl took a deep breath. 'As I explained,' she began calmly, nodding towards Hilary beside him, 'the cameras I used weren't exactly "specialist", but they would have been more than adequate for the job in hand if only the thief had gained access by the gate or the garden wall – as anyone would have reasonably expected.'

'Well,' said Radcliffe, 'I didn't hire "anyone" for this job, did I? I hired you, and I expected you to come up with results.'

Pearl gazed towards the top of the high garden wall before inspecting the soil in the shrubbery bed below it, which appeared quite undisturbed. 'It's a mystery . . .'

'Clearly,' said Radcliffe, unimpressed.

Pearl turned to him. 'I mean, how the thief could possibly have entered the garden to steal these items and not be caught on my cameras. I positioned them so that they would get a clear head shot.' She thought to herself. 'Does anyone else have access to your house?'

Hilary shook her head then said: 'Only my cleaner. But Hilda's almost seventy and I can't imagine she would risk creeping into the house in the middle of the night in order to steal a set of lingerie she could quite easily take at any other time. Besides,' she went on, 'she suffers from arthritis and has problems cleaning my kitchen shelves, let alone reaching the height of the rotary drier.'

Pearl shook her head slowly. 'I just don't understand it . . .' she said, glancing up at the surrounding houses that overlooked the Radcliffes' garden.

Ratty huffed. 'I haven't paid you a retainer for you *not* to understand. I still expect you to come up with a solution to this . . . "mystery". That's what a detective is meant to do, isn't it? Or are you more adept at finding lost pets and bicycles?'

'Peter,' said Hilary, admonishing her husband.

'What?' he declared, unabashed.

Embarrassed, Hilary lowered her voice. 'There's no need for sarcasm. You know as well as I do that Pearl has solved a number of crimes in our town – and some far more serious than my lost underwear.'

'It's not lost!' said Radcliffe. 'It was purloined, pilfered, stolen . . . and the culprit is still out there somewhere, no doubt laughing at us all because he's got away with it! If that's not serious, I don't know what is.'

Pearl spoke calmly. 'We don't know for sure that the thief is a man.'

'True,' Radcliffe agreed. 'For all we know, it could be a pantomime dame, because you're failing in your job, Pearl. We've had no proper communication throughout this entire case and you incited my wife to sacrifice even more items – and for what? We are none the wiser for your efforts – such as they are. I've got a good mind to write a review for your company, which, I assure you, will do Nolan's no favours.'

As he glared at her, Pearl considered handing Ratty back the cheque he had given her as a retainer for the case, before she remembered it was, in fact, made out to the Whitstable Carnival Committee, at her own request, and with the carnival still in dire need of funds. For a hundred and twenty years, the annual event had taken place every summer, but it was quite possible that without further substantial donations it might cease altogether, so Pearl bit her tongue.

'I'm sorry,' she said finally.

'I should think so too,' said Radcliffe, taking advantage of Pearl's humility. 'I have no doubt that you are far more interested in helping DCI McGuire with his murder case, but I would remind you that a crime is a crime – and I hired you first.' He paused for full effect before: 'I don't expect you to let me down again.'

Pearl took a deep breath and resisted the temptation

to explain to Ratty, in no uncertain terms, that she was no errant schoolgirl in need of a dressing-down from a pompous headmaster. Instead, she held her nerve and said: 'You'll receive an update soon.' Then she stepped across to the Radcliffes' garden gate, opened it, and with some considerable relief, escaped into the alley on the other side. Once there, she paused for a moment, checking the gate to note that it was firmly locked, then she shrugged to herself and set off towards home, duly chastised but also deeply frustrated that she was failing so badly with the Radcliffes' case. She had a feeling that if this continued, Ratty would never let her forget it.

Later that afternoon, after ensuring that everything was in hand for the evening service at the restaurant, Pearl headed home to Island Wall and was just about to open her front door when something caught her eye. Nathan was in his front garden, saying goodbye to a visitor who was partially obscured by a topiary hedge. Judging by his flamboyant clothes, Pearl was sure it was Max Sanchez. Hesitating for a moment, she looked more carefully and saw that it couldn't have been anyone else but the King of Tap. Max was dressed in white linen trousers with his signature red braces over an open-necked shirt, and was holding a panama hat in his hand, which he used to wave to Nathan before stepping into a classic red MGB convertible. After gunning the engine, Max drove off towards town, while Nathan stared after him, waiting, it seemed, for the car's engine to fade into the distance before he turned and saw Pearl standing behind him at his garden gate.

'Sweetie . . .'

'Max?'

'Who else?' Nathan smiled. 'He just happened to stop by. If I'd known you were home I'd have asked you over – especially as he was wondering how the investigation was going. As am I.' Nathan carefully dead-headed a slug-ravaged blossom on the navy-blue agapanthus in his front garden while Pearl stared in the direction Max had taken. 'What did he have to say about it all?'

Nathan gave a small shrug. 'There's not much love lost between Max and Tanya Ballard,' he said knowingly. 'In fact, dear Max seems to think if she hadn't returned here, then maybe none of this might have happened.'

'Oh?'

'Well, he has a point; the dance school's been ticking along quite uneventfully for years, then the Ballards arrive and suddenly there's a gruesome murder – of an innocent young woman.'

'Yes,' said Pearl. 'Innocent in both senses – the one person who can be ruled out as killer.' She glanced at Nathan, who gave her a stern look.

'You surely don't think Max had anything to do with it?' On Pearl's silence, he protested: 'Oh, come on. Max is an old friend. And he was also very fond of Florrie, from what I understand.'

Pearl looked back at him. Nathan read her look. 'I don't mean in that way,' he said bluntly. 'The girl joined his tap class at one point – and Max happens to be a very good teacher. He cares about his students – and makes an effort to get to know them.'

Pearl considered this, recalling Vivian's earlier comment about Max being the one to tell her that Florrie Johnson had been in foster care. Seeing her look so thoughtful, Nathan asked: 'How's your police detective getting on with this?'

'He's not,' said Pearl flatly. 'And he needs to.' Nathan looked back at her and Pearl explained: 'He could be transferred from Canterbury.'

'Far away?'

Pearl nodded. Nathan took this in, then asked: 'Would you . . . consider going with him?'

'How could I?' she asked helplessly. 'I have Mum, Charlie, the restaurant . . . Besides,' she added, 'I'm not sure McGuire would want me to. Things work . . . the way they are.'

'Your relationship, you mean?' said Nathan. 'With no commitment?'

Pearl failed to reply and Nathan decided against pressing her.

'Well,' he said, 'that's one consolation – for me, anyway. And I guess if he doesn't want to be shunted off he could always resign.'

'And do what?'

'He's a man of many talents, sweetie, especially on the dance floor.' He waited for Pearl's reaction. Finally, she smiled. Relieved, Nathan went on. 'If the worst came to the worst he could become Whitstable's new Tango King. According to Max, this murder has brought Tanya Ballard more publicity than ever – and she's still without a dance partner – unless Tony makes a sudden recovery.'

Pearl was pondering this when Nathan asked innocently: 'Limoncello?'

Pearl shook her head. 'Another time.'

'Any time,' said Nathan, leaning forward to give Pearl a kiss.

Leaving Nathan to his agapanthus, Pearl headed off and reached her front door just in time to hear her landline ringing. Hurrying inside she picked up the receiver.

'I was just going to try your mobile,' said McGuire.

Pearl took her new smartphone from her pocket, her smile fading as she noted: 'Good thing you didn't because I'm out of battery. Strange,' she mused, 'I thought I just charged it in the car.' She put the phone securely on charge and went on to ask: 'What's the news on Jack Harper?'

'I let him go.'

Shocked, Pearl sat down. 'But . . . he was making a statement?'

'He did,' said McGuire. 'And by the time he finished, I knew for sure I didn't have enough to charge him.' He paused. 'I've been trying to reach you all day. Harper has a cast-iron alibi for the night of Florrie Johnson's murder. He was definitely playing at The Pilgrims Rest Hotel.'

Pearl frowned. 'Are you sure you checked that out properly? Arrival and departure times . . .?'

'Of course,' said McGuire, before he stared out of his office window to see floodlights suddenly illuminating the city walls across the road. Once upon a time, the lights had all shone white – but now they were multicoloured, making the old stone walls and ramparts look like something better placed in Las Vegas.

'I've released him on bail,' he went on. 'There's no chance of him doing a runner and I can keep tabs on him. And be sure I will.'

Hearing the resolve in McGuire's voice, Pearl remained silent for a moment.

'Are you still there?' he asked.

A pause followed before Pearl finally replied. 'Yes.'

'Good,' said McGuire, 'because whatever's happening with this case – with Welch or your customers or clients, tomorrow night I'm taking you for dinner.'

'Are you?' asked Pearl, unsure if she might have just imagined this.

'You can count on it,' said McGuire, as he raised his first smile of the day.

Chapter Eighteen

Pearl watched Dolly investigating the shrubs and bushes in her garden, rooting around foliage and separating stems of bamboo before she finally turned to Pearl and announced with great concern: 'It's been days now. And I'm beginning to think the worst.'

Pearl began tentatively: 'You mean—'

Dolly broke in: 'Cat-napped!'

Judging from her expression, Dolly was completely serious, but nevertheless Pearl felt the need to check: 'Mojo?'

Dolly nodded balefully. 'I've been reading about it online. Do you realise how many pets are stolen each year?'

'Plenty of cats and dogs go missing,' Pearl replied. 'But plenty are also found. In fact, I started up the detective agency with the proceeds of that reward I received after I found Mr and Mrs Caffery's Wheaten Terrier, remember?'

Dolly's eyes suddenly widened as an idea dawned. 'Then it's down to you to find Mojo!'

'What?'

'You're meant to be a detective.'

'And I am,' said Pearl defensively. 'But I'm *not* a pet detective.'

Dolly looked affronted. 'I see,' she said. 'So you're quite prepared to spend valuable time looking for Hilary Radcliffe knickers, but none on the potential kidnapping of a much-loved family member?' Dolly snatched a handkerchief from her smock and gave a snort that resembled a trumpeting elephant.

'Oh, come on,' said Pearl, 'there's no evidence that anyone's run off with Mojo. And besides—' She broke off, just in time to stop herself from suggesting that no one, other than Dolly, could possibly want to spend more than a few minutes in the company of the querulous creature – *or* expect anyone to offer money for Mojo's return.

'*Besides* what?' said Dolly, pressing Pearl to continue.

'I was going to say,' Pearl went on, 'that kidnapping usually involves a ransom – and nobody has made any demands for Mojo, have they?'

Dolly shook her head.

'Well then,' said Pearl, 'I'm sure there's no third party involved in this. As usual, he'll turn up of his own accord . . . sooner or later.'

'How much later?' said Dolly, her bottom lip quivering as she went on: 'I know he can be difficult, but so can I – and we understand one another. The house just isn't the same without him.' She dabbed her eyes with her handkerchief and Pearl moved forward and placed an arm around her mother's shoulder.

'I'm sorry,' she said gently. Torn, she now admitted: 'I know how much he means to you and—' She broke off, then decided: 'You're right – I can help. How about you design a poster and I'll get copies of it up all over town?'

'Good idea!' said Dolly, suddenly enthused. 'I've got some excellent photos of him. I could come up with something really eye-catching. Here . . .' She stepped quickly into the conservatory and pulled an old album down from a bookshelf. Leafing through it, she gazed wistfully at one particular photo that showed Mojo sunbathing in one of Dolly's window boxes, crushing a bed of narcissi.

'What do you think?'

Pearl eyed the image, knowing it summed up Mojo's character perfectly – a spoilt old tom, who, in Dolly's eyes, could do no wrong.

'Perfect,' said Pearl. 'I'm sure we'll get him back in no time,' she added, hoping she would have more luck in tracing her mother's recalcitrant feline than she had managed, thus far, in finding either Hilary Radcliffe's lingerie or poor Florrie Johnson's killer.

A few hours later, after Dolly was finally happy with her poster design, Pearl managed to print off a handful of copies before her printer cartridge ran out of ink. Nevertheless, she had enough to begin an appeal for information – and for an excuse to visit Ballard's School of Dance, which had opened its doors for the first time since Florrie Johnson's murder. Entering by the front door, Pearl spent a few moments in the empty reception, checking the school's class timetable in her hand before she headed across to peer through the glass panels in the swing doors. In the studio she saw Max Sanchez taking his tap pupils through their paces to a melody Pearl recognised from one of Dolly's favourite Busby Berkeley films, *42nd Street*. Originally performed by squads of pretty girls in white fur-trimmed dance suits, Pearl noted Max's chorus line consisted of a few overweight housewives and an elderly couple who had clearly mastered the shuffle-ball-change tap steps some decades ago – without losing any enthusiasm for the routine. Max's voice rang out across the studio.

'And two! And three! And four!'

He wore a shiny black top hat and a pair of black-and-white tap shoes with which he was beating out a strict rhythm on the parquet floor along with some syncopated taps from the silver-handled cane in his hand. As the music reached its final crescendo, Max threw his top hat up into the air, allowing it to turn twice, before catching it firmly in his grasp. Pearl almost applauded but managed to stop herself in time and instead waited patiently in the foyer as the class ended and Max's pupils began to file past her and out of the building.

Taking a poster from her bag, she then waited for the class teacher, who was the last to leave, switching off the studio lights before he caught sight of Pearl. Brought up short for a moment, Max recovered and offered a smile, which Pearl returned. 'I hope you don't mind,' she began. 'I couldn't help but admire your performance there.'

'Mine – or my class?'

'Both,' said Pearl. 'Everyone looked very focused and professional.'

At this, Max gave a small nod in polite acknowledgement of her compliment. 'That's good,' he said. 'It's one thing to be a dancer – it's another to teach someone else how to dance.'

Pearl said nothing as she watched Max reach for his jacket and panama hat before he asked: 'I'm guessing you're not here just to spy on my class?'

'You're right,' said Pearl, producing two posters from her bag. 'My mother's cat, Mojo.' she explained. 'He's gone missing and I wondered if I could possibly put one of these posters up in your reception? You never know,' she added, 'someone here may just have seen him?'

Max shrugged and offered another smile. 'Go right ahead,' he said, indicating a large noticeboard on the wall. 'I'm sure Irene won't mind.'

Pearl pinned one of Dolly's posters to the board and asked: 'Don't you mean Tanya?'

Max looked back at Pearl who added: 'She and Tony are in charge of this place now, aren't they?'

'They may have taken over the school,' said Max, getting into his jacket, 'but I expect Irene will still be doing most of the work – under orders, of course.'

Pearl considered him. 'You're no fan of Tanya's.'

Max smiled. 'Tanya has enough fans,' he said, 'and an indulgent aunt. But she could do with some honest advice sometimes.'

'And that's your job?'

He turned to her and gave a casual shrug. 'My "job" is to be the Bojangles of this place.' Seeing Pearl's lost look, he went on: 'You never heard of Bill "Bojangles" Robinson?'

Pearl shook her head. Max pointed to a framed photograph on the wall showing three giant shadows projected on to the backdrop of a stage, reflecting the movements of a lone figure – a black tap dancer wearing a tight check jacket, light-coloured trousers, a bowler hat and white gloves. Max tilted his head towards the photo and explained: 'Bill Robinson was an extraordinary man. Tap dancer, actor, singer, and the most famous and highly paid black performer of his time in my country. He started out in the minstrel shows and then made his name on Broadway, Hollywood and TV. He was the first African-American to headline a mixed-race Broadway production.' Still staring up at the man in the photo, Max went on. 'His most famous routine was The Stair Dance, an unbelievably complex sequence in which he'd tap dance his way up and down a staircase.' He frowned as he considered something. 'Some said he was just . . . an Uncle Tom figure, dancing for the establishment. But Bill persuaded the Dallas Police Department to hire its first black policeman and during the last war he lobbied the President for fair treatment of black soldiers. He also managed to stage the first integrated public event in Miami.' He looked back at Pearl for a response.

'An amazing man.'

Max gave a nod. 'When he died, the schools in Harlem closed for a half-day so that kids could listen to the service – it went out over the radio.' His expression darkened. 'But he died a pauper.' Max paused again then looked at Pearl. 'The king is dead. Long live the king.'

'The King of Tap,' said Pearl, remembering.

'Not me,' said Max. 'Compared to the real Bojangles, I'm just an old hoofer.' He began moving towards the door. Pearl followed him.

'But . . . you also teach,' she said, 'brilliantly – from what I saw of your class.'

Max considered this. 'A stop-gap,' he said. 'Just a short-term plan.' Again, he went to move on.

'For two years?'

Max now halted in his tracks but failed to look back at Pearl, who explained: 'Nathan mentioned it.'

'And Nathan's right,' Max admitted. He heaved a heavy sigh and went on: 'There's no point in hiding the fact that if any of us could still be treading the boards, hoofing with the rest of them, we would be. But the truth is none of us are – not Madame Gleaves from the Royal Ballet or I, the King of Tap, or even, for that matter, the tango stars: Tanya and Tony Ballard.'

'Yes,' said Pearl. 'You mentioned that Tanya had pushed Tony too far with his knee injury.'

Max looked back at her and said knowingly: 'I'd say it's more than his knee that's keeping them from the tango circuit.'

Max allowed Pearl to exit before him, after which he locked the door and tested the handle to make sure it was secure.

'Like what?' asked Pearl.

Max left a pause before explaining. 'Dance is like acting,' he began. 'You have to inhabit the role. Whatever it is, you have to feel it – live it. An actor does that with words but a dancer needs music. There are some dances you can fake – but never tango – not when you're so close there's barely a whisper between you.' He held Pearl's gaze for a moment then slipped his panama hat on his head. 'If you ask me, there was something else stopping Tony from carrying on with that tango demonstration the other night.'

'Are you saying . . . he's faking this knee problem?'

Max paused then explained: 'That was real enough. Tony had surgery, did his convalescence and rehab and then he suffered some nerve damage. It happens. But let's just say he's been . . . "convalescing" for a very long time.' He fixed Pearl with a look and leaned closer to her as he added: 'I'd say the reason for that is that Tony Ballard no longer has the nerve, or the desire, to dance with his wife.'

With that, he began to make his way across the sunny forecourt to where his red MGB sports car was parked. Pearl quickly followed behind him. 'But . . . you don't know that for sure.'

'You're right,' said Max with a casual shrug, 'I don't.

But I understand the language of dance. Without the passion those two once had they're nothing more than the kind of dancers you might expect to find on top of a music box.' He opened his car door.

'And Florrie?'

At Pearl's question, Max froze. She moved to him. 'You knew her well, didn't you? She was once in your tap class.'

Max turned slowly to face her. 'What if she was?'

'Nathan said you were fond of her.'

Max looked down for a moment. 'And he's right,' he said finally. 'She was a good kid.'

'But not a child,' said Pearl. 'She was a young woman – the same age as my waitress, Ruby.' She paused. 'Florrie turned twenty last Saturday – the day she died.'

Max looked pained to hear this. 'I . . . didn't know.'

'It seems not many people did,' Pearl explained. 'But it was the reason I was here at the dance school that night, with Ruby, to drive the girls to Canterbury.'

'To see Jack play?'

Pearl frowned at this. 'Why d'you say that?'

'Because I know he plays piano in a bar on Saturday nights.'

'At The Pilgrims Rest Hotel?'

Max gave a nod but said nothing more.

Pearl asked: 'Was Florrie involved with him?'

Max looked shocked by the suggestion. 'Of course not – Jack's married. He's a nice guy – caught up with his music *and* his wife, but . . .' He took a moment before explaining.

'Look, Florrie loved music and I just thought . . .'

'What?'

Max Sanchez seemed to fight something in himself before continuing. 'The kid had no family. No one.' He paused. 'I understand that: what it's like to be an outsider? I grew up in Miami but my old man was a soldier back in Cuba. He'd fought on the side of the dictator, Batista, so after the revolution he and my mom fled to Miami and settled there. They say you can be anything you want in the States, *if* you work hard enough, but I guess you get used to being a soldier so my dad joined the US army. He ended up in Vietnam.' He gave an ironic smile. 'So proud of defending his new country.' He paused. 'In sixty-eight, when I was seven years old, he got sick – multiple sclerosis. The doctors said it was down to the Agent Orange he'd been exposed to in the war – the chemical he'd been using to deforest the jungle.' He seemed to struggle with memories for a moment before he went on: 'He was looked after at a Veterans' facility and my mom worked hard to keep us all. As a kid, I used to dance for money. Bojangles.' He paused again. 'When she died. I kept dancing. In the Land of the Free. Now I'm here.' He gave Pearl a look – the final punctuation mark for their conversation before he turned back to his car once more.

'Why?'

With a look of surprise on his face, Max turned. Pearl took a step closer. 'Why are you here, in Whitstable, of all places?'

As though reflecting on this, Max turned away for a

moment, before finally looking back to Pearl. 'You mean
. . . how can I feel comfortable in a little English town like
this where I can probably count on the fingers of one hand
the number of people who actually look like me?'

'That's not what I meant—'

'I know,' said Max, finally offering Pearl a smile.
'Maybe I've got too used to playing the outsider. For most
of my life I never felt like I really fitted in anywhere.'

'Except on stage?'

Max shrugged. 'It makes a good home for those of us
who need one.'

'Like this school – for Florrie?'

'Maybe,' said Max, noting Pearl staring at the sign
above the door.

'You locked up just now,' she said. 'Does everyone who
works here have a key to the school?'

Max shrugged. 'As far as I know. There are days when
there are no back-to-back classes,' he explained. 'Like
now, for instance.'

'And no full-time receptionist?'

Max shook his head. 'Florrie used to fill in.'

'Like the other night at the tango class?'

Max nodded. 'Sure. She would do whatever Tanya
asked.' He looked up again at the image of Tanya and
Tony on the new signage above the front door. 'Florrie was
very trusting,' he said softly. 'Maybe too trusting.' He gave
a dark look, then took off his panama hat before tossing it
on to the back seat and starting up the car. Looking back
at Pearl, he slipped the MGB into gear then drove off the

forecourt and on to the road, where Pearl heard the car's engine disappearing into the town. A moment later Pearl took the Ballard's School of Dance timetable from her bag and double-checked that Vivian's ballet class wasn't due to start until seven. Reassured that the building was now empty, Pearl walked to the side of it and followed the same path she had taken on the night of the murder. This time, she noted that the bank of six windows at the side of the building were all closed, as was the back door, which she and Ruby had found unlocked on the evening of Florrie's death. Looking in the opposite direction, Pearl saw that the rear area of the school was bordered by a low fence, beyond which was a tall privet hedge. Walking across to it, Pearl also noticed that a gap in the same fence allowed her to step straight into the old recreation ground and swing park that was used by local children in the daytime and by youths at night. Staring straight across the 'rec', as it was known locally, Pearl also noted that Tanya and Tony's apartment block was visible in the distance, on the other side of the area, just beyond the swing park. Although it was probably a twelve-minute walk using the pavement, heading on foot from the Ballards' home across the rec would barely take five minutes.

Chapter Nineteen

Parking in Canterbury was always at a premium, especially on a warm summer evening when the city was filled with tourists, so Pearl took the bus into the city, a journey of just twenty minutes, which, at this time of year, was particularly pleasant as it transported her along the winding Blean Road, cutting a path through verdant countryside. Nearing the city itself, garden trees provided striking contrasts of colour before spires finally rose in the distance out of a heat haze. The Norman cathedral dominated the landscape, inspiring visitors with the same sense of awe it had conveyed to so many throughout the centuries. Famed for Thomas à Becket's murder, the city had become one of the most visited pilgrimage sites in the medieval world – with Chaucer's *Canterbury Tales* continuing its fame. Alighting at the sixty-foot-high Westgate Towers at the entrance to Canterbury, Pearl checked her watch and headed on, not to the restaurant, nor to McGuire's riverside apartment, but towards the

Marlowe Theatre – a modern architectural contrast to the great cathedral, and one that drew as many to its productions as the cathedral attracted to its services.

Pearl looked on as crowds mounted the theatre's steps for the evening performance of a new play, and she paused for a moment, allowing herself to imagine that if she and Ruby had only arrived at Ballard's School of Dance half an hour earlier on that fateful evening, Florrie Johnson might still be alive, having celebrated her birthday here in Canterbury, as she had expected to do. Pearl took a deep breath and turned away from the theatre, heading instead towards the inconspicuous exterior of the Pilgrims Rest Hotel. Pearl had never crossed its threshold until now, but having done so, she found herself in a charming sixteenth-century building – the ideal place for an overnight stay after catching a show or exploring the city's attractions.

A young woman at reception offered a welcoming smile. 'Can I help?'

As Pearl looked around, she heard piano music softly playing. 'Your bar?'

The receptionist nodded and indicated the way through a half-open door and Pearl stepped through it into a busy dining area and cocktail bar. In a far corner Jack Harper was seated at a white baby grand piano, playing the haunting melody of Cole Porter's 'Night and Day', its pulsing Latin American rhythm evoking the aching desire for an absent lover. Hotel guests sipped drinks and continued their conversations and meals while Jack played on – engrossed in the music. Finding a bar stool, Pearl ordered an Espresso Martini, and stared again towards the piano area where Jack Harper looked as if he might be anywhere else than a busy city hotel. The barman prepared Pearl's drink with care, garnishing the cocktail with fresh coffee beans before presenting it to Pearl. She sipped it then tipped her head towards Jack and whispered: 'Wonderful music.'

Taking Pearl's payment, the barman leaned on the bar to agree with her. 'Yeah,' he said, 'Jack's cool – and very popular. We usually get a full house on the nights he plays.'

'Wednesdays, Thursdays and Saturdays?' asked Pearl.

The barman nodded again. 'Regular as clockwork. He never misses a session and he's always here right on time.' He offered a smile and moved off to serve another customer just as the Cole Porter number came to an end. As applause rippled around the bar, Jack appeared to remember where he was and acknowledged the response with a polite smile before picking up a tall glass of pale beer that was waiting for him on the piano. Taking this as her cue, Pearl wandered across to him.

On catching sight of Pearl, Jack Harper seemed confused – as though he recognised Pearl, without being able to place her.

'Pearl Nolan,' she said, reminding him. 'The Whitstable Pearl?'

Momentarily, Jack's expression clouded before he glanced anxiously around the busy room and asked: 'What is it you want?'

'A word?'

Jack frowned, pressured. 'I suppose I could take a quick break between songs.'

'It won't take long.'

Taking a deep breath the young man reluctantly indicated a quiet corner by the door. As he sat down, Pearl joined him, noting he continued to look away from her as if he'd rather be somewhere else. After a pause, she spoke. 'Laura came to see me.'

'She told me,' Jack said curtly, before taking a sip of his beer.

'The police took you in for questioning—'

'But released me,' he said quickly.

'On bail?'

Jack looked warily at Pearl. She offered him a sad smile and explained: 'It's hard keeping a secret in Whitstable.'

'Obviously,' said Jack, accepting this.

Pearl began again, framing her words very carefully. 'Laura's probably told you that apart from the restaurant, I also have a small detective agency.' She took one of her business cards from her bag and handed it to Jack, who stared down at it. He nodded once more but remained silent.

'Irene Taylor is very concerned about her niece, Tanya.'

'She may well be,' said Jack dully before: 'But *I'm* "concerned" I could be framed for a murder I didn't commit.' He turned to Pearl and held her gaze.

'Florrie Johnson's murder,' said Pearl. At that moment, a middle-aged couple walked past, heading towards the door with theatre tickets in their hands. Jack waited until they had exited, before he turned again to Pearl.

'I didn't murder anyone,' he said in an urgent whisper. 'I couldn't have done it. I was playing here that evening.'

'And you told the police that,' said Pearl, adding pointedly: 'eventually.'

Jack paused then rubbed his brow before trying to explain. 'Look, they cautioned me. I was worried about saying the wrong thing. I asked to see a solicitor and when he came, he told me I didn't have to answer any questions and that I should be careful.' He looked away as if the conversation was over, but Pearl spoke up.

'Because you'd been seen disposing of a backpack containing poems and a note to you written by Florrie?'

Jack turned to meet Pearl's stare. 'How do you know that?' he asked, his eyes narrowing with suspicion. 'Did Laura tell you – or the police?'

Pearl fought a battle with herself and finally owned up. 'I happened to see you on Sunday morning after Florrie's murder, heading through town—'

'You mean . . . you followed me?'

Pearl nodded. 'To the railway bridge. I could see something was wrong. The way you looked that day, especially at Prospect Field just before the train came?'

At this, Jack looked away, wiping his face with his hand as if trying to mask his emotions. Pearl continued softly, 'You liked Florrie, didn't you?'

Jack's head snapped back sharply. 'Liked her?' He

frowned in irritation. 'Of course I liked her, there was nothing to dislike. Even Tanya liked Florrie.'

'Tanya?'

Jack gave a nod. 'She doesn't care much for anything or anyone except . . . tango – and Tony.' He took a deep breath. 'Florrie was just a girl.'

'With a crush on you?'

For a moment Jack said nothing, then admitted, 'Maybe.' He gave a weary sigh. 'But there was nothing between us. She just had a way of . . . trying to engage you about the things she knew you really cared about. She only ever talked to me about music – nothing more.' He looked troubled. 'She did it at the restaurant the other day, remember? The tango music that was playing? She was always keen to know more. It was a nice thing about her. It would have been cruel to ignore her.' He gave a defeated look.

'The note,' said Pearl. 'She was thanking you for the time you spent with her at Prospect Field. You went there the morning after she died. You could easily have got rid of that, and Florrie's poems, somewhere else – but you went there. Why?'

Jack shook his head and pushed his long fair hair back from his face. 'To be honest . . . I really don't know. I didn't want Laura to find them. I couldn't let that happen – especially after Florrie had been murdered. I realised what I had in that bag was . . . incriminating – damaging – but not just with the police.' He broke off for a moment. 'I know I'm innocent but . . . I couldn't allow Laura to suspect that anything might have happened.'

'Between you and Florrie?'

Jack nodded. 'There was nothing going on, I swear. Florrie just asked me to meet her at Prospect Field one afternoon . . . about a week ago . . . and to bring my guitar.'

Pearl frowned at this but Jack explained: 'She wanted me to play some of my music for her, that's all. Songs I'd composed for a musical. I had some free time. So I did.'

'You . . . sang them for her?'

Jack shook his head. 'I'm no singer,' he explained. 'But I played – like I'm doing tonight – but on my guitar. Florrie sat and listened. It was a sunny afternoon and it's peaceful up there. It was a nice thing to do. But then . . . a few days later, just as she was leaving the school and I was coming in to start work . . . she handed me an envelope and smiled. Said she'd explain properly another time.'

'And the envelope contained . . .?'

'The poems and the note.' He shook his head at the thought. 'When I heard she'd been murdered, I realised how it would look, especially to Laura, and . . .'

'You felt the need to get rid of them.'

Jack looked pained then nodded. 'I should've done that straight away but there was so much going on – hospital appointments for Laura, the lunch at your restaurant then the tango class and . . . suddenly Florrie was dead. Murdered. I panicked. I didn't know what I was doing that morning. There was no real plan. I was just upset.' He shook his head. 'She was murdered on her birthday, did you know that?'

'Yes,' said Pearl. 'She told you?'

Jack nodded. "Said she was coming to Canterbury to celebrate with a friend and that she'd pop in here before a concert at the Marlowe. I thought I might get a chance to talk to her about the poems and the note but . . . she never arrived.' He paused, then: 'The next morning I knew why.'

Pearl took a moment to absorb this. 'Who told you?' asked Pearl. 'About the murder.'

'Irene,' said Jack. 'She called everyone and broke the news. Looking back, I think I was in a state of shock . . . but . . . then I thought about the poems . . . the letter . . . and I just wanted to get it all out of our apartment. I wasn't thinking straight. I thought of cycling down to the quay and chucking it all in the sea but then I realised the tide was out. Next thing, I left home and found myself heading to Prospect Field. I was still trying to work out the right thing to do. But when I got there, I felt even worse. It just reminded me of when I'd been there with Florrie and played for her. Then I thought about Laura and . . . I started to cross the railway bridge and I heard the train coming . . . the beat tapping out on the rails . . . it was like . . . someone tap dancing. My heart started pulsing in my chest . . . I realised what might happen.' He fixed Pearl with his gaze. 'I don't want Laura to lose our child. That's all that was in my mind at that moment – and I kept repeating it to myself with the rhythm of the train . . . I thought about everything we'd been through right up until that point – it's been so awful for her.'

'And for you,' said Pearl gently.

Jack shook his head slowly. 'No, not for me. Because throughout it all, *I* still had Laura – but *she* only had this emptiness inside her . . . a yearning.'

'For a child.'

Jack nodded. 'It took her over. Physically she was still there – we were still together – but . . . inside she was somewhere else, disappearing slowly, day by day, bit by bit.' He stared into the distance then returned his attention to Pearl. 'And then it all came together for us, it was happening. Laura was pregnant – and I had her back with me again. Everything was going to be fine, if she could just get through the pregnancy without losing this baby.' He looked at Pearl. 'Then Florrie was murdered . . . and I found myself standing on that railway bridge. It seemed so easy for me to simply . . . erase it all.' He fell silent, then grabbed his beer and took a mouthful before he went on. 'The train came – and went – and that seemed to bring me to my senses. I realised I needed to go home, back to Laura . . . but I still had Florrie's poems and the note she'd written. I crossed the bridge and then I saw the bin right there by the golf course fence. It was like an answer to a prayer . . . I threw the whole bag into it and ran down across the golf course to the sea.'

Pearl remained silent for a moment as she reflected on this.

'And I found it.'

'And the police came,' said Jack.

Pearl suddenly felt a burden of responsibility. 'How is Laura?' she asked with concern.

'Her doctor says she's doing okay but . . . she's still upset . . . about everything.'

'Everything?'

Jack bit his lip and then explained. 'Look, Laura's always been . . . insecure,' he began, 'it's probably down to her childhood. Her parents split up when she was young and she could never really rely on her dad – he disappeared out of her life and . . . Well, she always seems to think she's going to lose me, too.' He looked at Pearl. 'Laura's ten years older than me,' he added, 'but I couldn't give a damn about that. I've always told her she can trust me.'

'And she does,' said Pearl. 'She believes in you. She told me she doesn't think you're capable of murder.'

Jack Harper took a deep breath on hearing this. 'And you?' he asked finally, staring at Pearl, willing her to respond, but before Pearl had a chance to do so, someone else spoke.

'Jack?'

The hotel barman was standing before them. He gave a smile and tipped his head in the direction of the piano then tapped his watch. 'Last ten minutes.'

'I'll be right there,' Jack replied, quickly finishing his beer before the barman took his empty glass. Getting up from his seat the young man looked back at Pearl and said: 'I have to go.'

Pearl nodded and watched as Jack Harper headed back to the white baby grand piano. Applause greeted him, rippling around the bar once more before the young man began to play – another Latin rhythm – this time a bossa nova. As the opening chords sounded of the sixties song 'The Girl from Ipanema', an idea suddenly came to Pearl. She picked up her bag and hurried out of the bar.

Chapter Twenty

McGuire was sitting in the Italian restaurant across the river from his Canterbury apartment. For a Wednesday evening it was surprisingly busy, but he had managed to book a riverside table, outside on the veranda, close to the jetty from which tourists were ferried on the Great River Stour. He stared across the water towards his own bedroom window, then up at a cloudless blue sky – no rain forecast – a perfect summer's evening. On the red gingham tablecloth before him was a small vase of sweet peas – summer flowers Pearl used in her own restaurant – but tonight she wouldn't be cooking, she'd be enjoying a meal – with him.

McGuire had arrived early and ordered himself a Peroni, which he hoped would allow him to unwind from a stressful day, shedding the tensions of this case – if only for a while – so that he could focus on his evening with Pearl. His hand curled around the ice-cold glass before he picked up the beer and sipped it. In the same moment, the restaurant door opened and McGuire looked up expectantly to see . . . not Pearl, but a group of animated American tourists commenting on how quaint the riverside veranda looked with its vine-covered trellis. They hurried on towards the jetty, where they produced tickets before clambering into one of the rowing boats that would transport them on a river-boat trip through the city. Settling into the craft, they were soon spirited away by a young student wearing a straw boater who pulled hard on the oars. As they disappeared up the river, McGuire now glanced towards the restaurant's interior and saw only his own reflection staring back at him from a glass door. Blond and with high cheekbones, a strong jaw and bright blue eyes, McGuire knew he could easily be mistaken for a Scandinavian tourist instead of an exiled Met police detective, but now, for the first time, he no longer felt like a DFL – he felt as though he belonged and that he could remain here, with Pearl, if he could only solve this case.

He took another sip of his beer and reviewed his day: no forensic clues to go on and no clear suspects, other than a young man observed by Pearl trying to dispose of incriminating evidence. Jack Harper had kept his silence during those first police interviews – like so many other suspects McGuire had dealt with over the years. Most of the time they were hardened criminals, guilty as sin, but knowing how to play the system, the cat-and-mouse game during which their silence would force McGuire and his team to battle against a ticking clock in order to come up with enough evidence to secure a criminal charge. McGuire had failed to do so in this instance and he took another sip of beer, reflecting on this, feeling the alcohol hit the spot, giving him the courage to believe that things might change soon – if only he could get a decent lead. But there was a bitter irony in the fact that he had returned from Hampshire convinced he wanted Pearl nowhere near his cases – only to find he now needed her help just to remain in Kent . . . and in her life. However hard McGuire tried to separate Pearl from the inherent dangers of his work, she always found her way into the midst of it. What did she get in return? Certainly McGuire knew Pearl deserved far more than he had ever been able to offer her. Troubled, he set down his glass, then suddenly became aware of a certain floral perfume – the delicate fragrance of lilies. Before he could turn, McGuire felt Pearl's lips on the back of his neck and she quickly appeared beside him, smiling, her eyes burning with excitement as she explained: 'I've just come from talking to Jack Harper.'

'You've what?' McGuire's mind cleared as Pearl sat down and explained.

'The Pilgrims Rest Hotel. I took advantage of the fact that he's playing there tonight. Three times a week, remember – Wednesdays, Thursdays and Saturdays?'

McGuire saw his case encroaching on his evening with Pearl, but nevertheless heard himself ask: 'And?'

'And . . .' said Pearl, trailing off as she picked up her menu and scanned it, distracting herself for a moment as she added: 'You know, I've been waiting to sample the food here for a long time?'

A waitress came across and took an order from Pearl for a glass of Pinot Grigio. Still studying the menu, Pearl asked: 'Have you seen anything you fancy?'

Staring across at her, McGuire noted she was wearing the freshwater pearl earrings he had given her that so matched the colour of her eyes. 'Yes,' he said softly.

Looking up, she saw him smiling at her. 'Me too,' she replied, holding his gaze before she put down her menu as the waitress brought her drink and took their food order.

'Calamari,' Pearl decided, 'and the seafood linguine.'

Looking across at McGuire, Pearl found he was still staring at her. 'I'll have the same,' he said idly, handing his menu to the waitress.

Pearl picked up her wine glass. 'You could have gone for something else,' she said admonishingly.

'You're the expert,' he replied, before qualifying: 'when it comes to food.'

'But not crime?' She eyed him as she touched McGuire's glass with her own. McGuire failed to reply and they sipped their drinks – after which Pearl smiled. 'I see you finally found time to shave?'

'Specially for you,' said McGuire, losing himself in the simple pleasure of sitting across the table from her. He reached for her hand, noticing that, as ever, she wore no rings on her fingers – partly from habit: when she was cooking at the restaurant she didn't want jewellery to finish up in one of her dishes, but also, as McGuire had come to learn, because Pearl's style was simplicity itself. In fact, whatever she wore and whatever she did to herself, she always looked strikingly beautiful. He took a deep breath and allowed curiosity to get the better of him.

'So, what happened?' he asked. 'With Harper?'

Pearl set down her glass and leaned towards McGuire. 'Everything he told me makes perfect sense. On the day after the murder he was upset, in shock – as was everyone – but he left home that morning with the backpack, thinking about his meeting with Florrie on Prospect Field. He swears there was nothing to it – as far as he was concerned – he was just playing some songs for her on his guitar.'

McGuire looked sceptical. 'If it was all so innocent, why didn't he come clean to me at the outset?' He stared sidelong at her. 'Have you thought that by keeping quiet like he did, he gave himself just enough time to come up with the story he's spun you?'

'If it *is* a story,' said Pearl. 'It could well be true – and you said yourself he has an alibi for the night of the murder. Playing at the same hotel?'

McGuire shrugged and sat back in his chair. 'The times check out.'

'And you're absolutely *sure* about that?'

'He arrived a few minutes before six.'

'The barman told me Jack's very reliable – he's never late.'

McGuire produced his phone and scrolled through it for some notes. 'I told you – the autopsy confirmed the time of death as no later than five thirty.'

Pearl frowned. 'But Jack arrived at the hotel by six and it's only a twenty-minute drive into Canterbury.'

'He didn't drive,' said McGuire. 'Harper doesn't have a licence and neither he nor his wife owns a car. He cycled into work that night – as he's done every other night.'

'Cycled?'

'That's right.'

'But at a push, you could cycle in to Canterbury in half an hour.'

'Not on the night of the murder,' said McGuire. 'Remember I told you there was an accident on Whitstable Road on Saturday night? It blocked both main routes into Canterbury via Harbledown and Rough Common, as well as creating jams on all the other main routes like Watt Tyler Way. We know Harper arrived in Canterbury with his bike because he was caught on CCTV near the Marlowe just after five fifty-five.' McGuire paused again. 'We also checked out the footage at both railway stations – no sign of him with a bike. And if he'd managed to get a cab to transport him – and the bike – into the city . . .'

'That would have been caught up in the jam too,' said Pearl, realising. She mused on this while McGuire sipped his beer.

'What else did you talk about?'

Still deep in thought, Pearl looked confused for a moment. 'How Jack felt on the day I followed him to the railway bridge – and the fact that he doesn't want his wife upset – especially at this time.'

'You mean, if she found out he'd been seeing the girl?'

Pearl nodded. 'Of course. But he swears he only met Florrie once – at Prospect Field – and all he did was—'

'Play guitar,' said McGuire, unconvinced. 'And you actually believe that?'

'Yes,' said Pearl.

'But what about the note . . . the poems?'

'No,' said Pearl, a slow smile spreading across her face. 'I realised something,' she went on, 'as I was listening to Jack play?' She leaned forward across the table again towards McGuire, as if sharing a secret. 'They may not have been poems at all.'

McGuire stared at her. Pearl shrugged. 'It's perfectly possible that what we *assumed* were poems were actually lyrics that Florrie had written to the songs Jack had played her. He told me the only thing they'd ever talked about was music . . . and something else he said made me think about what kind of girl Florrie was.'

'An orphan,' said McGuire.

'That's right. Like Ruby, Florrie had no family. Vivian told me that Florrie's mother had been a widow and that when she died, the girl had gone into foster care.'

'That's not strictly true,' said McGuire. 'We checked that out: Florrie's mother was actually a single parent. She died twelve years ago and there was no other family to bring up the child.'

Pearl became thoughtful. 'So . . . Florrie must have doctored that story for Max . . .'

'What do you mean?' asked McGuire, picking up on this.

'Vivian said that Max had told her this, and if he did, he must have been told, in turn, by Florrie.'

McGuire remained unimpressed. 'Maybe the girl preferred the idea of her mother being a widow.'

'Maybe,' said Pearl. 'She had no family and seems only to have been close to her work colleagues – and Ruby, of course.' She thought for a moment then: 'You know, what struck me was something Jack said about Florrie tonight: that she had a way of trying to engage you about the things she knew you cared about.' Pearl looked at McGuire. 'Maybe that was Florrie's way of getting some-one's attention – a kind of survival mechanism? She was a hard worker, loyal and, if you think about it, that kind of engagement is a form of flattery.'

'And Harper succumbed to it?'

'I think that could be reason enough for him to have gone to Prospect Field with her and played her some of his songs.'

'And she then went off and wrote lyrics to them?' asked McGuire, still doubtful.

'Why not?' said Pearl. 'She was trying to find a niche for herself. She may well have looked up to Jack Harper for his musical talent as much as she did to Tanya and Tony Ballard for their talent for dance. Besides,' she went on, 'if she and Jack Harper were lovers, why would she not have signed those sheets of paper "Florrie", instead of with her full name?'

McGuire considered this and smiled, admitting: 'You're good, Pearl.'

She returned his smile and whispered: 'I know.'

But her smile faded as McGuire sipped his beer and frowned. He raised an admonishing finger. 'There's still nothing to prove they *weren't* love poems,' he said, 'written to Harper because the girl was having a relationship with him.'

'True,' Pearl conceded, 'but his alibi removes him from the crime scene.'

'Right,' said McGuire, 'and it's still possible the killer mistook Florrie Johnson for Tanya Ballard . . . and that she was the intended victim all along.'

Pearl watched the lights of the restaurant playing on the surface of the river. 'It's so nice here,' she said softly.

'Yes,' McGuire agreed, allowing himself a moment to lose himself in her beautiful grey eyes.

Pearl paused, then: 'Irene Taylor suspects Tanya's husband. After all, Tony did have an affair – though it's clear Tanya's forgiven him and wants to move on.' She sipped her wine. 'Taking over the school seems to be part of that – but it may also be a way of getting Tony out of temptation's way.'

'You think he's a player?'

'Irene seems to think so. She's very protective of Tanya. She treats her more like her own daughter – and I think I know why. It's not just because Irene's childless herself and has grown to love Tanya, it's because Tanya's mother fell victim to the wrong kind of man in the States where she lived for so long. If Irene couldn't save her sister, maybe now she feels an even greater responsibility to save her niece – Tanya.'

'From her own husband?' asked McGuire. He shook his head. 'Tony Ballard may have cheated on his wife, but there's no reason to suspect him of wanting to murder her. He wasn't able to dance on the night of the dance class, remember? According to a statement, he was at home, incapacitated and in pain, when Florrie Johnson was murdered – *and* his wife was with him.'

'Yes,' said Pearl, sitting back in her chair. 'Handy.'

McGuire stared back at her. Pearl continued: 'Mutual alibis for them both—' She broke off as the waitress appeared with their starters. Pearl eyed the calamari, encased in a light tempura batter, before squeezing some lemon juice on to it and picking up her fork to try it. Closing her eyes she savoured it. 'Delicious.'

McGuire smiled. 'You were saying?'

'Well, from what I've been told, by Tanya and Max Sanchez, Tony Ballard had some kind of cartilage problem, which led to a knee replacement.'

McGuire picked up his cutlery. 'Right. And it's all been checked out.'

'But since the operation, there have been complications,' said Pearl. 'Some sort of nerve damage but . . .' She paused to enjoy another bite of calamari before she went on: 'Max Sanchez seems to think that wasn't the reason Tony ducked out of dancing with Tanya the other evening. It was something else.' She watched McGuire finishing his mouthful of food. 'Good?'

McGuire nodded. 'Excellent.'

Pearl smiled.

'Go on,' said McGuire, keen to know more.

'Well,' said Pearl, taking a sip of wine, 'Max thinks it's impossible to hide behind a dance like tango.'

McGuire frowned. 'What's that supposed to mean?'

'You should know,' said Pearl. 'He said it's far too easy to look insincere when you're dancing a tango – and *not* involved with your partner.' She held McGuire's look.

'That's crazy.'

'Is it?'

'It's just a dance.'

'You looked pretty convincing the other evening dancing with Tanya.'

McGuire noted her playful look. 'Part of the dance. Like I said before, it's all attitude – and choreography. You learn the steps. You don't forget. It's just routine.'

'And . . . is that how it felt when you were dancing with me?'

McGuire met her gaze and smiled. 'You know it wasn't.'

'Then maybe,' said Pearl, 'what Max meant was that for a couple who had danced together for so long – and so publicly – Tony Ballard simply felt he couldn't . . . fake it any more.' She sipped her wine again. 'Or maybe he feared Tanya might *realise* he was faking it?'

McGuire considered this. 'So, if Ballard used his knee as an excuse not to dance with his wife . . .'

'He may well have been physically capable of killing Florrie.' She smiled, speared a calamari with her fork and savoured it before she went on. 'He was meant to be under sedation when I arrived at the Ballards' apartment yesterday – before I met you on the beach? I was talking with Irene and Tanya on the balcony but Tony managed to get up while I was there. It was hot – so I'm sure the bedroom window would have been open – and if he wasn't sedated, he may well have heard us talking.'

'And what would he have heard,' asked McGuire, tucking into his own food, 'apart from Irene Taylor's suspicions?'

'Tanya's loyalty to him. She won't hear a word said against him.' Pearl thought for a moment before finishing her food. 'Two women,' she then said, 'Tanya Ballard and Laura Harper, each needing to believe in their men.' She reflected on this for a moment before the waitress returned to clear their plates. McGuire fixed Pearl with his gaze. She raised her glass to him and sipped her wine.

'Anything else?' he asked.

Pearl stroked the stem of her glass. 'Vivian Gleaves,' she began, 'still a bit of a conundrum. Like Max she was at the top of her profession at one time – at the Royal Ballet. She proudly told me that when I first met her at the restaurant. But she also told me she'd like to retire – move out of Whitstable to the countryside. D'you think that's a sign of growing old,' she asked, 'escaping to the countryside?'

McGuire shrugged. 'If it is, I'm still young,' he said.

'Yes.' Pearl smiled, 'I can't see you in tweed with a Labrador at your side.'

'And Max?' asked McGuire, trying to keep Pearl on track.

She shrugged. 'I need to do a little more research on him, but Mum refers to him as the King of Tap. He starred in lots of Broadway musicals.'

'And he's now working at a back-street dance school?'

'Yes,' said Pearl, frowning at McGuire's remark. 'But I think he's still very passionate about encouraging people to enjoy dance, though I'm not sure he feels the same about his new employers – or Tanya, at least. There's no love lost there. He seems to think Tanya's simply using the school as a means of self-preservation and a chance to stay in the spotlight.'

McGuire sat back in his chair and considered Pearl.

'And what do *you* think?' he asked.

Pearl held his gaze. 'Tanya's an attractive woman, a talented dancer and a loyal wife. Perhaps she's—' She broke off suddenly.

'What?'

'The perfect woman?' Pearl smiled. 'And she wants *you* to join the next tango class.'

McGuire looked at Pearl askance, unsure if she was joking.

'She went out of her way to give me that card of hers, remember? I'm guessing you still have it?'

'All part of the investigation,' said McGuire with a smile.

'And nothing more?' asked Pearl, unsure.

'No,' said McGuire firmly. Leaning across the table he kissed Pearl. When she opened her eyes, she saw the waitress had returned to their table with seafood linguine. At the same time, Pearl's phone began to ring. 'Sorry,' she said. Checking her smartphone, she frowned as she failed to recognise the number. 'I'm not sure who this is. D'you mind?'

McGuire signalled for her to take the call before he picked up a fork and tried his linguine. Pearl responded with surprise to a voice on the end of the line.

'Pearl, is that you?'

Pearl's eyes met McGuire's as she replied: 'Yes, Vivian. What can I do for you?'

A pause followed, as the faint sound of Tchaikovsky's *Nutcracker* played in the background on the line.

'Vivian?' said Pearl, checking she was still here.

'Sorry. I'm at the dance school,' the ballet teacher explained. 'Just getting some music together for my class.' She paused again. 'But . . . you did say to call if anything occurred to me?'

'I did,' said Pearl, her gaze locked with McGuire's as she held her phone closer to him so they could both hear. 'What did you want to tell me?'

Vivian took her time as she explained. 'What you said when we met . . . at St Edward's . . . about recognising Florrie from her tattoo?'

'That's right,' said Pearl. 'It wasn't until I saw the tattoo that I realised it was Florrie's body – and not Tanya's.'

Another pause followed, during which Tchaikovsky's glittering orchestral textures still sounded on the line, then Vivian spoke again. 'Florrie told me she wanted to get rid of it.'

'She what?'

McGuire noted Pearl's sudden interest in what Vivian now had to say.

'The tattoo,' Vivian went on. 'She was saving up to get it removed. I think that's why she may have been working so many extra hours.' She paused again, then: 'She wanted the tattoo gone because she'd tired of him and—'

Music suddenly blared – a blast of Italian accordion – as the sound system from the restaurant hit the speakers on the terrace and Dean Martin's voice began singing 'That's Amore'. Pearl waited until the volume was turned down before going back to the call, trying hard to hear Vivian's voice on the line. 'Vivian? Are you still there?' This time she heard no voice and no Tchaikovsky.

Pearl looked down at her phone in frustration. 'Damn!'

'What is it?' asked McGuire.

'My battery's died. What do you think she was going to tell me?'

McGuire picked up his own phone.

'I've got a number for her here. Eat your food – it's getting cold.'

He searched through his phone for a contact number, rang it and passed the phone to Pearl. She looked at him – expectant – then disappointed.

'Engaged.'

'Could be a poor mobile signal?' McGuire suggested.

Pearl frowned at this, dissatisfied. 'Could you get someone to check the line?'

McGuire took the phone from Pearl and was just about to make a call when a party of Italians burst on to the terrace. Sharing a look with Pearl, he got up to make the call. 'I'll be right back.'

In his absence, Pearl tried to return to her meal but her attention remained on McGuire, who was visible through the glass door, talking on his phone. She wondered if the operator had managed to put him through to Vivian and if so, what she was telling him – perhaps something else about Florrie's tattoo . . . What was it that she had been about to say? After a short while, McGuire returned.

'Well?' asked Pearl, impatient.

'There's no one on the line,' he said. 'Just music playing in the background.'

'*The Nutcracker Suite*?'

McGuire shrugged. 'Operator said it was something classical.'

At this, Pearl stared down at her meal, feeling her appetite suddenly leaving her.

'Did she say where she was?' asked McGuire.

A weighted pause followed before Pearl looked up slowly and nodded. 'The dance school.'

McGuire was instantly torn. Looking down at his own meal on the table, a lit candle flickering behind glass, lights playing on the river and Pearl sitting opposite him, he noted her own plate was now untouched. Making a quick decision he tossed his napkin on to the table and gave in to forces he could not control. 'Come on.'

Placing enough cash on the table to cover the cost of the meal, McGuire offered his hand to Pearl, who took it, allowing him to steer her quickly from the terrace, past a group of laughing Italians and the sound of Dean Martin's voice floating out across the river.

It took little time for McGuire to drive from Canterbury to Ballard's School of Dance. As he sped along the winding Blean Road, Pearl glanced at the detective's strong hands on the steering wheel, feeling protected in spite of all her apprehension. McGuire looked back at her with a reassuring smile – whatever they discovered, it would be together.

Dusk had fallen by the time they reached the crest of Borstal Hill where the sea lay spread out below them, red lights twinkling in the distance from the wind farm. Speeding through the centre of town, Pearl noted groups of drinkers smoking outside the local pubs, packs of teenagers play-fighting on the pavements, couples sauntering along – ignoring everything else but each other. Parking up on the forecourt of the dance school, McGuire exited the car and opened the passenger door for Pearl. She stared up at the new sign showing Tanya and Tony locked in a tango embrace while McGuire tried the school's front door – and found it unlocked. Sharing a look, Pearl and McGuire stepped into the dark reception, where the police detective took a handkerchief from his pocket and used it to protect any fingerprints on the light switch. Approaching the swing door to the main studio, they saw nothing through its window but a single light shining dimly in the far corner.

'She must have left?' whispered Pearl.

'Or she's out the back,' said McGuire. They shared another look. 'Come on,' he said.

Together they entered the studio, crossing the parquet floor in order to reach the rear door, which led to the dressing rooms housing wardrobe items and props. Before they could do so, as they neared the school's piano, McGuire put out his hand to stop Pearl in her tracks. Taking his view, Pearl suddenly saw a figure seated on the piano stool, slumped forward towards the keys. At first, it appeared as though Vivian Gleaves might simply be taking a rest from playing, but as McGuire stepped towards her, reaching out to feel for a pulse in her neck, a long trail of pink ribbon suddenly became visible. McGuire raised Vivian's head so that her face was exposed. Fixed in a rictus grin, the ballet teacher's lips were blue, her eyes bulging and bloodshot. Two pretty pink ballet shoes hung absurdly from her neck, tied there by their pink straps, which were sunk so tightly into the skin of Vivian's throat, they had robbed her of breath – and life.

Chapter Twenty-one

'What kind of hell's dungeon has that school become?' said Dolly, aghast. 'Two women brutally murdered . . .'

'I know,' said Pearl helplessly. She closed her eyes for a moment but could still see a clear image in her mind's eye of Vivian Gleaves slumped in McGuire's arms, her mouth gaping open but unable to articulate whatever she had been trying to explain to Pearl the night before.

'And you say she called you?' asked Dolly.

Pearl nodded. 'She wanted to tell me something.'

'Tell you what?'

'That's just it,' said Pearl in frustration, 'maybe now I'll never know. I lost contact with her on my phone.'

Dolly frowned, confused. 'The signal?'

Pearl shook her head. 'The battery. McGuire managed to get the line checked. It was still open but . . .' She trailed off.

'You mean,' said Dolly, 'Vivian was silenced just as you were talking on the phone?' She gave Pearl a baleful look. 'That means the killer must have been right there, listening.'

'I know,' said Pearl. 'Vivian was sorting out some music for a ballet class – alone – apart from whoever it was who killed her.'

'Strangled,' said Dolly, 'and with the ribbons of her own ballet shoes. Is this maniac trying to make some kind of statement?'

'If so, I don't know what it is,' said Pearl.

Dolly looked at her. 'That young man was only released yesterday,' she said ominously.

'Jack Harper?' said Pearl. 'Yes,' she agreed. 'But I saw him earlier in the evening – he was playing piano in the bar at the Pilgrims Rest.'

'And what time did he finish there?'

Pearl frowned. 'I don't know exactly. McGuire's still tied up – he's taking statements – but when I left the hotel bar Jack only had ten minutes left of his set.'

'Time enough to get back to murder Vivian Gleaves?'

Pearl's look was all the answer Dolly needed. She sighed. 'Poor Irene – and Tanya. This dance school was meant to be a new beginning for everyone, but now it looks as though the whole project is doomed. Jinxed.' She looked at Pearl again. 'And I know, in comparison, my missing familiar seems quite insignificant but . . . I managed to get some more of these printed?'

She handed a pile of posters to Pearl, showing the photo of Mojo sprawled in Dolly's window box with the word MISSING above the image and telephone details below.

'I put your agency number on these ones,' Dolly explained. 'I got a few crank calls from the others.'

'Oh?'

'Asking if I needed help finding my pussy?' She gave Pearl an arch look. 'They'll be less inclined to do that with the Nolan's number. And if anything *has* happened to Mojo, well, I'd rather hear the bad news from you than from a stranger.'

Pearl took the posters from Dolly just as her smartphone sounded. A man's voice boomed gruffly on the line.

'I don't know if you've been going out of your way to avoid me,' said Peter Radcliffe, 'or whether this is just another example of your lack of client care—'

'Peter,' Pearl broke in sharply, 'before you say another word, I think I should tell you there was another murder last night.'

'Another—'

'Yes,' said Pearl quickly, taking advantage of the councillor's shock. 'A teacher at the dance school. I spent much of last night giving a statement to the police, which is another reason why I'm behind with your case.'

'Well,' huffed Radcliffe, 'at least you admit you're behind. What I'd like to know is what you intend to do about it?'

Pearl's mouth dropped open. A murder in a small town like Whitstable was an assault on the whole community, but still Radcliffe was consumed with the issue of his wife's stolen lingerie, as if nothing else mattered. Pearl framed a response but, on second thoughts, decided she couldn't trust herself to give it. Instead, she simply said: 'Sorry – my phone battery's just running down.'

Leaving Ratty hanging, Pearl ended the call and looked at her phone like it was an unexploded grenade. Immediately, it rang again. 'Look,' she said, both startled and exasperated, 'I wish I'd never taken on your case because your attitude is just—'

'Pearl?' A woman's voice was now on the line. 'It's Irene. I need to see you. As soon as you're free?'

Straight after leaving Dolly, Pearl took the opportunity of distributing a few more of her mother's posters. The final one went up in Marty Smith's store, Cornucopia – a far more appropriate name for what had once been a modest little greengrocer's shop, Granny Smith's, belonging to Marty's father. Latterly, it had become a veritable emporium from which Marty sold all manner of exotic fruit and vegetables, as well as smoothies for his thirsty summer customers. Colourful posters showed produce from all over the world – pomelo, physalis, carambola, papaya, persimmon – but Marty had seen fit to take down one of his posters in order to exhibit Dolly's appeal for information concerning the missing Mojo – something Pearl appreciated Marty would perhaps not have done for anyone else.

'How's that?' he asked as he proudly surveyed the poster now tacked to his wall.

'Perfect, Marty. Thank you.'

Marty raised a smile and looked up at the photo of Mojo. 'I'm sure the old fella'll turn up sooner or later,' he said reassuringly, then: 'You know what us blokes are like.' He gave a lascivious wink, spoiling the mood for Pearl, who recognised there was always a moment in her conversations with Marty when she realised why she had never gone for more than one innocent dinner date with him. He was an attractive man with thick dark hair, green eyes that matched the colour of his Cornucopia T-shirt and a fit body honed by lifting vegetable crates all day. Still it came as no surprise to Pearl that Marty's relationships with women were usually short-lived and that the two-person kayak he had bought some years ago seemed only ever used by its owner – alone.

Now he leaned across the counter and took a quick look, left and right, before whispering: 'Reckon we've got a psychopath at work?' His thick dark eyebrows rose. 'The dance school murders,' he added. 'You know that's how they're being talked about?' He reached beneath his counter and slapped a copy of the morning's *Chronicle* newspaper on it. Pearl saw that it featured a recent photograph of Vivian Gleaves with another earlier shot of her as a young woman in costume for a Royal Ballet performance of *Giselle*, wearing a mid-length georgette skirt with a headdress of flowers in her hair. Pearl recalled how proud Vivian had been of her early career. Now she began to wonder if she would still be remembered for it – or whether her fine reputation as a dancer would be eclipsed by the horrific way she had been strangled with the straps of her own ballet shoes.

'These are senseless murders,' said Pearl, still feeling frustrated by her own lack of progress with this case. 'There doesn't seem to be any connection between the two dead women – apart from the dance school.'

Marty shrugged. 'Like I say,' he went on knowingly, 'probably some nut-job on the loose. Someone with a thing about dance shoes – our own Boston Strangler?'

'Florrie Johnson wasn't strangled,' Pearl reminded him. 'I just can't seem to find a way through this,' she admitted in exasperation.

'Well,' said Marty, putting the newspaper back under his counter, 'that's not really your problem, is it? Not your responsibility, Pearl. It's the job of your copper friend – that's what he gets paid for.' Marty eyed her, then continued: 'He's certainly been practising his dance steps, judging by his performance at the class the other night. Sure *he's* not the one with a dance fixation?'

Pearl scoffed. 'You're not seriously suggesting that DCI McGuire might have been responsible for—'

'Think about it,' said Marty. 'It wouldn't be the first time a copper did the crime.' He leaned closer and whispered, 'Perfect cover for a psychopathic killer?' He raised his eyebrows still further. 'You should watch your step – or his.' Marty gave her a knowing look but Pearl had heard enough. She gathered the remaining posters from his counter.

'Thanks for putting this up for me,' she said, keen to leave the shop and Marty's inferences behind.

'Any time!' Marty called cheerily. 'Hope you find the little fella soon. *And* the killer, of course.' He gave another irritating wink before Pearl headed for the door.

Once out on the street, Pearl took a deep breath as she stared across at the old Playhouse where a new billboard poster was being glued into place. It advertised a forthcoming production – a murder mystery titled *Without a Clue*. The words seemed to resonate for Pearl with the way she felt in that instant – until her attention was caught by something else. At the side of the Playhouse, in Kemp Alley, Pearl noticed two figures talking animatedly – a man and a woman. Finding herself having to squint against the early-morning sun, Pearl moved quickly behind a Cornucopia van that was parked outside Marty's store. Concealing herself behind the vehicle, she now peered across the road and found she had not been mistaken. In the shade of the alley, Jack Harper's wife Laura was deep in conversation with Tony Ballard. It looked to be an intense exchange, but after a short while, Tony seemed to be considering something Laura Harper had just told him, before he finally gave a nod. After this, Laura quickly reached out and grabbed Tony's hand, putting it to her lips and holding his gaze for a moment, before she finally turned and hurried away – out of Kemp Alley in the direction of Harbour Street. As Pearl continued to look on, she saw Tony Ballard appeared frozen, lost in thought, until he headed off in the opposite direction, back along the alley and away from the High Street – without showing any signs of pain. Once he had finally disappeared, Pearl considered what she had just seen before taking out her phone and dialling a number.

'Irene? It's Pearl Nolan. I just finished what I had to do for Mum and I'm on my way to you right now but . . . I wondered if I could ask you a quick question – in strictest confidence?'

Chapter Twenty-two

Twenty minutes later, Tanya Ballard was pacing back and forth in the living room of her aunt's bungalow on Marine Parade. Her long dark hair hung loose on her shoulders and Pearl could see she was on the verge of tears.

'Why are these murders happening?' she asked. 'And why is this killer targeting my school. First poor Florrie . . . now Vivian. If it's me they're trying to get—'

'I don't believe it is,' said Pearl firmly. 'This time there's no chance the killer could possibly have confused Vivian with you. After all, she was much older and you couldn't have looked less alike.'

'That's true,' Tanya admitted, before looking to her aunt for an opinion.

Seated in a comfortable armchair, Irene Taylor turned to Pearl and said ominously: 'That's not to say Tanya isn't still in danger.'

'But from whom?' asked Pearl. 'And why?'

At this, Irene got up and walked slowly to the window. Her silence spoke volumes, and it was left to Tanya to reply. With tension written on her face, she said: 'You know how Aunt Irene feels about Tony. And I know he betrayed me, but I'll never believe he's capable of murder.'

It was clear she was convinced of this, but Irene Taylor now turned and braced herself before announcing to Pearl: 'He wasn't at home last night when Vivian was murdered.'

'Aunt Irene—' said Tanya reproachfully, but Irene Taylor spoke over her.

'It's no secret, Tanya. The police already know – they've taken statements.'

Tanya was silenced.

'Where was he?' asked Pearl.

Tanya took a deep breath and explained: 'We've . . . been in touch with Tony's specialist, who recommended more exercise – nothing weight-bearing – just . . . a daily swim.'

'And he went swimming last night?' asked Pearl.

Tanya nodded. Pearl gave this some thought before responding: 'Okay. Well, the fitness centre will be able to confirm that he was there – they operate a ticket system that shows the time of arrival.'

Irene shared a look with Tanya.

'What is it?' asked Pearl.

'Tony didn't go to the pool,' Tanya admitted. 'He would have been recognised by everyone, especially after that recent newspaper story, and besides, he hates chlorine and prefers to swim in the sea. He left home just in time for high tide.'

Pearl thought about this for a moment. 'Around six thirty?'

Tanya nodded.

'And d'you happen to know where he went?'

'Yes,' she said. 'He always swims near the lifeguard station at the foot of Tankerton Slopes.' She looked hopefully at Pearl. 'I'm sure one of the lifeguards would have seen him?'

Pearl shrugged. 'I'm sure they wouldn't. During the school summer holidays the lifeguards work seven days a week, but from ten until five, so they would have been off duty by the time Tony arrived on that stretch of beach.'

Pearl glanced out of the window and saw a host of sparrows fluttering down to land on Irene Taylor's bird feeder on the front lawn. Looking back at Tanya she asked: 'What was Vivian Gleaves doing at the school last night? She didn't have a class, did she?'

Tanya looked to her aunt for an answer. 'No,' Irene replied. 'But she'd mentioned needing to prepare some music for her Christmas performance.'

'*The Nutcracker*?'

Irene nodded. 'Usually Jack would have done that for her but . . . well, there's nothing "usual" about these times. Maybe Vivian lost trust in him after he was arrested for police questioning.'

Pearl looked between the two women. 'Is there . . . anyone you can think of who had reason to want Vivian dead?'

'Of course not,' said Tanya, shaking her head in confusion before she finally admitted: 'But then I don't know anything any more.' She slumped down into a chair and put a hand to her brow before she looked directly at her aunt and added: 'Apart from the fact that I do trust Tony.' She fixed Irene with her gaze.

'Yes,' said Irene, 'you've always trusted Tony. And he abused that trust, Tanya, you admitted that yourself.'

'I know,' said Tanya, increasingly stressed. 'But that was different. We were having problems. I was pushing him . . . nagging him . . . I know what he did – he betrayed me – but he was sorry. And I forgave him. I know it will never happen again.'

Silence fell before Pearl asked: 'What happened last night, Tanya? After Tony went swimming?'

Tanya shrugged. 'Aunt Irene came over at about six. We had more accounts to go through. She left about . . . half an hour before Tony came back just before eight.' She paused. 'Look, I'm absolutely certain he'd been swimming. His hair was wet, and so were his towel and swimsuit.'

'Then he *has* to be innocent,' said Irene, with a look to Tanya that made plain she was being ironic.

'Why don't you just come right out and say how much you hate Tony?' asked Tanya.

'I don't care about Tony,' said Irene with increasing frustration, 'not after what he did to you. But I do care about you and why you feel such a need to protect him. For heaven's sake, Tanya, there's a murder investigation going on. Two members of our staff have been murdered and Tony has no way of confirming his movements last night, other than your assurance that he returned here *looking* as though he had been swimming? Do you know how ridiculous that must sound to Pearl?'

Suitably wounded, Tanya was stunned into silence. Pearl tried to intervene. 'Irene,' she began calmly, 'why don't we hear what Tanya has to say—'

'Because it will just be more of the same,' said Irene in exasperation. 'Why don't you tell her what you saw earlier today?' she asked suddenly.

'Not now,' said Pearl firmly as she noted Tanya's suspicion.

'Why not?' snapped Irene. 'Go on. Ask Tanya what you asked me on the phone.'

Pearl remained silent but Tanya saw the look Pearl gave to Irene – admonishing her to keep quiet.

'What did you ask my aunt?' Tanya asked.

'It doesn't matter,' Pearl replied, keen to drop the subject, but Tanya came closer as she insisted: 'It matters to me. What was it you saw?'

Irene Taylor ignored Pearl's silence and answered for her. 'Pearl asked me if there was any reason at all why Tony would want to meet up with Laura Harper.'

Tanya looked confounded. 'Jack's wife?' She looked again to Pearl. 'Why would you ask that?'

'Look,' began Pearl, reluctantly. But Tanya spoke over her. 'Why?' she demanded.

Again it was Irene who replied. 'Because Pearl saw them together, this morning, in Kemp Alley by the Playhouse.'

'Is this true?' said Tanya.

Reluctantly, Pearl nodded.

Tanya Ballard betrayed some apprehension before asking: 'Well . . . what were they doing?'

'Talking,' said Pearl.

'Deep in conversation,' said Irene, qualifying, 'at the end of which, Laura kissed Tony's hand.'

At this, Tanya turned automatically to Pearl, who felt both conflicted and caught off guard. 'Is this true?' asked Tanya again, her voice almost a whisper this time.

Pearl saw the woman before her was no longer proud and confident but diminished by fear and disappointment. Feeling defeated herself, Pearl said gently, 'I'm very sorry.' Picking up her bag, she headed for the door.

Irene Taylor followed quickly after her, catching up with Pearl in the hallway. 'Pearl, wait!'

At the front door, Pearl turned back to Irene and spoke in a fierce hushed tone, 'I told you in confidence.'

'I know but—'

'No buts, Irene,' said Pearl firmly. 'I know what you think of Tony Ballard, but why would you possibly humiliate Tanya like that?'

At this, Irene Taylor seemed suddenly to come to her senses and her expression softened into a terrible sadness. She shook her head slowly, but with no suitable answer forthcoming, Pearl turned and headed away.

The meeting with Tanya and Irene haunted Pearl throughout her shift at The Whitstable Pearl, but once it was over, she prepared a cooler bag of food items and set off purposefully up the busy High Street. The pavements were still teeming with tourists staring into shop windows or huddling in groups as they consulted maps for directions. Reaching the old Oxford Street railway bridge, which marked the main entrance to town for traffic arriving from London, Pearl glanced up at the plaques on its parapet which recorded the names of the various railway companies that had once operated this line. A few years ago, another piece of work had joined the plaques on the bridge: a local urban masterpiece by a graffiti artist known as Catman had mysteriously appeared on the brick abutment. It showed a deep-sea diver, laden with shopping bags, and the slogan SHOP LOCAL above his head. Although the identity of Catman continued to remain a mystery to most people in town, Pearl had made it her business to discover the name of the young artist – who turned out to be a friend of Charlie's. Now, Pearl only wished she could come up with a name for the killer responsible for what Marty had dubbed 'the dance school murders'. Heading under the bridge, she turned the corner, passing the Labour Club, where a large red banner was still strung from an upper window following a recent election, then she crossed the well-kept lawn towards Windsor House. The tower block's spacious ground-floor area was traditionally used as a local polling station but it also housed a veritable squadron of mobility scooters for its more senior residents. Pearl took the opportunity of pinning one of Dolly's posters to the noticeboard in the lobby then she quickly took the stairs to Ruby's flat on the first floor and rang the bell. The young waitress answered the door with a towel wrapped around her head.

'Pearl . . .' Surprised to see her boss on the doorstep, Ruby nevertheless welcomed Pearl through a narrow hallway and into the kitchen.

'I should have called first,' said Pearl. 'I didn't mean to disturb you on your day off.'

'S'okay,' said Ruby. 'I just took a shower.'

Pearl realised it had been some time since she had visited Ruby in what had once been her grandmother's flat. Vestiges of Mary Hill were still apparent – a teapot with its hand-knitted cosy sat alongside a modern French cafetière like the ones Pearl used in the restaurant. Ruby sat down and gestured for Pearl to do the same before broaching: 'I . . . heard there's been another murder. A teacher at the school?'

'That's right,' said Pearl. 'I just wanted to check you're okay – and to bring you this.'

She handed the cooler bag across. Ruby looked inside and identified the contents: 'Lasagne . . .?'

'And more trifle,' said Pearl.

'Carry on like this and I'm going to need a bigger uniform.' Ruby managed a smile before getting up to settle the food into her small fridge. As she did so, Pearl noticed that the kitchen was as tidy as the girl always left Pearl's restaurant; perhaps a sign of a need for order following a chaotic childhood of her own. Knowing that Ruby's mother had been involved with drugs and a New Age traveller lifestyle,

Pearl now wondered if an unstable childhood had provided an easy point of contact between Ruby and Florrie Johnson – both girls had been finding their way after a difficult start in life. A few framed photographs on the kitchen dresser revealed Ruby's progress. One image showed Pearl's waitress wearing a Santa hat at The Whitstable Pearl staff lunch last Christmas. Another showed her with her gran at the local bingo hall, which had since been transformed into a cavernous pub. There was also a photo of Ruby with Florrie Johnson, two girls posed together on the beach outside the Old Neptune, their smiling faces bathed gold in the late-afternoon sun. Florrie's arm encircled Ruby's shoulder, her hand hanging loose – exposing her tattoo. Pearl's gaze lingered on this as she asked: 'Did Florrie ever mention anything to you about her tattoo?'

Turning back, Ruby saw Pearl was staring at the photograph.

'The lightning strike, you mean?' She closed her fridge door and shrugged. 'Only that she wanted to get rid of it.' She sat down and went on: 'She said she was sorry she'd ever had it done and . . . she was glad it was only small because otherwise it would cost more to remove.' She glanced at the photo and added: 'She knew she was going to need a few sessions to get rid of it completely.'

'So she definitely wanted it removed?'

Ruby nodded. 'Oh, yeah. She was saving up, putting some of her wages away every week.'

'And . . . did she ever say why she didn't want the tattoo any more?'

Ruby gave this some thought and then shrugged. 'Not really . . . just that it had been a mistake.' She glanced at the photo again. 'She really loved it at first but I s'pose she just got fed up with it. It happens a lot with tats, that's why I haven't had one done.' She gave a sad smile. 'Florrie had her heart set on getting something new.'

'Did she say what that was?'

Ruby shook her head. 'No. She said she'd surprise me and that she'd explain after she'd got it done.' She looked down for a moment. 'She won't get to do that now, so I s'pose I'll never know.' She paused. 'Is it important?'

Pearl looked thoughtful. 'I don't know, Ruby. But it was important enough for Vivian Gleaves to call me last night.'

'The teacher who was murdered?'

Pearl nodded. 'Can you remember when Florrie had that tattoo done?'

'Sure. Last summer. Just before the Oyster Festival.'

'So . . . around the third week of July?'

Florrie nodded. 'She'd just started work at the school and was taking some dance lessons.'

'Tap?'

Ruby nodded again. 'She did it for a while – then gave it up.'

'Why?'

'To be honest, I don't think she was very good at it. She made me laugh, because one week she went to the class wearing dungarees and said she felt like a tap-dancing plumber.' She smiled, then explained: 'It's a bit fogey, isn't it? Tap dancing. Florrie was really into current music, chart sounds . . . mainstream stuff.'

'Did she ever say anything to you about her tap teacher?'

'The American guy?'

'Max Sanchez.'

'Not really, but she was dead impressed that he'd been in lots of stage musicals. She said she'd found clips of some of his shows on YouTube and she used to watch them and say how cool he was. But . . .' She paused and wrinkled her nose. 'Well, he's getting on a bit now, isn't he?'

Pearl smiled. 'He still looked pretty fit when he was taking a class the other day.'

Ruby returned Pearl's smile and took the towel from her head, rubbing it against her damp hair.

Pearl picked up her bag and said: 'I'd better let you get on.'

Ruby smiled. 'Thanks. If I don't get the straighteners out soon, it'll be a right frizz.' Pearl paused for a moment then asked: 'Did Florrie mention to you that she was going to dye her hair?'

Ruby shook her head. 'No.' She looked pained. 'So, it was like a . . . double shock . . . finding her at the school that night?' She looked up at Pearl, who nodded.

'I understand.'

Ruby frowned. 'Florrie went to a lot of trouble getting her outfit ready for the tango class . . . we both did. It was a bit of fun.'

'She was wearing the rose in her hair that night.'

'Yeah, that's right.'

'So, in a way it would have made more sense for her to have dyed her hair for the class – to complete the whole image?'

Ruby shrugged. 'Maybe she only got the idea that night – to go dark?'

Pearl took this in as she headed into the hallway. As she opened the front door, Ruby spoke again. 'So . . . the police have let the pianist from the school go. Jack, is it?'

'That's right,' said Pearl. 'Jack Harper.' She looked back at Ruby and asked: 'Who told you?'

'No one. I just saw him in Harbour Street earlier.'

'He lives there,' said Pearl, 'with his wife. Harbour Buildings – it looks a bit like a castle?'

Ruby nodded and Pearl hesitated for a moment before turning back again to ask: 'What was he doing?'

Ruby shrugged. 'Nothing, just cycling past – on a racing bike. Why? Is it important?'

Pearl took a moment to consider this. 'I'm not sure, Ruby. It could be. See you tomorrow.' She gave her waitress a hug and left.

Pearl stood on the lawn of Windsor House for a moment, feeling the warm sun on her face as she thought about what she had just heard. Then she reached for her phone and dialled McGuire's number. Predictably, she got his voicemail. After the beep, she left a message: *Call me as soon as you can. I need to ask you something.*

Chapter Twenty-three

By late afternoon that same day, the sky had suddenly clouded, bringing an unexpected chill to the air as Pearl walked along Tankerton Slopes, an area that in Edwardian times had attracted visitors who preferred more genteel coastal surroundings to the industrial oyster fishing shores of Whitstable. Gazing out to sea, the estuary waters had been transformed from a deep blue to a slate-grey hue – the kind that was seen everywhere these days on fashionable house exteriors. Perched on the horizon, the Red Sands army fort was still visible in the haze – seven steel towers that had sat eight miles offshore since the Second World War, when the fort had served as an anti-aircraft defence, housing weapons, munitions and over two hundred soldiers in an attempt to block the passage of enemy planes on their way to London. Decades later, the structure had been commandeered by pirate radio stations, a group of local DJs spinning singles in the same bleak quarters in which soldiers had once risked their lives. Now the towers rusted on their old steel supports, orbited by pleasure craft and an old Thames sailing barge that operated day trips from the harbour.

Pearl headed towards an old telescope that stood near the pair of cannons and the pitch-pot beacon. Slipping a twenty-pence piece into its slot, she watched a circle of daylight appear in its lens. The telescope offered a good view as far as the Red Sands fort, but Pearl focused much closer in to the shore where a kite surfer was performing backflips on the stiffening breeze. A kayak was also visible; perhaps, thought Pearl, it might contain Marty Smith, enjoying a break after a hard day at Cornucopia. Fishing boats were already out on the high tide, one moored to a buoy that was directly in line with the empty lifeguards' station. On the beach, families were already packing up to leave, trying to deal with grizzling children. Only one figure was visible in the sea – cutting through the water with smooth confident strokes, oblivious to the change in weather. The swimmer was wearing goggles, legs kicking up behind, creating surf in the flat grey estuary water. The figure looked at home in this setting: streamlined, efficient, like a shark, thought Pearl. The telescope lens faded to black and Pearl now made her way down to the shore. Spotting a towel and a beach bag resting on a timber groyne, she moved across to them and waited. After a few minutes, the swimmer headed in to shallow water, finally standing upright on the shell-encrusted estuary bed. Tony Ballard emerged from the waves, his body looking tight, muscular and honed, in spite of his long convalescence.

Striding through the shallows, wearing black surf shoes, he stepped up on to the shore and slipped the goggles on to his head before making his way to the groyne, where he suddenly caught sight of Pearl.

She offered a smile. 'I thought it was you.'

Tony reached for his towel, drying his chest quickly before wrapping the towel around his neck as though it were a scarf. Pearl looked out to sea as she went on: 'I wish I could find more time to take a daily swim.'

Tony took a T-shirt from the beach bag and put it on before stuffing his goggles into the bag. 'Doctor's orders,' he said.

'That's right,' said Pearl. 'You've had quite a time of it lately.'

Tony looked at Pearl as though unsure what she meant. 'I was at the tango class the other evening,' she explained.

Tony ran a hand through his wet hair. 'Minor setback,' he said. 'But I'm working hard to get back in shape.'

'You're doing well,' said Pearl.

Tony looked at her again, this time with a glint in his eye. 'Buoyancy in the sea water,' he said, 'helps to take pressure off joints.'

Pearl nodded and watched Tony getting out of his surf shoes before he slipped on some casual loafers. As he looked back at Pearl, his eyes seemed to reflect the shade of the sea at that moment. He smiled finally. 'That was a great afternoon at your restaurant.'

'The calm before the storm,' said Pearl, 'considering what happened later – to Florrie and Vivian.'

'Yes.' Tony stared down at the pebbled shore, unable to avoid the subject any longer. 'Florrie was a sweet girl,' he said. 'Harmless, always wanting to help. Nothing was ever too much trouble.'

'She even helped you out of the studio that night. Your knee?'

Tony paused, then: 'That's right. Irene called a cab to get me home. Florrie was suddenly my nurse. A little . . . Florence Nightingale.' He seemed to consider this before grabbing a jacket from his bag. For a moment he appeared lost, and leaned back against the timber breakwater, gazing out to sea. Finally, he said: 'I'm guessing you're not here just to pass the time of day.' He looked back at Pearl. 'You're some kind of private detective, aren't you? That's why you were at the apartment the other day – with Irene and Tanya? My wife said you're helping the police with their investigation?'

Pearl gave a small shrug. 'We all have a responsibility to do that,' she said, 'to find whoever's committing these murders. I'm sure you want that too?'

'Of course.'

Pearl paused as she watched Tony packing his things into the beach bag before admitting: 'Vivian Gleaves called me last night just before she was killed. She wanted to tell me something, but someone decided to silence her.'

Tony spun round to face Pearl, his eyes narrowed. 'What did she tell you?'

Pearl paused. 'I haven't been able to make sense of it – yet.'

Tony considered this then swallowed hard. 'Look,' he began, 'I've given a full statement to the police; I've told them all I know.' He went on: 'I was here last night, swimming. When I got home Tanya was distraught. She'd just got the news from Irene.' He paused. 'I can only think . . . Vivian must have left the door unlocked at the school and someone came in and . . .' He trailed off.

'Who?'

'How should I know?' Tony frowned. 'This is as much a mystery to me as it is to everyone else.'

'Except the killer.' Pearl paused for a moment before framing the question she most wanted answered: 'What does Laura Harper have to say?'

'Laura? Why d'you ask that?'

Pearl took her time to reply, wondering whether Tony Ballard had been a good liar to have kept his affair from Tanya for as long as he did – or a bad one for allowing her ever to find out about it. She also weighed up whether to explain about having seen him with Laura Harper earlier or simply to leave him without a clue, which she now recalled was the title of the new theatre production at the local Playhouse.

'It doesn't matter,' she said finally.

As Tony Ballard pulled on some loose white shorts, Pearl noted the scar running vertically up his kneecap. He picked up his bag and heaved the strap across his shoulder.

'I wish I could help you,' he said, 'because there's no one who wants to see this killer caught more than me – and Tanya and Irene, of course,' he added.

'Of course,' echoed Pearl.

Tony managed a smile. 'And now, if you'll excuse me, I need a hot shower.'

Tony Ballard moved off, heading away to take a path leading up the grassy slopes. Pearl watched him go, noticing that, like earlier that day, he no longer appeared to be in any pain. Perhaps that was down to his swim . . . or to the sight of an attractive blonde who was heading down the path towards him at that very moment, walking a cute Labradoodle puppy. Pearl hung back to observe Tony giving the woman a charming smile as he looked across his shoulder to check the woman's progress down the path and on to the beach, before he finally continued on his way.

Pearl arrived home at Seaspray Cottage to the sound of her landline ringing. She rushed inside and picked up the receiver.

'Why can I never reach you on your mobile?' McGuire asked.

Pearl quickly plucked her smartphone from her pocket and saw it had died. 'Sorry,' she said. 'It's this new phone. There must be something wrong with the battery, so I'll take it back to the shop tomorrow and get it checked.' After putting it on charge, she asked: 'How are things going?'

'They're not,' confided McGuire as he paced in the privacy of his office. 'I've hit a wall. Forensics have finished their work at the school but there are no new leads and

I'm still waiting on the autopsy for Vivian Gleaves.' He paused. 'Another woman dead.'

Pearl heard the weight of responsibility in his voice. 'That's the fault of the killer, not you,' she said. Sitting down quickly to open her laptop, she steered McGuire back to the facts: 'Cause of death was pretty obvious.'

'Yeah,' McGuire agreed. 'Strangulation. And preliminary examination shows the only other wounds on the body were self-inflicted: gouges in the neck caused by her fingernails as she tried to claw beneath the straps of those shoes.'

Pearl considered this before she put in an online search for YouTube.

'As with Florrie Johnson,' McGuire continued. 'It looks like the killer approached from behind . . .'

'While she was on the phone to me,' said Pearl, 'trying to tell me something about Florrie Johnson's tattoo.'

'But what?' asked McGuire.

'I don't know,' Pearl replied. 'She . . . said something about Florrie wanting to get rid of it – which Ruby confirmed this afternoon.'

'And you think that's important?'

'It may be,' said Pearl. 'Apparently Florrie was planning to replace the lightning strike with another design, but what that might have been, I just don't know.'

McGuire stared up at the whiteboard on his wall which he used for displaying ideas and trying to find any possible connections between what might have been safely established so far. In a serious crime like murder, a central police computer program called HOLMES 2 helped to collect and connect links between people, places and events, but McGuire's recent training course had also underscored a need for good data insight, especially because so much information was gathered these days it was easy to miss opportunities to understand it all. Software was being designed to help with 'data mining' – analysing and making sense of any links to a crime – as well as pointing up what could be important anomalies within patterns. Digital time-event charts could also illustrate graphically the chronology of activities of a victim, or suspect, enabling McGuire and his team to focus on specific incidents and gain a potential new area of interest or lead. McGuire had nothing against progress and welcomed anything that helped him in his job, but he doubted that anything so sophisticated could come up with more than he was actually viewing on his whiteboard at this point in time: photographs of Florrie Johnson and Vivian Gleaves; details about the staff at Ballard's School of Dance, as well as the building itself, including shots of all access points, and the 'weapons' used: the stiletto heel of a dance shoe and a pair of ballet pumps.

McGuire considered all this and finally admitted to Pearl, 'I'm beginning to taste the Cornish sea air.'

'Don't be so defeatist,' she insisted. 'We can do this – we just need one good break. Besides,' she went on, 'you won't get a decent oyster stout in Cornwall or hold on to that fit body of yours with pasties.'

McGuire raised a smile then considered the photo

on his whiteboard showing a young man leaning over a railway bridge. 'You know . . . the only real lead we've ever had on this case was Jack Harper ditching a bag containing Florrie's poems—'

'Strictly speaking,' said Pearl, breaking in, 'you mean disposing of a backpack containing Florrie Johnson's song lyrics.'

'*If* they were song lyrics,' said McGuire. 'He may have been seeing the girl – and you and I both know why he wouldn't want his wife to find out.'

'Because she's pregnant,' said Pearl. 'She told me she and Jack were keeping quiet about it until the next trimester. And I don't blame her, considering what she's been through to get pregnant.' She became thoughtful as she admitted: 'I happened to see her this morning with Tony Ballard.'

McGuire looked away from the photo. 'Doing what?'

'Talking. In fact, they looked like they were engaged in some intense conversation – after which she took his hand in her own and kissed it.'

McGuire frowned. 'Why didn't you tell me?'

'I tried,' said Pearl. 'I called you but I couldn't get through, so I'm telling you now.'

McGuire nodded. 'Okay. So what d'you think that was all about?'

'I don't know,' Pearl confessed. 'But I wish I did – and I also wish I hadn't asked Irene Taylor about it – because I did so in confidence and she then went and told Tanya.'

'Fireworks in the Ballard household?'

'I hope not,' said Pearl, troubled, 'because they might just spread to the Harpers and I don't want to cause any more problems for Laura.'

'More problems than being married to a killer?'

Pearl failed to reply and instead typed the name 'Max Sanchez' into the YouTube search box on her laptop. She watched a number of links appear.

'You . . . said you wanted to ask me something?' said McGuire.

'I do,' said Pearl, clicking on one of the footage links as she went on. 'Ruby told me she saw Jack Harper today in the High Street.'

'Glad to hear he's still around,' said McGuire, sitting down at his desk and closing his palm around the rubber-band ball.

'He was on a racing bike.'

'So?'

'So . . . on the evening I saw him at the Canterbury piano bar he told me that as soon as he heard about Florrie's murder, he thought of cycling to the harbour and dumping those papers in the sea – until he remembered the tide was out.'

'Which is why he went to the railway embankment.'

'That's right.'

'I don't see what you're getting at . . .'

'Jack Harper's out on bail because you haven't enough evidence to charge him,' Pearl went on.

'And I can't charge him,' said McGuire, 'because

he can account for his whereabouts on the evening of Florrie's murder.'

'Tell me again why he couldn't have made it to Canterbury on time?'

'Traffic,' said McGuire wearily. He got up from his desk and stared out of his window, watching three police cars enter the car park below. 'There was a major RTA that evening,' he said. 'A lorry overturned and the roads were blocked till after seven o'clock. Harper couldn't possibly have murdered Florrie and made it from Ballard's dance school to The Pilgrims Rest Hotel just before six – even on a racing bike – the roads were impassable and he couldn't have done it in time by trying to cycle on the crowded pavements either.'

'Which is why he may have taken another route.'

McGuire picked up on this. 'What route?'

'The old Crab and Winkle Way,' said Pearl. 'It's what's left of a six-mile railway line that used to carry passengers from Canterbury to Whitstable harbour on a steam locomotive called the *Invicta*.' She paused for a moment then went on, 'It passed through two ancient woods and my dad used to tell me stories about how the goods trains slowed down so that crews could check pheasant traps and pick mushrooms.'

'Pearl—'

'Hear me out,' she said quickly. 'The line was closed seventy-odd years ago but it's still accessible – as a cycle route. You can pick it up in Whitstable, pass through those same woods and, although there's a sixty-metre climb, you only hit that coming the other way *out* of Canterbury. It's possible Jack Harper made it to the hotel, cycling on the Crab and Winkle line, in *less* than half an hour – and then returned home by road much later – after the traffic had cleared.'

McGuire remained silent for a moment. 'Why did no one on my team tell me about this?'

Pearl smiled to herself. 'Aren't I on your team?' she asked. 'I told you I followed Jack along the railway embankment because something didn't seem right to me that morning? He was wearing gloves – on a hot day.'

'And he'd have needed them,' said McGuire, 'in order to dispose of Florrie's poems, or lyrics, without leaving fingerprints.'

'But what if they were cycle gloves?' said Pearl. 'That would fit with what he told me about wanting to cycle down to the harbour to dispose of everything in the sea. But he was upset, panicked . . . so he went to Prospect Field – the place where he and Florrie had met one afternoon – and where he had played guitar for her.'

McGuire took a moment to absorb this then wandered back to his whiteboard. 'So . . . if he did take the Crab and Winkle route on the evening of Florrie's murder, he doesn't have an alibi after all.' He stared again at the photo of Jack Harper – this time with new eyes. 'You're a genius.'

Pearl failed to reply as her attention was suddenly caught by something she had just seen on her laptop screen.

'Pearl . . .?' McGuire heard only faint music on the line. 'What're you doing?'

'I'm watching Max Sanchez dancing a tap routine,' she said softly, almost to herself, as she viewed Max, dressed in the same outfit that Bill 'Bojangles' Robinson wore in the photograph at the dance school, as he executed his own version of The Stair Dance, tapping out a syncopated rhythm with his spat-style tap shoes.

'Why?' asked McGuire, confused.

'Because Florrie Johnson used to be in Max's tap class, and today Ruby told me that Florrie used to watch Max's performances online—' She broke off suddenly. 'There are notes here,' she went on, 'below the clip? It seems Cuba's very proud of Max Sanchez. His parents were originally from Havana and . . .' She trailed off again, then realised: 'Mum always refers to him as The King of Tap but in his home country he's known as *Pies de Rayo*.'

McGuire shook his head. 'What the hell's that supposed to mean?'

'It says here it's Spanish . . .' she paused. 'For "Lightning Feet".'

McGuire took this in. 'Florrie Johnson's tattoo was a lightning strike . . .'

'That's right,' said Pearl hurriedly. 'And the night Vivian called me, she was trying to tell me about the tattoo . . . how Florrie wanted to get rid of it? She was saving up to have it removed, working all the hours she could get at the school . . .'

'What are you saying?' asked McGuire, trying to focus on the important point. 'That Sanchez is involved with these murders – or Jack Harper?'

Pearl shook her head in frustration. 'I'm not sure. It's so easy to get put off track just by looking at things from the wrong—' She broke off as an idea finally came to her.

'From what?' asked McGuire. 'What're you thinking?'

'Vivian Gleaves . . .' said Pearl. 'When I went to see her at St Edward's School she talked about ballet . . . how it's a strict discipline and needs . . . attention to detail.'

'So?'

'She said she was "good at detail" – that it was her "forte". And the other day when she was in the restaurant, we talked about the absence of clues in Florrie's murder and she said it was like a missing piece of choreography . . . She said, sooner or later, someone would come forward with a piece of information and . . . something seemingly trivial might make everything clear?'

'Someone,' said McGuire. 'She could've been talking about herself?'

'Yes,' said Pearl. 'If she *was* good with detail . . . Vivian may well have noticed more than was good for her. She told me she wanted to retire, remember? To a nice little place in the countryside . . . *if* she could "stretch to that".'

'Blackmail,' said McGuire, making sense of this. 'Didn't you say Max Sanchez was in the restaurant with her that day?'

Pearl's gaze shifted back to the image on her screen. 'That's right,' she said slowly, another thought dawning: 'and . . . Max was footing the bill.'

Pearl suddenly looked away from her laptop screen to the window, which offered a clear view straight out to the horizon. Suddenly, things became clear. 'Of course . . .' she said to herself. 'I've been so stupid . . .'

'Pearl?'

Springing to her feet, she made a sudden decision. 'I have to go and do something.'

'Do what?' McGuire demanded.

'Make something right,' she said, grabbing her bag. 'There's no time to lose. But I promise I'll explain later.'

'Pearl!' But McGuire heard nothing more on the line. Staring at the phone in his hand, he realised she had gone.

Chapter Twenty-Four

Pearl headed directly to Harbour Buildings, the unusual castellated building at the end of Harbour Street, which, at one time, had marked the entrance to the town for passengers arriving on the Crab and Winkle railway line. A businessman by the name of Fred 'Biscuits' Goldfinch, who had once sold sea biscuits from his grocery store, was said to have risen to the challenge of trying to make something of the odd triangular piece of land by sketching a plan of the building on the inside of a cigarette packet – a design as eccentric as 'Biscuits' himself. Pearl reached the building's heavy front door and rang the bell, hoping that Peter and Hilary Radcliffe wouldn't suddenly appear at the Old Captain's House across the road and begin taking her to task for neglecting their case. For a moment or two, as she waited for a response, she stared up at the decorative shields on the outer wall of Harbour Buildings, which included one dedicated to the old town council: a wheel with twelve spokes to represent the dozen councillors at that time – of which 'Biscuits' had been one. Harbour Buildings itself was represented within another shield, together with the Invicta horse, the symbol of Kent, which signified the county's invincibility. As Pearl looked up at it, she took heart – and a deep breath – hoping she wouldn't be defeated by this case. Laura Harper's voice finally sounded on the entry-phone speaker.

'Who is it?'

'Pearl Nolan. Can I speak to you?'

'Me?'

'It's very important.'

A pause followed before a buzzer sounded. Pearl pushed open the heavy front door and made her way quickly upstairs to the Harpers' apartment. There, Laura Harper looked apprehensive before opening the door wider and allowing Pearl inside. Jack Harper was standing in the living room, as though braced for bad news.

'What is it?' he asked.

'I need to talk to you both,' Pearl explained, glancing around to make sure Laura had followed her in, while at the same time noticing dishes on a table: a half-empty pasta bowl and plates.

'Sorry,' said Laura. 'We just had a bite to eat before Jack heads off to play at the hotel.' She nodded to her husband, who responded by helping her to clear the table. As the couple ferried dishes to the kitchen, Pearl glanced out of the window across Harbour Street to another triangular piece of land, Starvation Point, its name echoing a time when hungry seamen desperate for work would congregate there in the hope of being hired for a voyage. Pearl tried to control her own sense of desperation – an overwhelming need for information to put an end to this case.

Returning from the kitchen, Jack gestured for Pearl to take a seat at the table and Laura followed, the couple sitting close together as if for protection.

Pearl focused on Laura and said: 'I happened to see you today, talking to Tony Ballard.'

Jack turned quickly to his wife, surprise written on his face. Pearl went on, 'Can I ask what it was you were talking about?'

Laura sat in silence. Jack frowned. 'Laura?' he asked. Still she remained mute.

Pearl continued to hold Laura Harper's gaze as she went on to explain: 'I believe you were asking Tony for a favour.'

At this, Jack Harper seemed incredulous. 'What kind of favour?'

Laura turned to him and read the suspicion in her husband's eyes.

'I . . . think it would be better if you explained,' said Pearl gently.

Under pressure, but reassured by Pearl's look, Laura Harper finally nodded. 'All right, it's true.'

Jack looked stung and Laura closed her eyes for a moment before she pushed back the blonde fringe from her forehead and explained. 'I'm glad you know,' she said, 'because I can't sit back and do nothing, Jack.

I need to help. I may be pregnant but otherwise I'm fit and well, and I can't go on seeing you having to do everything.'

Jack Harper shook his head in confusion. 'I don't understand.'

'You were asking Tony Ballard for work?' asked Pearl.

Laura nodded then hung her head low, allowing her long Alice in Wonderland hair to fall across her shoulders. 'I told him we were both devastated about losing Florrie but . . . I could help finish off the work she had been doing with the wardrobe and props.' She looked at Pearl and explained: 'I still help out at the Playhouse, so it would be easy for me. A couple of hours in the evening, two or three times a week? I could get a lot done – especially on the nights Jack plays in Canterbury.' She turned and looked guiltily at her husband. 'I thought perhaps . . . you'd never even need to know.'

'Laura . . .' he began admonishingly, but Pearl spoke over him.

'And what did Tony say?' she asked quickly.

Laura shook her head. 'He . . . wasn't keen on the idea. Said it wasn't up to him, because he doesn't make those kinds of decisions, but . . .' She trailed off, conflicted, before continuing: 'I didn't want to ask Tanya or Irene first because I couldn't be sure either of them would keep this from Jack.'

Pearl asked: 'So you asked Tony instead . . .'

'For a chance to prove myself,' said Laura quickly, 'that's all.'

Pearl took a moment to absorb this. 'And . . . you were grateful.'

'Of course.' Laura paused. 'I knew there was a chance he was just humouring me – but I had to try. And I wanted him to *know* I was grateful for even listening to me.'

At this, Pearl looked away again out of the Harpers' window, this time down into the street below where a young couple were just passing by, pushing a small child in a buggy. Pearl wondered how many times Laura Harper had seen such a sight from her window and dreamed that one day, she and Jack might be walking their own child on Harbour Street.

'Why didn't you tell me?' asked Jack, wounded.

'Because I didn't want to worry you,' said Laura. 'You've been through so much . . . and what with being arrested . . .' She turned to Pearl, trying to explain further.

'The police have finished their work at the school, so I told Tony I could go in this evening, after Jack went to work. There are no classes and I could make some headway – and hopefully a good impression. I said I wouldn't need payment – and Tony could just treat it as a trial run – and put in a word for me with Irene and Tanya.' She gave a weak smile but Jack was unappeased and shook his head.

'I don't know how you could have done this without telling me?'

Pearl spoke up on Laura's behalf. 'Laura just wants to help.'

'That's right,' said Laura. 'I need to, because if the school closes we'll never survive.' She paused, then: 'I've taken you away from your music for long enough.'

As Jack considered this, Pearl thought for a moment. 'Did Tony give you a key to the school?'

After a pause, Laura nodded. 'It was kind of him to give me a chance. I was so pleased I actually kissed his hand.' She looked sadly between Pearl and Jack.

'Can I have it?' said Pearl. 'The key?'

Laura frowned, torn. 'I'm not sure, I—'

'Please,' said Pearl, holding out her hand. 'It's important, Laura. Trust me.'

Still Laura Harper hesitated, then she shook her head slowly. 'I can't. I promised him I'd take good care of it.' She looked to her husband. After a moment, Jack reached into the pocket of a jacket hanging on the back of his chair and paused for only a moment before making a decision and tossing a set of keys to Pearl. 'Take mine.'

At precisely the same time, McGuire was hurrying along a corridor at Canterbury Police Station, pulling on his jacket as he spoke on his mobile to Dean at The Whitstable Pearl.

'And she hasn't been back since this afternoon?' The detective waited for Dean's reply, which was just what he feared: Pearl hadn't been seen at the restaurant since lunchtime and wasn't due to work that evening.

'Okay,' said McGuire swiftly. 'If you hear from her, please tell her to call me, would you?' Ending the call,

McGuire found himself staring at two lifts that could ferry him to the ground floor. He punched one of the call buttons, then the other. Red lights indicated that the first lift was on the fourth floor and the other stuck at ground level. Neither was moving, so McGuire stepped forward and slammed both buttons again, managing to relieve only some of the frustration he felt at not being able to locate Pearl. The first lift finally arrived and McGuire stepped into it, knowing that in a few minutes he would literally be speeding his way to Whitstable. It was clear Pearl was up to something, probably following her gut instincts as usual, but McGuire's own instincts warned him something was wrong. He was desperate to find her – and fast.

The day was dying when Pearl made her way across the old recreation ground. Ahead of her, at the playground, a child's swing, caught by the evening breeze, creaked on rusting hinges. The area was desolate, with no one to observe Pearl but the odd herring gull scavenging for scraps in litter bins – until she heard a young man's voice. Turning quickly, she saw a group of youths had just entered the swing park from the beach. Slugging cans of lager while play-fighting like cubs, they failed to notice Pearl as she made her way towards the boundary hedge between the rec and Ballard's School of Dance. A small section of police tape, still affixed to a fence, was flapping noisily in the wind as she reached the rear door. Taking Jack Harper's keys from her pocket, she found one that fitted the lock – and steeled herself before entering.

Closing the door softly behind her, Pearl failed to turn on the hallway light and instead used a small pocket torch to make her way to the dressing room – the same room in which Florrie Johnson's body had been found. In spite of the heat insulation created by the stores of props and costumes lining the walls, Pearl felt a sudden chill running through her as she stepped inside. Glancing around, she tried to imagine Florrie's state of mind on the evening of her death – full of expectations for her birthday celebration, she was happy in her job, had lost weight and her newly coloured hair was the same shade as Tanya Ballard's – a shade that seemed to reflect the dark passions of a dance called tango. Staring around, Pearl guessed it must have been a thrill for the girl to be working in this room, filled as it was with all the costumes she had been cataloguing, making note of the laced-bodice dresses and flowered headdresses for performances of the ballets *Giselle* and *Swan Lake*, and the top hats and canes like those used by Max Sanchez in his tap class. But most of all, the greatest temptation for Florrie was clearly Tanya's tango dress – scarlet and black – two colours that, in the natural world, so often signalled dangerous creatures. Pearl remembered a time when her son Charlie had been fascinated by reptiles – snakes, in particular – like the black mamba, the most dangerous snake in the world, and the red spitting cobra, venomous and cannibalistic. Pearl found herself looking at Tanya's dance costumes, all of which were black and red – colours which, if aligned in a certain striped pattern on a snake's body, could signal if the creature was either harmless or deadly . . .

Moving on, Pearl now searched further and discovered a selection of wigs and hairpieces – bright copper ringlets, an exotic turban and black pigtail and a long blonde wig, perhaps for a performance of *Cinderella*. Lifting the wig from its stand, Pearl studied it and an old adage came to mind: 'blondes have more fun'. Was that true – or just a clever slogan from a hair company to tempt women to try a lighter shade? For decades, blonde women had enjoyed their own special Hollywood glamour but they had also been depicted as being dizzy and immoral – the archetypal 'dumb blonde'. But long blonde hair could also signify a childlike innocence, as with Laura Harper's style. The hairpiece in Pearl's hands was so very different from Pearl's own long dark curls – so fair it seemed almost as though it had been spun from flax . . .

Pearl had never once tried to colour her own hair, but now she set down the torch on the dressing table, pinned up her dark curls, and slipped on the wig. Overcoming her tension, she sat down and tried again to put herself in Florrie's place, imagining how the girl must have felt on that fateful night: apprehensive and yet excited that, no longer a teenager, she was on the brink of rediscovering herself as a young woman with a new image. Pearl leaned forward and switched on the light bulbs that surrounded the make-up mirror. In its reflection, she saw a stranger staring back at her, recognisable only by her moonstone-grey eyes. On the dressing table before her, among pots of stage make-up, pan-stick, brushes, sponges and combs, Pearl saw a pair of dressmaker's scissors. Picking them up, she paused before cutting a neat fringe in the wig just above her eyes. The sharp blades made easy work of it, but as Pearl set the scissors down, she knew with all certainty that if she was right about something, she could finally solve this murder, and that if she did so, McGuire would stay. Staring at her reflection, she now waited. Something told her she wouldn't have to wait for long.

Chapter Twenty-five

McGuire pulled up outside Seaspray Cottage, leapt from his car and rang Pearl's doorbell. With no response, he stood back on the pavement and looked up at Pearl's leaded bedroom windows – but saw no sign of life. Heading quickly into Starboard Light Alley he ignored the old yawl that lay moored alongside Pearl's home and headed directly into the garden to peer through the windows of Pearl's beach-hut office. Seeing her empty desk McGuire suddenly felt an acute sense of loss. Whenever he was working at the police station in Canterbury, it was easy to imagine Pearl either at the restaurant or here at home – always on hand to help. But now she was gone – seemingly vanished – and something didn't feel right.

Making his way to the kitchen door he found the key that Pearl kept beneath a heavy pot of red geraniums – in spite of all his advice for her not to do so. This time he was grateful Pearl had ignored him. Unlocking the door, he entered, closing it firmly behind him before taking a moment to note Pearl's well-ordered kitchen. He smelt the sweet fragrance of fresh herbs drying on the window ledge, mingling with the aroma of home-baked bread, before he lingered at a noticeboard covered in Pearl's bold handwriting – showing reminders of upcoming community events and birthdays. Three recent days were circled in red pen – Friday, Saturday and Wednesday – each featuring McGuire's name and an exclamation mark noting the importance of Pearl's dates with him.

McGuire moved on quickly into the living room, where he caught sight of a light flashing on Pearl's open laptop. Tapping the return key, the screen flashed into life to reveal a YouTube page showing footage of a performance by Max Sanchez – The Stair Dance. The text beneath it included, as Pearl had mentioned, Max's Cuban nickname, *Pies de Rayo*. Reflecting on this for a moment, McGuire then pulled his phone from his pocket, before he suddenly noticed Pearl's smartphone was still charging on a shelf. Frustrated, he was beginning to feel what he had come to recognise in his job as 'the chill': an anticipation of bad news. He stared helplessly around the room, his attention drawn to a small framed photo taken during a trip he had made with Pearl to Bruges. A carriage ride had transported them through the city's fabled streets to the Belfry of Bruges, where he had learned that Pearl was scared of heights. It had taken some effort on McGuire's part to persuade her to climb the three thousand steps to the very top, to be rewarded by a spectacular view across the city, but she had done so – because she had trusted him to keep her safe. In that moment, McGuire was suddenly reminded that there had been a life for him before his arrival in Whitstable and a life after. He had tried to draw a convenient line between the two, a barrier to hold back difficult emotions connected to the first: the loss of a woman he once loved and his failure to save Donna and to cope with that truth. But now it seemed those same emotions were seeping through, like seawater through the pierced hull of a ship, threatening to destabilise him with a weight of guilt and grief, as well as the fear of having to return to all he had tried to escape – a new fierce dread of losing the person he needed most. McGuire picked up the framed photo and stared hard at the image of Pearl's smiling face as he whispered: 'Where the hell are you?'

Pearl was still seated at the make-up mirror in the dressing room of Ballard's School of Dance, listening acutely, but hearing only silence, punctuated by the sudden scratching of seagulls' claws as they landed on a skylight in the roof. After a moment, the birds flew off again – and silence returned. Pearl took a deep breath and tried once more to channel Florrie Johnson's feelings on that last evening of her life – in this same room – thrilled with her new hair colour and full of anticipation for the evening ahead with Ruby. They had been about to head to Canterbury for a birthday concert – but not before hearing Jack Harper play in the piano bar of The Pilgrims Rest Hotel. Perhaps

Florrie had been planning to use the occasion to explain to Jack about what she had recently given him. If Pearl was right, Florrie would have been explaining that the verses were in fact lyrics she had penned for the songs Jack had played for her at Prospect Field one sunny afternoon. Perhaps the girl saw this as a suitable gift to him, but there might also have been a hope on her part that Jack would view this as a musical collaboration, inviting her to join him on future compositions.

Pearl knew this was nothing more than a hunch on her part, but it was one she had formed from what little information she had been able to glean about Florrie – a girl whose musical preferences, according to Ruby, were for something more current than stage musicals featuring the kind of tap dancing for which Max Sanchez was famous. Florrie had transferred her interest from Max to Jack Harper, perhaps because the girl had seen a way to seed her own ambitions. What was it Ruby had said – that Florrie had been 'finding her feet' since she had left the care system? Just like Ruby, Florrie had been on her own, keen to know how Ruby had coped after her grandmother's death. Ruby had told her friend that Pearl had helped with getting the flat put into Ruby's name, as well as giving her the job at The Whitstable Pearl. *That was like having family again,* Ruby had told Pearl. *I think Florrie must have felt the same about the dance school.*

So, thought Pearl now, Ballard's School of Dance had become Florrie Johnson's own Whitstable Pearl and the staff here were her own 'family' – at least that was the way she had viewed them – except one member might have been considered by Florrie as a 'partner'. That, thought Pearl, was no doubt what Vivian Gleaves had been about to tell Pearl when she had been silenced, strangled, and perhaps with the nearest thing to hand in an opportunistic killing – the straps of her own ballet shoes. That single act had prevented Pearl from discovering what Florrie Johnson's new tattoo might have shown. Could it have been linked to her association with Jack Harper? Certainly, Florrie had once confided in Max, her former tap teacher, about her family circumstances and her time in the foster care system – and it had been Vivian Gleaves who had told Pearl this – a sign perhaps that while Vivian seemed to distance herself with a haughty disdain from her colleagues at the school, she had been observing and storing information about them – something that may well have sealed her fate.

Pearl stared at her reflection in the make-up mirror, framed by light bulbs, and couldn't help but think of the Alice in Wonderland style of Laura Harper's long blonde hair. Laura had experienced an unhappy family life – something she was keen to put behind her and erase with the creation of a happy family of her own . . .

A sound suddenly broke Pearl's train of thought. Listening carefully once more, she was sure she had just heard the soft click of the back door closing. Silence followed – then footsteps began slowly approaching.

Pearl braced herself . . . and then heard the sound of a doorknob being turned. More footsteps followed before a figure emerged from behind a clothes rail, reflected in the dressing-room mirror. Irene Taylor stopped in her tracks, having to pause to recover from her own shock before she murmured, 'Pearl . . .?'

'Surprised I wasn't Laura Harper?' said Pearl.

Irene looked momentarily confused but finally nodded as she said falteringly: 'Why yes. Your . . . hair, it's . . .'

'Blonde,' said Pearl. 'And as much of a surprise as Florrie's dark hair must have seemed on the night of her murder.' She paused. 'A case of mistaken identity? Or maybe not.' Getting up from the mirrored dressing table, Pearl turned to face Irene as she asked: 'Why are you here?'

Irene appeared to struggle for an answer before she finally admitted: 'I . . . knew you had worked out what had happened.'

'As you wanted me to?' asked Pearl, aware now that something didn't feel right. Sensing this, Irene spoke quickly – and confidently. 'It's gone on long enough,' she said. 'I want it to end – now – I want to give myself up.'

'For the murder of Florrie Johnson and Vivian Gleaves?' Pearl tilted her head to one side and took a step closer. 'Why?' she asked. 'Why would you want to kill Florrie and Vivian?'

Irene remained speechless before managing to frame a few words. 'Does it matter?' she asked. 'I'm telling you now; I need to talk to the police.'

'Then do it,' said Pearl simply. 'You have DCI McGuire's number. You told me yourself he gave it to you so you could call him if anything occurred to you. You have your phone with you, don't you?'

Irene nodded mutely and took a hand from her pocket. In her palm lay her mobile phone. Pearl took it from her. 'Here,' she said, scrolling through the contacts until she found what she was looking for. 'Here's his number. Call him and tell him where you are.'

Pearl offered the phone back to her. Irene's mouth simply gaped open as Pearl continued to call her bluff. 'Take it!' she ordered.

Irene's trembling hand now reached for her mobile but before she could make the call, a warning suddenly sounded in the room. Someone else entered, startling Irene so that she dropped her mobile on to the dressing table as a voice spoke.

'Don't say another word.'

Tanya Ballard stepped slowly out of the shadows near the door and Irene moved quickly to her niece. 'You shouldn't have come—'

'But I had to,' said Tanya calmly, her eyes fixed on Pearl as she continued to come forward. The faint smile on her lips froze then disappeared. 'Whatever my aunt's told you – she's lying.'

'Tanya . . .' said Irene, pained.

Pearl spoke over her. 'Why would she do that?'

'Why else?' said Tanya flatly. 'To protect me.'

Pearl remained silent for a moment, then: 'She's always protected you.'

'Not this time,' said Irene, putting herself between the two women.

Tanya sighed wearily. 'It's no use,' she said. 'Don't

you see, Aunt Irene? This is like some . . . strange dance. We've been going through the motions, just like me and Tony.' She paused again as she looked at Pearl. 'But now it's almost over.'

Irene shook her head. 'No,' she said. 'I've always been honest with you, with everyone – especially your mother.'

Anger flashed across Tanya's face before she quickly turned away. 'Why do you always have to mention her?'

'How can I not?' said Irene. 'I tried so hard to get her away from all those who wanted to take advantage of her . . . to use her. I wanted to do the same for you. I still do. It's *all* I want.'

Tanya clamped her hands against her ears. 'Stop it!' she yelled. 'It's too late, don't you see?'

Irene was silenced. Pearl spoke up. 'You're right, Tanya,' she said, taking a step forward. 'I know what happened. I knew before I even got here this evening.' She fixed Tanya with a look. 'You murdered Florrie Johnson. Here in this room. And I know why: jealousy.' Pearl moved closer as she went on. 'A young girl infatuated with an older man – as Florrie had been with Max – and then with Jack . . . But now it was your husband she had really fallen for, and that stirred all those feelings in you again – the same feelings you had to deny in order to forgive Tony, to move forward and come here, to Whitstable, and get him out of temptation's way . . . only to have him tempted by a young woman who was naïve enough to think she had found . . .' Pearl paused again, '. . . a partner.'

Tanya spat venom. 'Tony is *my* partner!'

'Your dance partner,' said Pearl. 'Tanya and Tony. But now he wants his freedom, doesn't he?'

It was Irene who responded. 'Please,' she begged. 'Tanya's suffered enough—'

'*Suffered?*' said Pearl, cutting in. 'What about poor Florrie? To have died in this room the way she did?' Pearl tore off the blonde wig and shook out her own dark hair as she turned back to Tanya. 'The truth,' she demanded. 'What did you hear on the evening of the dance class when you got home to find Florrie still there in your apartment with your husband? When you learned that Tony's pain that night was faked?' She paused. '*What* did you see?'

Tanya Ballard remained stock-still, staring off into the distance, strangely unfocused, as though she was trying to make sense of a scene playing out before her.

'Dancing,' she said softly, frowning as though confused. 'They were . . . dancing together, in my home. Tony was holding her in an embrace . . . an *abrazo*. And Florrie was looking up at him so adoringly.' Tanya's expression suddenly hardened. 'But she didn't know him. Not like I do. She'd never gone through all that I have with him. It was *my* hard work, *my* determination, *my* ambition that got us where we were – that made him what he is today – Tony Ballard. He's nothing without me – but he could still demand half of everything – everything we'd earned – as well as this dance school, which Aunt Irene has worked so hard to hold on to – for me . . .' Tanya glanced around the room as though finally remembering where she was, then she looked to her aunt – but this time Irene Taylor had no response for her. Unable to hold her niece's look, she dropped her gaze to the floor.

'I watched them both,' Tanya continued, 'a talentless girl, fawning over my husband that night, and I went back out of the apartment . . . and pretended I hadn't seen a thing. I took the lift all the way down to the ground floor, and I rang the doorbell as if nothing had happened. I said I had forgotten my key and Florrie pressed the buzzer on the entry-phone to let me in.' Tanya took a step forward and stood at the dressing table as she went on: 'When I stepped back into the lift I saw my reflection in the mirror – just like now – but I didn't recognise myself. It was like . . . I was looking at someone else . . . I was playing a role, wearing a mask?'

She frowned suddenly then went on. 'The apartment door was open and Florrie was standing there, flushed, but acting as though nothing had happened. When I walked into the lounge I saw Tony was lying on the sofa, pretending to be in pain . . . But he wasn't. He could dance with Florrie – but he couldn't dance with me—' Tanya broke off, swallowing hard before she went on. 'I told the girl she could go home and that I would look after Tony – my devoted husband – but Florrie kept asking me how she could help?' Tanya shook her head slowly. 'She was always so willing . . . so ready to help . . .' Her lips tightened at the thought. 'So, I said she could do that the next day by staying until six to log the wardrobe.' Tanya paused and looked at Pearl. 'She went, leaving me alone with Tony. He took something to help him sleep while I lay awake, telling myself that we could get over this. I'd forgiven him once before and I could do it again. For the sake of our future. The school . . .' Her face clouded. 'But then there was Florrie. I realised I would have to get rid of her. Sack her.'

'And that's why you went to the school the following evening?' asked Pearl.

Tanya nodded. 'I didn't tell Tony. I gave him something to help him sleep and then I ran quickly, across the recreation ground to the school. I took Florrie's wages. I was going to pay her off. Get rid of her – once and for all. I knew it would be a shock for the girl but . . . When I got there, I found she had a surprise for me. She had dyed her hair, just like mine.' Tanya touched her own dark hair as she considered this. 'The strange thing was . . . she looked just like me at her age – when I was young and full of dreams . . .' She trailed off.

'What happened?' asked Pearl.

'I knew,' Tanya began, 'that Florrie didn't just want to steal my husband . . . she wanted to steal my life.' At this, Tanya Ballard began pacing, agitation rising as she continued. 'So I played along with her, I told her, right there and then, that she could wear my dress. She was so pleased. So happy to be taking *everything* I had—'

'Tanya—' Irene Taylor tried to speak over her niece but Tanya shouted her down.

'No! You don't know what it's like,' she cried, 'losing everything. You've never had what I had – and you never will.'

Irene recoiled, as though stung by a viper. Tanya slumped down at the dressing table and hung her head for a few moments before slowly looking up again. 'She was sitting right here,' she whispered, 'wearing my dress, when she asked me how I did my make-up. And so I showed her . . .' She stared down at the pots on the dressing table, her fingers stroking them as she went on. 'I told her how I apply it – every little stroke. She was so pleased . . .' She trailed off.

'And then?' said Pearl.

'Then I went to get my tango shoes for her . . .' Tanya paused. 'She couldn't wear the dress without shoes, so I asked what size she took. "Five!" she called back. My shoes are four – but I lied and told her they would fit. I couldn't disappoint her, could I? She was still painting her face when I came up behind her, putting on some blusher, smiling, pleased by what she saw in the reflection . . . telling me this was the best birthday present ever . . . and I knew what she was thinking . . . how she could take over my life . . . and the only man I've ever loved.' Tanya tilted her head to one side before her fingers curled around the scissors lying on the dressing table. Looking in the mirror she continued: 'I raised my arm and swung it out, forward and then sharply back, just like I would do in a tango spin . . .' Pearl's eyes remained fixed on the sharp scissors in Tanya's hand as she executed the move – the scissors remaining frozen in mid-air in front of Tanya's own face. 'Suddenly there was resistance,' she explained. 'It wouldn't move – it was . . . stuck . . . embedded . . .'

As Tanya took on a confused look, Pearl asked: 'And Vivian? She had plans for her retirement, didn't she? Before you silenced her.'

Tanya looked back at Pearl.

'Vivian,' she said. 'The prima ballerina. The prima donna. So graceful, so dignified, you'd never think she could stoop so low as to become a cheap blackmailer? She didn't really care about Florrie – only how much she could get from me to keep silent!'

'Tanya . . .' said Irene, trying to calm her, but Pearl continued to push for answers.

'She knew?'

'She knew enough,' said Tanya bitterly. 'She was a nosy woman – always watching everything and everyone. Storing it all up for future use.' She looked at Pearl. 'She phoned me and told me to meet her here at the school. Said she had something important to tell me – then out she came with her sly suspicions . . . about Florrie's tattoo. She knew the girl had got it done when she was impressed with Max, so when Florrie told her she was getting it removed and replaced with something special, Vivian guessed why.'

'A new tattoo for a new love,' said Pearl.

'What did Florrie Johnson know about love?' Tanya exploded. 'I told Vivian she couldn't threaten me with her suspicions. I told her to do her worst!'

'You called her bluff,' said Pearl calmly.

'Of course!' said Tanya. 'I thought she would do the smart thing, forget her demands and try to hold on to her job but instead she picked up the phone . . .' Tanya trailed off at this memory, while a thought suddenly came to Pearl, who backed slowly towards the dressing table, her fingers searching for something behind her as she spoke quickly, trying to distract Tanya.

'Vivian called me,' she said.

Tanya nodded slowly. 'Yes, she was taunting me,' she explained. 'I let her go on, talking to you on the phone, then I went to walk out, to leave her, but . . . her ballet shoes were right there, next to the music centre. She was turned away from me, having trouble with the phone line . . . *The Nutcracker Suite* was playing in the background . . . It . . . was so easy to silence her.'

At this, Irene Taylor moved quickly forward – perhaps to silence Tanya, or to comfort or contain her, but Tanya's senses were too keen and alert – in the next instant, she held Irene at bay with the scissors in her hand.

'You can't do anything about this, Aunt Irene,' she warned. 'I know you want to – that's why you tried to put the blame on Tony instead of me. You knew, didn't you?'

Irene stared at her helplessly but remained silent.

'And I defended my husband,' Tanya went on, 'until today, when you told me about . . . Tony and Laura. Now I blame him too. I hate him. I hate this school!' She looked around in desperation. 'I have nothing. Nothing at all – but you?' Anguish written on her face, Tanya stared at her aunt, while continuing to hold her at bay with the sharp scissors in her trembling hand.

Pearl spoke softly. 'There's nothing between Laura and your husband,' she said slowly. 'Laura Harper is pregnant. She loves her husband and all she ever wanted from Tony was a job.'

'You're lying,' said Tanya, shaking her head in disbelief. 'Tony said the same tonight but . . . he was lying too.' Her expression hardened. 'Why on earth would I believe him now?'

'Because it's true,' said Pearl. 'I misunderstood what I saw – I told your aunt in confidence, expecting she might have an answer for me.' She turned to Irene. 'You shouldn't have broken that confidence. That's why I'm here now, to take responsibility.'

'Dressed like Laura?' asked Tanya, confused.

Pearl nodded slowly. 'I realised you would come here tonight – once Tony told you that Laura would be here – as I'm sure he did. But he was only giving her a chance, that's all. You both misread his intentions.' Pearl turned to Irene. 'You may well have thought the same and come here to protect Laura? But more than that, you wanted to protect Tanya as you've always done – this time by taking the blame for her.'

Tanya shook her head. 'That won't be necessary,' she said starkly, turning sharply to face Pearl, the scissors now aimed at Pearl's face.

'Please, Tanya, don't do this?' Irene begged. 'You're my family. You're all I have.'

Tanya shook her head as her face softened with sadness. 'I . . . don't deserve you.'

'You do,' Irene insisted. 'And we can make this right. Come here . . .' Irene took another step forward, her hands outstretched, intent on taking the scissors from Tanya's grasp. A moment passed and Tanya looked almost tempted to hand them over. 'You're right,' she said suddenly, 'we *can* make it right.' But her body snapped back towards Pearl as she realised something. 'There's only one other person who knows what really happened.' She paused, her head cocked to one side as she continued to stare at Pearl. 'You.' She took a step forward and Pearl instantly recoiled.

'Tanya, please!' yelled Irene, but this time Tanya shoved her aunt roughly aside. Emboldened by Pearl's retreat, Tanya made another move towards Pearl, who stepped back again, but this time Pearl felt herself losing her balance, stumbling back across a costume hamper. She let out an involuntary cry as Irene Taylor's mobile phone flew from her hand, skidding across the floor to lie too far from her grasp. As she realised this, Tanya Ballard filled Pearl's frame of vision, her expression set, the sharp blades of the scissors aimed at Pearl's throat as she closed in before making a sudden lunge—

A scream went out – not from Pearl or from Irene Taylor, but from Tanya as the scissors suddenly clattered to the parquet floorboards. She was struggling, spitting, fighting for freedom like a wild animal, her arms pinned back by someone much stronger than her.

McGuire spoke hurriedly to Pearl. 'Are you okay?'

Coming to her senses, Pearl nodded slowly, registering McGuire's relief as he continued to restrain Tanya Ballard tightly in his grasp. Pearl now reached for Irene Taylor's mobile phone and finally ended the call she had managed to make to McGuire.

Chapter Twenty-six

Max Sanchez was sitting across from Pearl in Nathan's stylish lounge. Sliding glass doors were open on to the garden and a wind chime softly sounded on the warm breeze. 'Someone once said,' Max began, 'that "tango is a sad thought danced". That has resonance for Tanya Ballard,' he added. 'I had her down as a control freak, maybe even a narcissist, but I never reckoned on her being a killer.'

Pearl considered this. 'Looking at her childhood: all the insecurity . . . Losing her mother at such a young age—'

Max broke in quickly: 'Nothing excuses murder.'

'I know,' said Pearl, 'and I'd never want to do that. After all, Florrie also had a tough upbringing. And maybe that's why she needed someone to look up to – to "partner". First you, Max, then Jack Harper – and finally Tony Ballard.'

'There was never anything between us,' said Max firmly.

'Not on your part,' said Pearl. 'But Florrie was infatu-ated with you at one time – with your talent? Hence the tattoo.' She thought for a moment. 'I never realised the significance of that until I found out about your Cuban nickname.'

'*Pies de Rayo*,' said Nathan, entering from the kitchen to set a bowl of pistachios on his coffee table for his guests.

'Tanya was devastated at Tony's affair but she forgave him,' Pearl went on. 'She loved him. She needed him. But she'd clearly never got over his affair and must have been watching him like a hawk. On the night of the dance class she went home after the demonstration and saw Florrie dancing with her husband . . .' She paused. 'We'll never know exactly what it was Tanya heard – perhaps only some harmless flirting? But after Tony's affair, she didn't need much to fire her jealousy and suspicion. All she needed was to see them dancing together – in an embrace. An *abrazo*. Something Tony could no longer do with Tanya. The next day, when she found Florrie had dyed her hair, just like her own, Tanya knew, instinctively, the girl was trying to take her place. Perhaps it was then that she realised she had never truly forgiven Tony for his affair – and that he was capable of having another.'

'So,' Nathan began, 'the evening after that first tango class, on Florrie Johnson's birthday, Tanya encouraged the girl to try on her own dress and when she was busy at the dressing-room mirror she went to fetch her dance shoes—'

'And killed her,' said Max balefully.

'But why murder Vivian too?' asked Nathan.

'Blackmail,' said Max. 'She tried to do the same to me; told me she had something important to say about Florrie's murder and got me to take her to lunch. When she started asking me if the police knew what Florrie's tattoo signified, I guessed what she wanted. She'd hinted enough over her lobster Thermidor.'

Nathan frowned. 'Why didn't you tell the police? Or me or Pearl?'

Max shook his head. 'I guess I didn't trust you enough to believe me.'

'Max . . .' began Nathan, but Pearl's look silenced him. She turned back to Max and said softly: 'Blackmail's an ugly crime – especially when it's aimed at an "outsider".'

Max's gaze met Pearl's and he nodded slowly. 'Yes. So I kept quiet, kept my head down – and decided to ignore Vivian.'

'So she then went to Tanya,' said Pearl. 'She arranged a meeting at the school and put it to her boss that it would be wise to increase her wages or she might just have to mention to me about having known that Florrie was about to change her tattoo in honour of her new "partner".'

'Tony Ballard,' said Nathan.

'Vivian knew that was motive enough for Tanya to dispose of her young rival and she may well have elaborated what she knew, but Tanya had to resist blackmail because the demands seldom end, and that night, Vivian put more pressure on her by calling me just to show Tanya she wasn't bluffing.' She paused. 'She turned her back . . .'

'And Tanya made her move,' said Max.

'She used the nearest thing to silence Vivian,' said Pearl.

'The straps of her own ballet shoes,' said Nathan. He took a deep breath. 'And Laura Harper?'

Pearl explained: 'I realised that if *I* could misinterpret Laura's meeting with Tony—'

'So could Tanya,' said Max.

Pearl nodded once more. 'Not only that, I'd unwittingly given Tanya good reason to do so when I'd confided in Irene about seeing Laura and Tony that morning near the Playhouse. Irene broke my confidence and told Tanya, so I knew I needed to do something to protect Laura – to get her out of harm's way. She's pregnant – with a longed-for baby. At that moment, I could only think of drawing Tanya out by putting myself in Laura's place.'

'You could've got yourself killed,' said Max. 'If you hadn't managed to get your hands on Irene's phone—'

'I know,' Pearl agreed. 'It was a huge gamble.'

'A *dangerous* gamble,' began Nathan. 'If your policeman hadn't picked up the call . . . if he hadn't already been in Whitstable, looking for you—'

'I know,' Pearl repeated, stressed. 'I was lucky.'

'Lucky if he ever forgives you,' said Nathan. 'I feel exactly the same.' He smiled slowly. 'Though I do, of course, forgive you. Because I can't live without you, sweetie. So I got you this.' He reached into a drawer and took out a brand-new smartphone. 'You'll never be out of touch again.'

Pearl looked up and saw Nathan's smile was still in place before he gave her a peck on the cheek and made a sudden decision. 'And now I think we need a drink,' he announced, feeling the need to lighten the mood.

As he turned away, Pearl asked: 'Limoncello?'

Nathan shook his head as he moved to his drinks table. '*Mojitos!*' he said. 'Made with Max's finest Cuban rum.'

Pearl watched as Nathan placed crushed ice into three tumblers followed by a mix of mint, sugar and lime juice and finally a few hefty slugs of white rum before he began mixing the drinks with a long cocktail spoon. Handing the drinks to Pearl and Max, he picked up his own and smiled.

'Cheers.'

'*Salud!*' said Max.

Pearl touched their glasses with her own before taking a sip.

'Do you know,' she began, 'this has to be the finest *mojito* I've ever tasted?'

A short while later, as she headed home, Pearl crossed Island Wall to the beach, where she paused to gaze out towards the coast. She never tired of Whitstable's seascape, which remained ever-changing like a gallery of beautiful paintings – each one different and unique. Tonight the sky was a fierce scarlet, reminding Pearl of Tanya Ballard's tango dress – and its deadly owner.

Music sailed on the air from the Old Neptune pub, a young man singing along to a guitar accompaniment, background music perhaps to a pub full of customers engaged in their own conversations, reminding Pearl of the piano bar at The Pilgrims Rest. She thought suddenly of the Harpers – a young couple, expecting a much-loved child, struggling to survive against all the odds while still holding on to a dream, as Pearl herself had done for many years while bringing up Charlie. She had worked so hard to build up her restaurant, looking forward to the day when she might be able to revive an old dream and return to an abandoned career as a detective – a dream fulfilled with her own agency. She took a deep breath and headed on along the beach to her cottage, opening the gate and heading through it into her sea-facing garden. The evening air was laden with the heavy perfume of lavender and jasmine, and she felt relaxed and calm – the effects of Nathan's *mojito* – so much so that she was suddenly caught off guard and totally unprepared for the figure that stepped out of the shadows.

'You're back, then?'

Pearl felt her heart leap out of her chest at the sight of the man before her. Over two metres tall, with a grimy face and clothes that stank of fish, whelk fisherman Ned Rumball lifted a creel-shaped lobster basket in his gnarled hands and said: 'Found in my whelk hut!'

Inside the basket, a creature lay sprawled on what looked like a bed of clothing. Peering closer, Pearl recognised the animal's surly stare.

'That's Mojo . . .' she said, stunned. 'What was he doing in your hut?'

The fisherman shrugged. 'Search me. I've been out at sea and got back to find he'd made himself at home. Been comin' and goin' through a crack in the weatherboard.'

Pearl frowned, suddenly suspicious as she peered into Ned's creel. 'What's that he's lying on?'

'Looks like someone's washing,' said Ned, before adding quickly: 'And before you ask, it ain't mine!'

With that, he shoved the creel on to Pearl, together with one of Dolly's crumpled posters, then headed off smartly along Pearl's garden path as he called back: 'And you can return that creel tomorrow!'

Pearl watched Ned disappearing along the prom, a dark silhouette against the fiery sky, before she heard an unhappy growl from the basket in her hand. Now on his feet, Mojo was giving his limbs a welcome stretch, while revealing his 'bed' to be a selection of exclusive underwear – covered in paw-prints and stinking of whelks.

Chapter Twenty-seven

'He's *such* a good boy,' said Dolly, cooing over Mojo, who was perched on a large satin cushion on Dolly's sofa like a precious trophy.

'A good boy?' said Pearl, incredulous. 'After what he did to Hilary Radcliffe's underwear? No wonder I didn't see anything on my surveillance cameras. I positioned them high but he must have leapt up from below, from the lawn, and snatched everything from the line with those sharp claws of his – taking the pegs down at the same time.'

Dolly smiled. 'He's a clever old tom,' she said, before something dawned on her. 'He did it once before, you know, to an old petticoat of mine? Nothing quite as fancy as Hilary Radcliffe's knickers, but I reckon he must have a thing about satin—'

'Why didn't you tell me!'

'Because I forgot,' said Dolly. 'I've only just remembered.'

'What sort of cat steals underwear?' Pearl exclaimed.

'Not "underwear",' said Dolly, 'you said yourself Hilary's smalls were high-quality lingerie. And Mojo won't be the first, you know,' she added defensively. 'I once read about a Tonkinese called Brigit who stole eleven pairs of underpants and more than fifty socks.' She frowned. 'I never thought for a minute my boy would do something like that again but . . . well, Hilary's underwear must've been a bit too tempting for an old tom – didn't it have a few feathers on?'

'Not by the time I returned it.'

'But you gave it all a good wash?'

Pearl shook her head. 'No, I did not. The last thing I needed was for it to go missing from *my* washing line. And I certainly didn't admit to the Radcliffes that the real thief was Mojo.' Pearl glared at the errant feline.

'Well, I won't say if you don't,' said Dolly. 'And I'm guessing the Radcliffes will never venture near a whelk stall, so they won't get to hear about this from Ned Rumball.' She smiled. 'By hook or by crook, you got there in the end, Pearl. You always do. And you've also escaped Ratty giving you a bad review and demanding his retainer back.'

'Yes,' agreed Pearl, relieved. 'His payment's been safely delivered to the carnival committee, who have offered us a principle float next year.'

'How wonderful!' Dolly beamed.

Pearl asked tentatively: 'I . . . wonder if the dance school might take one.'

Dolly gave a rueful look and a loud sigh. 'If only she had never come back.'

'Tanya?'

Dolly nodded. 'And that faithless husband of hers. It's amazing how one young woman could have inspired such jealousy. But Florrie probably wasn't aware of her power over the male species.'

'Not all men are capable of being led astray,' cautioned Pearl. 'Florrie's crushes may have flattered them – Jack Harper, Max Sanchez . . .'

'Tony Ballard?' said Dolly.

Pearl shrugged. 'I'm not sure anything ever happened between Tony and Florrie – beyond a dance in the Ballards' apartment after that tango class. But his affair had scarred Tanya—'

'Unhinged her, don't you mean?' said Dolly.

'Maybe,' said Pearl, 'so when she saw them dancing together that night, she was able to see something that wasn't there . . . or rather,' she added, 'something to come.' She paused. 'Will Irene ever reopen the place, do you think?'

Dolly gave a sad look. 'I hope so. The school's been her life. And I realise she obstructed the police by failing to tell McGuire all she suspected, but then so did you. You went off to that dance school alone, remember?'

'There wasn't time. I was following a hunch—'

'Straight into harm's way,' said Dolly with a knowing look. 'Thank heavens you managed to hit the call button on Irene's mobile. If McGuire hadn't listened in, who knows what might have happened?' She paused. 'I can't say I blame Irene for being loyal to her family, though.

Whatever happens, I'm going to stay in touch with her – I might even take up some lessons . . .'

'You can't,' said Pearl. 'You're a "slave to that disc" of yours, remember?'

'I know,' said Dolly. 'Which is why, at this stage in my life, I shall attempt nothing more strenuous than a gentle waltz.' Dolly smiled, then eyed Pearl and took her daughter's hand. 'Promise me you'll never put yourself in danger like that again?' She went on: 'You should've shared your suspicions with McGuire and let him deal with it.'

'I know,' said Pearl, conflicted, 'but I couldn't be sure I was on the right track until I arrived at the school, and even then we still needed a confession.'

Dolly felt for her daughter. 'Have you talked to him?' she asked gently.

Pearl shook her head. 'Not properly. He's busy con-cluding the investigation, and though his superintendent had planned to transfer him, I'd be surprised if he's not in line for some kind of commendation. After all,' she added, 'he not only discovered a murderer, he saved my life.'

Before Dolly could respond, Mojo gave a loud mew, sounding much like a grumpy baby. His owner jumped to attention. 'Time for his supper!' Dolly said. 'And just look what I've got for my boy tonight . . .'

Moving quickly to her fridge she took out a large cooked fish which Pearl instantly recognised.

'Sea bass!' said Pearl, shocked. 'That was on my menu today.'

'Yes,' smiled Dolly, 'leftovers. I'm sure you'll be pleased to know you have one more satisfied customer this evening.'

And with that, she set the sea bass in a bowl for Mojo, who looked back at Pearl, offering what appeared to be a blink of triumph, before tucking into his fish supper.

On her way back home to Seaspray Cottage, Pearl stopped in her tracks as she recognised a figure resting on one of the timber breakwaters. Her heart pounded in her chest at the sight of McGuire and she took a moment to watch him from afar, wondering how long he had been there. He was dressed casually in a white shirt and jeans, a pair of deck shoes beside him as his feet dangled in the shallow waves. Dolly's words echoed in her mind along with those of Nathan: *Lucky if he ever forgives you* . . .

Pearl took a deep breath and gathered her thoughts before putting a hand to her hair to try to tidy her long dark curls. She then headed across, and coming up behind McGuire she spoke softly. 'That view beats Cornwall.'

McGuire turned and saw her. 'I wouldn't know,' he said simply.

Pearl sat down close beside him. 'Are you . . . likely to find out?'

The detective paused before shaking his head slowly. 'Welch has decided to put up with me a little longer.'

Pearl felt instant relief. 'Well,' she said, 'if he can – I can too.' She smiled and expected McGuire to do the same, but instead, he held her gaze and an uncomfortable silence fell between them. 'Look, Pearl—'

She raised her hand to stop him – trying to make things easier for him while knowing a certain conversation couldn't be avoided. 'It's all right,' she began, 'I know what you're going to say.'

'Do you?'

She nodded. 'You're sick of me putting myself at risk . . . so why don't I just stick to running the restaurant and give up my agency?' She paused before adding: 'You've said it enough times before.'

'I know,' said McGuire gently. 'But I wasn't going to say it now. What would be the point when I know how much you've always wanted it?'

He looked at Pearl, disarming her so completely that she felt suddenly lost for words. Getting down from the timber groyne, McGuire faced her, placing his palms gently on her suntanned shoulders before he went on. 'You're a beautiful woman, Pearl. You're smart, hardworking, you have the respect of everyone in this town whose opinion really counts, and . . .' He suddenly trailed off and looked away, pausing before framing his next words very carefully. 'You really should be teamed up with a partner who's there for you one hundred per cent, who loves you and is able to protect you . . . every minute of the day.'

Pearl looked at him askance, unsure what McGuire was really trying to say, but unnerved by his serious expression and the fact that this wasn't the praise she expected for solving the case – or the reprimand she knew she had earned by going it alone and putting herself in jeopardy to do so.

'That's . . . what you want?' she asked tentatively.

McGuire held her look for a moment, his blue eyes scanning her face before he nodded slowly. 'It's what you deserve.'

McGuire's reply was delivered in a soft whisper but in that instant, Pearl felt blindsided, as though she had been dealt a hard blow to her solar plexus. She closed her eyes, blotting out the image of McGuire before her, framed by the seascape in the background, and in the next instant she was taken back to another day, shortly after they had met, when he had informed her that he would be returning to London, to the Met, where he belonged. It had been another summer's afternoon, just like this, a day on which she had felt, as she did now, that she had been set adrift, like a ship at sea. She had been clever with this case – but she had failed to see this coming. Her head began to reel as though she was suffering vertigo, perhaps from having climbed a tall building like the Belfry of Bruges – but without having McGuire there to talk her down.

'Are you saying—' She broke off, unable to speak further.

'Marry me.'

McGuire's words were spoken so softly, Pearl could hardly be sure she had heard them. She opened her eyes and asked: 'What?'

She saw he was staring straight at her. 'I said, marry me.'

'You're . . . serious?' she asked, suddenly suspicious. 'I mean . . . you didn't plan this, did you? No ring? No bending down on one knee?'

McGuire shook his head.

'But . . . you *are* serious?'

He nodded slowly. 'Deadly serious. Maybe I should've planned this but . . . all I know is I love you and I don't want to lose you.' He waited expectantly. Pearl opened her mouth to speak but found herself lost for words.

'What is it you want?' asked McGuire.

Recognising his need for an answer, Pearl braced herself and finally replied. 'Right now,' she began, 'I . . . just want you to hold me.'

McGuire took her firmly in his arms and Pearl laid her cheek against his chest, feeling his heart beating strongly. Looking up at him, she reached for his hand, kissed it then took it in her own before slowly holding it away from herself at shoulder height. Staring into McGuire's eyes, she kicked off her shoes and circled her toe in the waves. As she gave a slow smile, McGuire returned it, nodding slowly as he took three steps with her along the shore. Still caught in his gaze, Pearl felt the warmth of McGuire's hand against her skin, as he pulled her tightly to him, before spinning her around in the shallow waters of the incoming tide. Suddenly, without warning, she felt herself swooning, falling back, only to be rescued by McGuire's strong arms. A moment passed. McGuire pulled her to him and finally kissed her as the tide pushed hard against them. She looked up at him, breathless.

'Well?' he whispered.

A million thoughts suddenly entered Pearl's head as she considered her proud independence, the years she had spent failing ever to compromise, while waiting for Mr Right among a sea of Mr Wrongs, which had included, at one point, even the attractive but dull Marty Smith. She couldn't be sure of anything any more apart from the fact she was finally in the arms of the right partner – and couldn't bear to lose him. She heard the word falling from her lips.

'Yes.'

A moment passed before McGuire returned Pearl's smile and kissed her once more – but this time a trickle of applause suddenly sounded. Glancing around, Pearl saw a small crowd had gathered on the beach: couples, children, pensioners walking their dogs – all looking on and clapping what they saw. Pearl smiled and looked back at McGuire.

'Does this mean we're engaged?'

McGuire nodded slowly and pulled her to him again, never realising, until this moment, that all the evenings he had spent practising *ochos*, *pasadas* and *paradas* in a dance hall in Streatham would one day help him net the woman of his dreams – while Pearl now knew for sure that for all McGuire's reliance on procedure, his caution and predictability, he could allow passion to overtake him – and present her with the greatest surprise of all.

Acknowledgements

I am very grateful to many people who have helped me, in lots of disparate ways, with the completion of this book: the eighth Whitstable Pearl Mystery.

Firstly, I must thank all those connected with the Tankerton Dancing Academy, especially Helena Griffiths who, as owner of Whitstable's real-life dance school, welcomed me to join her wonderful adult ballet classes run by Linda Wood. Although these came to a premature end for me due to the Covid-19 lockdown, the idea of a fictional dance school, nestled somewhere in the back streets of Whitstable, formed the first seeds of inspiration for this novel, together with the fabulous tango routines on TV's *Strictly Come Dancing*.

I am also very grateful to my neighbour, Adam Skeaping, for his valuable information on all things technical, to Howard Stoate for medical advice, to Christine Mackenzie for help with location photographs, and to Roger Hext for some timely police research.

Warm thanks also go to three Kent-based novelists: fellow crime writer and real-life detective Lisa Cutts, for helping with more police research, as well as teaming up with me for some very enjoyable author events – as did the wonderful Broadstairs novelist, Jane Wenham-Jones. I'm also grateful to author and film screenwriter, Mark Stay, for his friendship and support in helping to promote my books via his excellent podcast series *The Bestseller Experiment.*

Although lockdown and Covid-19 precautions prevented so many book festival events and author signings from taking place in 2020, I'd like to thank my friend Victoria Falconer for managing to restage a Whitstable Pearl event as two lovely online features for Whitstable's literary festival, WhitLit. Thanks also go to all the hardworking staff at the independent bookshops: Harbour Books in Whitstable as well as Top Hat and Tales in Faversham and the wonderful Whitstable coffee shop Blueprint – all of whom managed to sell my books by mail order during lockdown.

I remain ever grateful to Dominic King of BBC Radio Kent for inviting me on to his show to talk about this series and for a special feature that examined my use of music in the Whitstable Pearl Mysteries with a fantastic contribution from Daniel Leeson Harding, the Director of Music Performance at Kent University, and the wonderfully talented mezzo-soprano, Michelle Harris. I also thank Canterbury-based musician and composer Luke Smith for the magical evening I spent listening to him playing TV crime themes on a white baby grand piano, which gave me the inspiration for Jack Harper's performance in the book.

I must also thank Tony Wood, Richard Tulk-Hart and all at Buccaneer Media and Acorn TV for demonstrating such unwavering commitment to creating a television series, *Whitstable Pearl*, adapted from my books, which will air in 2021, starring Kerry Godliman as Pearl Nolan.

And my gratitude goes, as ever, to my publishing director and editor, Krystyna Green at Little, Brown Book Group for having faith in these novels in the first instance – and to my agents, Michelle Kass, Russell Franklin and Tishna Molla, for their unswerving support.

Finally, huge thanks and appreciation go to all those who enjoy and support my Whitstable Pearl Mystery novels – because, as we all know, an author is nothing without readers.